MW01277952

KISS OF THE DEATH ADDER

PUBLISHING HOUSE

GABRIOLA, BC CANADA V0R 1X4

Copyright © 2022, H.B. Dumont.
All rights reserved.

KISS OF THE DEATH ADDER
ISBN 978-1-990335-01-3 (PAPERBACK)
ISBN 978-1-990335-02-0 (CASEBOUND)
ISBN 978-1-990335-03-7 (EBOOK)

PRINTED ON ACID-FREE PAPER THAT includes no fibre from
endangered forests. Agio Publishing House is a socially
responsible company, measuring success on a triple-bottom-
line basis.

10 9 8 7 6 5 4 3 2 1c

DEDICATED TO JUDY

Noir Intelligence Series

The Black Hat
Spine of the Antiquarian
Kiss of the Death Adder

KISS OF THE DEATH ADDER

BOOK THREE
of the
Noir Intelligence Series

A Novel

H.B. Dumont

CHAPTER 1

"Herr Rafael Blosch was about to reveal unknown details regarding the mysterious *Quer* when he was fatally bitten by a death adder that had crawled up through a dank, discoloured cavity in the floor of his sweltering desert cell," Daan Segers, the director of the European Union Intelligence Unit, announced in an exasperated voice.

At that pronouncement, a church-like stillness filled the room while profanities faintly rolled off tightened lips. The frustration of those assembled was magnified because they appeared to be on the verge of uncovering critical intelligence about the enigmatic *Quer* that had been imprecisely perceived on their radar, like an apparition sensed but not seen. The kiss of the death adder had ensured that Herr Blosch would take that crucial intelligence with him to his anonymous grave.

The *Quer* was an olden society conceived when Celtic and Druid cultures dominated much of what would become Western Europe. The original seven members were *patres familias* – male owners of family estates, although not Roman citizens. Today, the *Quer* had tentacles reaching into financial institutions and political capitals of major nation states, most notably the European Union. Their rank and file were deadlier and more ruthless, with a reputation for greater savagery and tenacity than any Sicilian Mafioso.

"The law of unintended consequences," Paul Bernard muttered. His measured gaze assessed the level of preparedness for such news. "We have people in high places including government and police departments," he added somberly.

Daan held his focus.

After a brief silence, Paul continued. "Those were the last words Herr Blosch said to me as we were being gagged and hooded on the yacht. Perhaps with the revelation of Herr Blosch's death, a select few of these elite senior members of the constabulary and governance who may have been loyal to Herr Blosch and the *Quer* could be urged to transfer allegiances."

Alexandra Belliveau chimed in, "*Reculer pour mieux sauter –* we need to step back in order to take up a more strategic position from which we may re-engage." *In every adversity, there are the seeds of its opposite*, she mused. She had risen to become the top forensic psychologist in Europe by always meeting adversity with optimism. The untimely death of Herr Blosch proved the impetus for such a review of the facts and circumstances which she projected on the monitor of her mind.

"I agree," Daan re-joined the conversation. A chameleon-like change had transformed the retired general from briefly stoic to assuredly resolute. "With Herr Blosch's inopportune demise, it is absolutely imperative that we do whatever is necessary to apprehend the seventh and final member of the *Quer* who has maintained his cloak of secrecy. If that means contracting out to an external freelance resource – a centurion – to lure him out of hiding, we will consider that option."

This invitation triggered a hint of restraint among those colleagues gathered. Since its inception, members of the European Union Intelligence Unit had been carefully selected from citizens of the initial six member states and then only after a lengthy vetting process and meticulous levels of scrutiny. The sole purpose of the Intelligence Unit was to protect the European Union from internal and external threats to its political and economic stability. No external resource had ever been recruited since 1957 when the European Union had been officially formed as an adjunct to the Treaty of Rome, written by those six initial signatories.

"On a positive note," Daan added, "we have tentatively identified the seventh member of the *Quer*. I say 'tentative' because we compared names of the captured members with the original family names noted on the membership list. The one surname missing is Durand. Ironically, it is derived from the old French, *durant*, which means to endure or to last. He seems to be living up to his ancient family tradition. Intelligence suggests that his first name could be Baird or some derivative, but that needs to be confirmed."

The captured members of the *Quer* were still in safe custody in the Desert Springs Interrogation Facility. They had single-mindedly objected to their consigned wardrobes of fluorescent green coveralls and ankle bracelets. None, however, had demonstrated the potential to become as communicative as Herr Blosch. Perhaps with news of his death, they too might be persuaded to disclose yet unknown details about the *Quer* and its clandestine mandate. Then again, they might become even more resolute to keep their oath of silence, to not follow in Herr Blosch's footsteps. No member of the *Quer* in its long history had divulged any details of its existence or mission. Probably they would simply wait until eventually freed by their captors, who would then suffer the consequences of their misguided action.

The timing of this announcement could not have been worse for Alexandra and Paul. This was supposed to be the first week of their Mediterranean honeymoon. Instead, they were re-engaged with colleagues from the European Union Intelligence Unit at a discrete location. On the bright side, if you had to interrupt an amorous vacation, then Santorini, an island in the Aegean Sea overlooking the Caldera, was an ideal venue.

"May I suggest a possible external centurion to work with us not as a formal member of the European Union Intelligence Unit, but as a contractor," Paul suggested. Maintaining the security of the Unit and the anonymity of its members was paramount. By contracting this work, the policy of not offering any status close to permanent membership in the European Union Intelligence Unit to 'outsiders' would be strictly adhered to. "You may find my suggestion unorthodox but unusual circumstances dictate extraordinary measures."

Matthieu Richard, as head of operations for the EUI Unit, invited Paul to explain his proposition. "The floor is yours, *mon ami.*"

"As you are aware, I was approached last week when running the marathon in Palermo by a man who identified himself as the Armenian Turk. We confirmed that he had contacted me on behalf of Francine Myette. His real name is Aiolos Yusuf Dimir, codename Rakici. We don't know a great deal about him except that he may have been Turkish Military Intelligence. We can conclude that he is professional to the extent he knew I would be running in this marathon. I certainly did not make that information known.

"He and Francine Myette apparently first met when they were attending the University of Rostov in southern Russia. Her name at that time was Tatyana Sokolov, known as Tanya. We know much more about Francine. She is, or was, a Russian agent who had infiltrated French Intelligence. She is now supposedly more supportive of democratic philosophies, or at least less dedicated to communist doctrine. The Armenian Turk mentioned that Francine was open to engaging in conversations that could be of mutual benefit. I suggest that we accept Francine's invitation to enter into preliminary discussions as a start."

Alexandra joined the discussion. "It is interesting that Rakici refers to himself as the Armenian Turk rather than the Turkish Armenian. That suggests he sees himself as Armenian first and foremost, and Turkish as a result of some extraneous event or association, more than likely political. It is worth digging deeper into his character. Turkey has a reputation for working both sides of the fence, a Western NATO ally and an ally of former

Eastern satellite communist states of the USSR including Mother Russia. In contrast, Armenia entered a partnership with the Atlantic Cooperation Council in 1992 and a partnership with NATO two years later. That begs the question: Does Rakici perceive himself to be a NATO ally? Is he playing the field advantage? Or is he a survivor? Nothing wrong with that, subject to his true motivation and loyalties."

CHAPTER 2

"My intuitive response," Matthieu responded, "is that it's unorthodox. But, as you said, Paul, unanticipated circumstances could open the door to unconventional responses."

Alexandra looked at Matthieu, scanning him for the reason for his response, one way or another. Was his initial reaction to the nominee or the nominator? His focus remained on Paul in an attempt to understand his motivation in suggesting Francine.

Matthieu had only worked with Paul on one major case with the European Union Intelligence Unit. There he had come to respect and trust Paul's judgement. A decade earlier, they had walked similar turf while serving with the United Nations Protection Force in the Former Republic of Yugoslavia. Colonel Paul Bernard, as he knew him on that mission, had a PhD in biochemistry. Recently, he had been inducted as a Commandeur de la Légion d'Honneur at the Élysée Palace in Paris for notable courage and steadfastness when gathering evidence at scenes of war crimes and presenting it at the International Criminal Court in The Hague.

An interlude followed before Matthieu continued. This reaction was consistent with his modus operandi, which was to ponder before proposing a response. More often than not, he sought additional knowledge in order to shed light on all factors contributing to potential decisions.

"You met Francine Myette briefly while working on the Thon case but not Rakici." Matthieu let his observation settle.

Paul clarified his proposal. "My sense is that Rakici, the Armenian Turk, may be positioning himself on the periphery for some future benefit. So, we would need to factor him into the

Francine equation. He may be neither comrade nor adversary at this time, but simply a convenient link to an opportune solution."

Matthieu looked toward Daan who furrowed his forehead and nodded tentatively in agreement as he opened his mouth and then closed it without saying anything. Words unuttered had more power at that moment. Matthieu sensed there was something disconcerting about his superior's manner. Working closely with Daan for over a decade, he had come to realize that retired generals tend to deliberate strategically, without necessarily debating the details in a public forum.

Matthieu sought additional input. Dr. Alexandra Belliveau was a valuable source who had spent her career as a forensic psychologist working with the Police nationale and the Prefecture de Police in Paris. Paul alone referred to her as AV. There was a story behind that but Matthieu was not one of the privileged few who knew the reason, at least not yet.

"Alexandra, your thoughts?"

"Paul and I have talked about the possibility of Francine's involvement. She was trained KGB before transferring to FSB. She is utterly appalled and disgusted with her former employer because they murdered Capitaine Dominique Roland of the Police nationale. Francine and Dominique had been in an intimate relationship. I did not trust Francine when we first met but the context has changed since then. Today, my intuition tells me that her motivation to join forces with us may be genuine. I would support this recommendation with a codicil of caution. My preference would be to spend some time with Francine to gauge the level of her sincerity before we propose any business relationship."

Alexandra concluded her psychological assessment prophetically but with professional efficiency. "In the words of our KGB contemporaries, *doveryat i proveryat* – trust and verify. Francine would do the same. She would expect the same. If we proceed too quickly, she would become suspicious. If we dragged our feet, she would become guarded. It is a matter of professional balance, but balance from her KGB/FSB perspective, not ours."

"A guarded proviso," Paul added. "When you sub-contract to another gladiator, you run the risk of giving up control over some aspects of the mission, which may result in you becoming subservient to that gladiator in ways only the gladiator knows."

Matthieu glanced over at his superior who had been resting his chin against his steepled fingers in contemplation. Occasionally, Daan would merely ponder, sifting through the facts as they were related, not presenting any indication of his intentions. On other occasions, he would blink once slowly followed with a tic of a nod, denoting he was on the cusp of a decision, a forthcoming directive.

"In espionage parlance," Daan declared, "you either want to *only* be seen or *never* be seen by your target. We could employ Francine to only be seen by the truant final member of the *Quer*, Baird Durand, if we can be assured of her loyalty. His capture is our number one priority."

Daan waited for confirmation before continuing with his deliberation. They had reached a point when additional considerations were welcome. He scanned the composure and read the gaze of his team members. All nodded, agreeing with the priority level of this case.

"Second, we know that the old KGB is still after the code that Alexandra's mother, Maria Belliveau, developed when she was employed by French Counterintelligence. An interesting twist. We suspect that it is old KGB and not current FSB because of the vintage of the bug that was planted in Alexandra's apartment. The Russians are currently tracking Alexandra, and Paul by association, in hopes of finding the code. Using an appropriate disguise, we could employ Francine to manoeuvre invisibly, never seen by these old-guard KGB agents. It will be a delicate balance but I'm confident we could neutralize this obstinate and malignant Soviet menace, while minimizing the gladiator subservient factor which Paul correctly identified."

Again, Daan paused briefly to take a sounding before delivering his directive. Once a general, always a general.

"Contact the Armenian Turk via the hotel concierge he mentioned, Paul, and meet with Francine. Alexandra, you will work with Paul."

"Let me know when you have established contact, Paul," Matthieu promptly followed up. "We will have the Delta Team provide surveillance and security. The techies will wire you and ideally install cameras so we can analyze Francine's responses and demeanour. If Francine becomes aware of our surveillance, she will not be surprised. As Alexandra suggested, Francine would do the same and expect the same."

"Having you collaborate on this case is the least I can do for interrupting your honeymoon!" Daan whispered to Alexandra and Paul in his customary light-hearted manner and with a sheepish chuckle. He was well aware of how cherished holiday time was, but emergencies usurp personal schedules.

"This will cost you another all-expenses-paid weekend in Liechtenstein," Alexandra replied with equal levity as she and Paul left Daan and Matthieu to debrief. As with all missions, they would debate the pros and cons of each scenario, particularly the contingencies and exit strategies. She had not met Rakici, the Armenian Turk, so would need to depend on Paul's assessment, however brief. They had both met Francine when working on a previous case but their engagement had been limited to across-the-table appraisals. Introductions had been brief and formal. Communications had been restricted to the formal exchange of business cards devoid of handshakes which would have provided the opportunity for reinforcement of tacit intuition, a strength that Alexandra had perfected as a forensic psychologist.

"Walk with me," Daan invited Matthieu. "I think better on my feet amid the hustle and bustle of morning traffic. We can grab a coffee at the kiosk on the way out."

Once on the sidewalk, Matthieu murmured to Daan. "When Paul suggested that we consider Francine as the centurion, you seemed a bit distant about his nomination." He let his observation hang as an open-ended question.

The impenetrable din of street-level commerce muffled his enquiry and would do the same for the ensuing response. Matthieu savoured the aroma as he sipped his cappuccino while awaiting Daan's reply. He too had been tutored in the richness of patience.

"I have full confidence in Paul's suggestion," Daan affirmed. "I thought that it was audacious but brilliant, typical Paul. That's why I hired him, in addition to his astute intellectual perspectives. My apologies if I gave you the wrong impression. I was debating whether we could also employ Francine to deactivate the Russian threat to the code. That would be a bonus. And now there is the wild card that has popped up on our radar: Rakici, the Armenian Turk, and his relationship with Francine."

⊣ ⊢

WITH A DISCRETE BOW, THE concierge acknowledged Paul's note addressed to Rakici requesting a meeting with Francine. The text was terse but to the point just like Rakici's initial introduction to Paul when running the Palermo marathon.

"I will ensure that your communiqué is passed along, *monsieur.*" The concierge appeared unfazed by the seemingly vagueness of Paul's request as if such actions were routine beyond Hollywood movie scripts of heroes and heroines, protagonists and antagonists leaving clandestine communiqués to arrange a romantic rendezvous.

Paul reflected on his mission in Sarajevo when he was employed by the United Nations Protection Force. He had worked alongside a Russian major who was also employed with the UNPROFOR. They were comrades in arms on this Balkans mission because their respective politicians had deemed it so. Yet barely five years before, they were pointing guns at each other across the Berlin Wall because their politicians had decided they were enemies.

This New World Order had caused a change in ethos on both sides, albeit a tenuous one. Enemies and Allies of both World Wars barely twenty years apart had hoisted military standards and alliances at the stroke of the political pen. In previous centuries, a royal marriage of convenience or a divorce could bring about violent wars lasting decades or fragile peace treaties spanning a few years. In the final analysis, it all boiled down to interpersonal relations. The Cold War had allowed for peace among former enemy agents from the East such as Francine and Rakici and from the West such as Alexandra and Paul. The foggy ground in between defined the nebulous landscape. Likewise, one could argue that France's loyalty to the ethos of the Western NATO Alliance under President Charles de Gaul's leadership was also hazy.

Today, there was room for additional shifting of alliances based on perceived common agendas. Paul concluded he had worked with a former enemy, a Russian major, in the Former Republic of Yugoslavia. Accordingly, he could now work with a former Russian enemy agent and her Armenian Turkish associate. In the immediate situation, they would be neither avowed enemies nor fervent friends, but simply associates working under the cloak of finding a possible solution to a thorny problem that, if unresolved, could result in continuing unfavourable results for all. It was in their mutual interest to work toward a common solution. When they first met at the Palermo marathon, Rakici had explained Francine's motivation to meet within that collaborative context. Paul was open.

CHAPTER 3

"The paradox of misfortune," Alexandra muttered. "Some die while others benefit from death. Both you and I have been recognized and advanced in our chosen careers on the heels of misfortune, the murders, or untimely deaths of others." *The obliqueness of death,* she mused.

"It's a function of living outside our normal lives, whatever normal is or was," said Paul in acknowledgement of the fact. As an only child growing up in Montigny-lès-Metz, "normal" meant a protected middle-class household with both parents at home for dinner. He was neither spoiled by being given anything that money could buy, nor did he want for anything either. Death was not a foreign concept. His father, being a police officer, spoke openly of his experience in dealing with all aspects of law enforcement including the seedier side of society. Both his parents encouraged a balanced discussion to ensure he would not remain too naïve. Nor would he be traumatized by constant news of social violence. As a result of the family environment, he gained a keen interest in science and a desire to learn about biochemistry as it applied to human health.

Death was seen as a normal part of life. Mortality resulting from violence, or what Alexandra referred to as the obliqueness of death, had its own norm. It might appear senseless to those who exhibited lower levels of emotional intelligence, yet logical to the scientific mind of the rational Mr. Spock from the television program *Star Trek.* Thus, Paul understood Alexandra's perspective. It wasn't that he was devoid of emotion. He knew about love and hate, happiness and sorrow. He'd had experience dealing with severe stress resulting from overwhelming emotional and physical trauma.

The paradox of misfortune was a reality for which everyone needed to take responsibility. His late wife, Suzette, made the choice to drive while impaired. His eldest son, Yvon, had drowned because of choices he had made while using and trafficking illegal drugs. They had both failed to consider the consequences of their reckless actions. In contrast, his younger son, Jean, had followed in Paul's footsteps and had become successful as a result.

Alexandra reflected on the disquiet that had assured her survival on occasions when heightened situational awareness was needed. She re-evaluated the knowns and, more importantly, the unknowns of their current mission, ever conscious of the intervening variables in this ominous environment. She sensed nothing that would cause her imminent concern but her *shrew*, her intuition, continued to remind her that invisible eyes were watching, and concealed ears were listening, in addition to instinctual senses scanning. On the eve of his being poisoned by an old KGB foe, their previous CIA associate, Tom Hunt, had encouraged both Alexandra and Paul to remember the imperative of situational awareness. Her intuition had never been wrong. It was only the misinterpretation of her intuition that left her in the lurch when she dismissed the subtle signals.

Her upbringing was different from Paul's in some respects although similar in other ways. She never knew her father as a child. She was raised by her aunt and uncle because her mother was constantly travelling as a French Counterintelligence agent. From a young age, she had learned to accept responsibility and appreciate the consequences of her decisions. A deep desire to understand how and why individuals made decisions had drawn her to the world of forensic psychology. She became an expert at understanding others, but less expert in analyzing the motivation for some of her own decisions.

When she had asked her mother what it was like to grow up in the shadow of the Second World War, she was advised sternly that she needed to remain close-lipped. Only later did she learn her mother and grandmother had been members of the French Resistance, the *Maquis*. "You simply did not talk about what went on back then," they had warned her on several occasions. The dutiful Alexandra never did talk about it until after her mother's funeral. Even then, she contemplated the paradox of misfortune as it related to death in the context of her mother's career, in addition to her own life.

In truth, Alexandra was a lioness, a natural protector of her pride. She had demonstrated proficiency as a predator who could track a common criminal, a serial killer, a demented sociopath, or a deviant terrorist. She was a woman of many disguises and equally of many personalities to be adopted as circumstances dictated. She took full responsibility for the consequences of those decisions, some of which had contributed to the end of her first marriage to André.

Paul had become aware of some of her masks but certainly not all. Other clandestine innuendos he might perceive but she would follow her mother's advice not to talk about such matters for safety's sake. There were unknown eyes scanning and prying ears ready to pilfer secrets.

"You're rubbing your amulet. Talk to me." Paul's voice was hardly more than a warm whisper. He had seen her on other occasions hovering in these cognitive spaces shrouded in the mist of enquiry. One characteristic of her personality he had learned to consider when engaging in conversation with her was patience. Her default mode was to ponder before expressing her thoughts.

"In the fullness of time," she said philosophically, "if you serve the system like Herr Blosch did, you are rewarded. He did well because he understood the depth and dimensions of fealty. He had faithfully served the corporate elite of the *Quer*. Together, all members and associates of this nefarious organization, including Herr

Blosch, had benefitted financially from their malicious exploits over millennia. In the past few decades, they had profited from the carnage of the Third Reich and its successor." Alexandra carefully gathered her thoughts. "Herr Blosch paid the ultimate price. What is next?"

"Our mandate is to gather intelligence," Paul reminded her. "Enforcement falls primarily to other agencies. Welcome to the New World Order where there are different rules for different circumstances. Your mother and her colleagues helped define the parameters of this ever-changing arena of the Cold War and how to manoeuvre within it. You and I, Francine and Rakici, and a host of other unknown players have inherited this toxic playground. Once in, there is no turning back. George Smiley, John le Carré's fictional career spy with the British Secret Intelligence Service, realized that truth after he attempted to retire. When called to account for past deeds, he realized that full retirement was beyond his reach. We entered with eyes wide open!"

"Let's look at the players and their methodology," Alexandra proposed. "The *Quer* learned to adapt and improvise, to strategically manoeuvre into known and emerging enclaves when it was to their advantage and, of necessity, to survive. They continue to adapt as circumstances dictate."

Paul agreed. "True. They had perfected the art and science of the chameleon and its distant venomous cousin the Komodo dragon, each adopting successful strategies, one more passive than the other but both successful, given their hostile environment."

"Another factor," Alexandra proposed solemnly, "was the driving ethos of the *Quer* and the Thousand-Year Reich which continues to amass extraordinary wealth, thereby ensuring an almost limitless capability to buy loyalty, tenuous as it may be. This equated to absolute influence and control. Everyone had a price in order to evade the ultimate consequence – untimely and often sudden death."

Paul added, "By chance and inheritance, we have acquired considerable prosperity. Regardless of whether you define it as clean or tainted, we are now in the crosshairs of someone's sniper rifle. There are always consequences!"

"Fair enough. What's our exit strategy?" Alexandra asked, not as a rhetorical question but a fundamental approach. "Like the *Quer,* are we able to retreat into unknown bastioned enclaves if circumstances warrant? There is a high probability that we will need such secluded sanctuaries sooner rather than later. Let's not forget Collette and Jean. As my daughter, Collette has inherited my world as I became part of my mother's world, without choice. And as your son, Jean cannot escape his father's exploits." With that pronouncement, Alexandra retreated into a dark solitude that Paul had witnessed on a few occasions. It was best to leave her to resolve it. His obligation was to stand sentinel.

While in these trances, she recited her mother's premonitions with the cautionary caveats, perhaps for reassurance that all would be resolved or as guidance that Alexandra would find the key: "Your roots are those of Charlemagne and your destiny is Merovingian. The truths of those times are masked in the mists of the Moselle. In them, you will discover your strengths and unearth the truths."

Paul pursed his lips and squinted into the distance, staring at nothing yet sensing a spiritual energy. "You are absolutely correct. There is a big difference between growing up within and inheriting an environment that had previously been foreign to you. What is your *shrew* suggesting?"

"There are a growing number of eyes upon us, some from the past, while others are current. Each has their own motivations and consequences. The immediate threat is twofold. The first is with

Baird Durand, the truant and final member of the *Quer*. We now know his name. What we don't know is the full extent of his potential for violence. We have to conclude he will live up to the venomous reputation of the *Quer*."

"No argument from me." Paul bowed in agreement. The paradox of both fortune and calamity, as Alexandra had prophesied, mandated constant surveillance or what he referred to as SA – situational awareness. It had kept him out of harm's way several times when serving with the United Nations Protection Force in Sarajevo and on the subsequent missions gathering evidence at scenes of war crimes.

"The second threat," Alexandra proposed, "has many heads like the mythical serpent, Hydra, whose lair was purported to be in the depths of Lake Lerna. The most prominent threat is the KGB. We know more about the old guard today but still not enough, because emphasis has shifted to its successor, the FSB. Some of these former adversaries are emerging as opportunist allies. We only have to look at Francine and Rakici, the Armenian Turk, gladiators with battle scars and honours in their own rights. We can only speculate about the extent to which they have been tested in the emerging post-Cold War arena. We do know they are survivors."

Paul nodded deliberately. "Not only just survivors but benefactors, due in part to their finely-tuned competencies in the tradecraft. I mentioned that Herr Blosch wasn't worried initially when we were taken hostage on the yacht because he was confident that senior members of the constabulary and governance, who were on the *Quer* payroll, would come to our rescue."

"And?" Alexandra's voice rose inquiringly. She sensed that what Paul was contemplating was one of these decision points that could have either a beneficial or disastrous outcome. What exit strategies would they need to develop?

"And as a vanguard, I think someone needs to make discrete

enquiries to find out if any of those members of the constabulary and governance, whose loyalty had been purchased by the *Quer*, could be convinced to transfer allegiance to the European Union Intelligence Unit. Their motivation would be to survive in their respective worlds that have mutated like a virulent virus. When you prostitute yourself for the almighty dollar, you abrogate your integrity, that ability to steadfastly adhere to moral standards. They have been bought once. They can be bought again. Their intelligence might offset the loss from Herr Blosch's unfortunate death."

"Are you suggesting that Francine would be the best resource to take on this task with or without Rakici?" Alexandra asked. "Best outcome – it would demonstrate the intent of their willingness to work with us as contractors. Worst case scenario – they warn the former financial benefactors of the *Quer* that the European Union Intelligence Unit is closing in on them. In addition, they inform the Kremlin. If the latter, they would fly their true colours not as disgruntled agents of Moscow but as still-active FSB agents."

"Best we find out sooner rather than later," Paul proposed. "If their intent is to defect, I surmise that Francine has greater finesse and diplomacy. In contrast, Rakici would attempt to manipulate his target. If unsuccessful, he might re-engage with guns blazing, so to speak. Either one would be perceived as being at arm's length of the EUI Unit if it backfired. Let's present this strategy to Daan."

Alexandra lingered, unsure of the optimal strategy. "We're missing something, but I don't know what. There's an unknown unknown. Invisible eyes are watching and less-than-plugged ears are listening."

CHAPTER 4

The concierge approached Paul. "A message for you, *monsieur*." Alexandra watched intently as he read.

"Rakici has suggested we meet in Thira later this evening. He'll have a mutual acquaintance with him," Paul noted in a tone that was both buoyant yet wary.

Matthieu's cell boogied across the table with the vibrations of the incoming message. "Meeting with our target after dinner in Thira. Exact location TBA. Need to be wired," Paul's text read.

Paul had complete confidence in Alexandra's proven ability to take the initiative with no prior notice and under the most stressful conditions. In the previous Thon case, she had manipulated Thon into revealing a fatal flaw in his sociopathic personality and *modus operandi*. That encounter ultimately ended Thon's murderous rampage at the hands of one of his supposed loyal Fourth Reich soldiers who, at the last minute, moved his pistol away from Alexandra to point it at Thon and end his life with one carefully aimed bullet to his head.

Through personal experience and lessons taught by her mother, a seasoned French Counterintelligence agent, Alexandra had become acutely aware that in the duplicitous world of espionage and intelligence, nothing exists in the absence of context. More importantly, intelligence and context could be misaligned when there were truths, partial truths, and make-believe truths.

Today, she sensed Francine was not motivated to harm either her or Paul. On the contrary, both she and Paul had been cordial when they first met despite their initial misgivings. In addition, they had been respectful and non-judgemental toward Capitaine

Dominique Roland of the Police nationale, Francine's intimate partner. Alexandra concluded that Francine having already been the target of a Moscow assassin, wounded, and now a possible defector, the probability of her having malicious intent was very low.

If there was a wild card, it would be Rakici, the Armenian Turk. He had contacted Paul at the Palermo marathon supposedly at Francine's behest. Now, he had set up this secret meeting. But who might be compensating him? A more pressing concern was whether they were providing backup to each other or had an independent set of eyes watching.

The most likely threat would come from a Moscow agent who might be tailing Francine to identify anyone meeting with her. Alternately, any threat could be another foreign agent, possibly Chinese, or private entrepreneur contracted to assassinate Francine and anyone associated with her including Rakici, Alexandra and Paul. In anticipation of the latter possibility, Daan had dispatched the EUI Delta Team as a protection force.

On a positive note, Francine had requested the meeting on the pretext that there could be mutual benefits in warming East/West relations and working as allies rather than enemies. Accordingly, Alexandra expected Francine to provide most of the conversation this evening with Rakici supporting her. If they switched roles as a strategy, Alexandra would continue to direct her enquiries to Francine. She needed to assess Francine's intent and integrity. As planned, she would leave the dialogue with Rakici to Paul, who would follow up on their initial brief encounter at the Palermo marathon.

What might Francine be thinking in anticipation of the impending meeting? Alexandra pondered. She anticipated that the persona on the other side of the table was an integral part of that planning process. She would rely on her intuition, her *shrew*. FSB agents had been taught to respond to interrogation by deflecting and lying convincingly when necessary. Alexandra would lean on her *shrew* to differentiate between what was closer to the truth, the partial truth and anything but the truth. She would rehearse equally for all scenarios.

At dinner, Paul and Alexandra discussed the probability of each of the unknowns. They then confirmed with Daan the presence of the EUI Unit Delta Force Protection Team.

Only at the last minute did Rakici confirm the location of the café where they would rendezvous. It was not the best-case scenario for the Delta Team, which had to scramble.

"I don't like it," Paul whispered to Alexandra. "They seem to have stacked the deck in their favour. We will have more agents, but one well-aimed bullet will quickly negate any numeric advantage. Thoughts?"

"Two possibilities. First, Francine and Rakici are being extra cautious in order to protect Francine. Second, they are testing our resources. Either way, they are nervous. But why? They have to anticipate that we will be anxious as a result."

Matthieu reassured Daan. "I have dispatched the 'ladies distraction members' of the Delta Force to escort Alexandra and Paul from dinner to the rendezvous café due to the increased level of uncertainty surrounding the meeting. These ladies will have the additional fire power with Uzi semi-automatic weapons hidden in their satchels in the event a major assault needs to be countered quickly."

"Good call," Daan confirmed. "At this crucial stage in the mission, neither Alexandra nor Paul could be replaced." *If both were killed, we would be back to square one. If either or both were killed, Yolina Lambert at the EU Commission in Brussels would be looking for a new leader to replace me,* Daan pondered. He had lost one too many agents on previous intelligence gathering missions and never fully recovered from the resulting sleepless nights or relentless nightmares. From experience, he knew that no amount of alcohol, regardless of its quality, could quell the debilitating flashbacks.

CHAPTER 5

"Francine, it has been a while since we sat across the table from each other. I would not have recognized you had it not been for your associate," Paul stated.

As discussed with Paul, Alexandra maintained eye contact with Francine with a polite glance to acknowledge her Armenian Turkish associate. Paul did the opposite. Neither couple appeared distracted by the existence of collegial backup.

"That it has," replied Francine. "A lot of turbulent water has passed under the bridge for all of us since Paris. I am indebted to you both for the respect and kindness you extended to Capitaine Dominique Roland. As you are aware, Dominique and I had both a professional and personal relationship."

"Different times. Similar affiliations. Different employers. Similar missions," Alexandra commented. "Your colleague, Rakici, mentioned to Paul that there may be mutual benefit from a renewed association. We are intrigued by your proposition."

Francine bowed in acknowledgement. "Yusuf and I go back many years. Suffice it to say, we have had a camouflaged working relationship but have enjoyed and benefitted from an informal supportive alliance."

Her deportment was relaxed, in contrast to when they had met at the initial briefing regarding the Thon case, which Dominique had organized in Commandant Parent's office at the Police nationale headquarters in Paris. Curiously, she seemed less perturbed by the formal gathering of those associated with the Thon investigation than she appeared today. Perhaps being wounded and then hidden in a series of safe houses during her recovery continued to weigh heavily on her mind.

Francine would not have ventured too far, certainly not to locations like Santorini where foreign eyes would be trawling through albums of memories of faces and body profiles they might have once seen but in a different context. Francine, no doubt, would do the same, despite all efforts to excise herself from the identity of her past with disguises and pseudonyms.

Alexandra smiled subtly and splayed her fingers upward with a gesture of measured openness. Although Francine maintained direct eye contact, she was conscious of Alexandra's affable body language. Francine reciprocated, while at the same time visually frisking both Alexandra and Paul for the threat of weapons. Her own scant evening attire revealed she was not concealing anything. She and Yusuf had arrived first, so neither Alexandra nor Paul could be sure that there were no weapons hidden out of sight under the table or beneath their chairs. It came down to trust factors which were veneer-thin.

"It's probably no surprise to you to learn that I have parted ways with my previous employer because they were complicit in Dominique's murder and my attempted murder. Hence, my change in appearance and loyalties. Betrayal is a fact of life in our trade but unforgiveable perfidy when you become a collegial target. Yusuf was there for me when no one else was. Some of your colleagues, I might add, provided me with a safe haven and support during my extended period of convalescence. For that gesture, I am eternally grateful."

"I grew up close to Moulins-lès-Metz where you were ambushed," Paul commented, all the while seeking Francine's perspective on the incident that left Dominique and one other dead, and Francine critically injured. He was watching Francine as much as Yusuf in an effort to assess their respective physiological responses. There was none, which was more telling than if either had reacted.

"It seems ironic that the assassin was perched behind the concrete fence and under the partial camouflaged shade of the weeping willow tree in the front yard of the residence that had once been occupied by the Nazi Commandant for the Moselle Valley District during the German occupation approximately sixty years ago," Francine replied.

Paul acknowledged her historical commentary with a brief nod, sensing that Francine was testing his familiarity with the background knowledge of the neighbourhood. He too was well versed in the art of repartee in an engaging tennis match of communiqués. The ball had changed courts.

Injecting questions into this routine ritual banter that tended to prompt dialogue among former adversaries and now possible allies, Alexandra got straight to the point.

"Where was the leak, Francine? Who knew you would be accompanying Dominique? Who knew about the third person in your car, Rudolf Heydrich? Who set you up and why? Was this an FSB assassination directive or an old KGB vendetta?"

"I'm not exactly sure," Francine admitted willingly. "Just before our departure from Paris, I met with my Russian handler. I had mentioned that I was accompanying Dominique at her request. I did not mention Rudolf because I didn't know anything about him, not even his name, or that he would be with us. It was at this meeting that I first got the sense my handler might have been holding back on me. But I could be wrong. He was oddly vague yet clearly aware of my intimate relationship with Dominique because he had directed me to engage with her. He had previously mentioned that the directive for this intimate liaison had come from our Moscow employer. In retrospect, I'm not sure the communiqué had come from the Kremlin."

"I'm curious. Why did Dominique ask you to accompany her?" Alexandra pressed.

Francine had correctly anticipated all the questions Alexandra had asked thus far. Her rehearsed answers were easy because they had been based on facts, not on fiction. "I don't know why," Francine replied in a neutral yet forthright voice.

"Did you ask her? Did you find her request suspicious?"

"In response to your first question, no. She had asked me to accompany her on other occasions before… asked me for my opinion. I didn't think her request was out of the ordinary, given our professional and personal relationship."

Alexandra maintained her muted, enquiring pose. In the silence lay the questions anticipated but not yet asked and the answers yet to be composed but not yet provided.

"I conclude that the leak was not within my immediate FSB realm, but I can't speak for former KGB colleagues. I don't believe Dominique was the joker in the pack either. I can't say the same for others in Dominique's policing house. My sources suggested there was a confederate in the French Intelligence network who was possibly working for a third party."

Francine's demeanour had not changed throughout her responses. She was a professional spy and a survivor of over twenty years in the tradecraft. Alexandra would have been both surprised and suspicious had she demonstrated any indication of stress.

"Could it have been Rudolf? Could he have been bugged by a third party?" Alexandra continued. Negative responses from Francine to her questions shortened the list of possible confederates.

"I've replayed this tape over and over. I just don't know." Francine was as forthright in her response as she had been to Alexandra's initial questions. "That is what bothers me the most. As I said, I wasn't aware of Rudolf before we left Paris. I only got to know a little about him from conversations en route to Moulins-lès-Metz."

"Was this an FSB operation?" Alexandra repeated.

Francine took an unhurried breath.

"I doubt it. They had too much invested in me. Until this incident, I had no serious intention of switching sides, although I admit the thought had crossed my mind on more than one occasion. If they had suspicions or proof, I would have been assigned to a new handler. Their policy would have been to turn me into a double agent, not kill me."

"So, what, then?" Alexandra probed. "What's missing in this equation?"

"I just don't know," Francine replied earnestly. "Not being in the know is fatal in the world of espionage." Her frustration was obvious. Her reaction was palpable. Her reply was straightforward.

The ball was back in Alexandra's court. She carefully considered her next move.

"As you may recall, I am a forensic psychologist. With your consent, I would like to hypnotise you to ascertain if you can recall any other details that might shed light on this incident."

Francine dwelled briefly on this request. She had undergone hypnosis as part of her training with the KGB in addition to sodium pentothal truth serum. Accordingly, Alexandra's request did not faze her. Further, she did not know any more than she had already related.

"Only if Yusuf is present. At this juncture, he is the only person I trust. I'm sure that you can appreciate my position. My life, perhaps all our lives, are in the crosshairs right now. Although Yusuf and I have been very careful to ensure we were not followed here this evening, there is always a possibility. This is why we did not tell you earlier of the exact location and time. We hope that it did not cause you undue inconvenience or anxiety."

Paul read Alexandra's request for endorsement as she rubbed her amulet. He slowed his breathing while nodding almost imperceptibly to signal his support of the path she had chosen to take.

"That's agreeable, Francine. Your compliance to undergo hypnosis will go a long way towards developing a trusting relationship with mutual benefit. I'm sure you can appreciate our position."

When pursuing other interviews with criminals, the suggestion of hypnosis tended to produce one of two responses. One was rejection, usually immediate, which suggested guilt or something to hide. The other was acceptance because the subject had nothing to hide or because they believed they were smarter than the hypnotist. Perhaps Francine had both nothing to hide and, through her own training as a Russian spy, was confident she could outwit Alexandra. Either way, information derived under hypnosis would add to the growing body of intelligence or, possibly, evidence.

Alexandra's primary motivation was to test the truthfulness of Francine's suggestion that working together could lead to mutual benefit after a reasonable level of confidence had been established. Only Alexandra would be able to make that assessment and only after thorough analysis of the explicit: the facts, and the intuitive exploration of the implicit, her sensation of the mind – her *shrew*.

Alexandra thought about her own training to become a forensic psychologist. On those occasions when she had been experiencing one of her sensations of the mind, a male colleague often quoted Joe Friday, the lead character in the American TV police detective series, *Dragnet* – "Give me the facts, ma'am, just the facts."

Alexandra knew that facts were essential and were derived from the science, but how you got the facts was a combination of both the science and the sensations of the mind. The latter, she knew, was wisdom older than consciousness itself.

This would not be the first time Francine had undergone hypnotism. The first time she was alone. She wasn't wholly certain of what Alexandra wanted. Was it to test her genuineness or her willingness to comply with requests, orders? Growing up in the USSR, her psyche was constantly fraught with suspicion and, as a result, tension. There was a dearth of collegial trust during basic training to become a KGB agent. Other cadets spied on you and you on them. Only the best cadets were chosen to advance. Success came from trusting only yourself; everyone else was your enemy. There would be only you in the field, no one else.

Yusuf seemed different somehow, as Dominique had been. Francine had developed trusting relationships with both. There was not only collegial confidence but personal trust that had been tested and found to be true. And now there was the duo of Alexandra and Paul. Francine understood Alexandra's motivation to hypnotize her in an attempt to find any lingering links or deep-seated clues regarding the ambush at Moulins-lès-Metz. When they first met, Alexandra had been collegial but understandably cautious. The wariness was mutual. But Francine had not picked up on any deceitfulness regarding Alexandra's intent. Nor had she sensed any deception in Paul's demeanour.

In a way, Francine envied Alexandra and Paul for their apparent mutual love and unquestioning devotion to each other, the way they subtly touched and naturally held hands. She had read about such relationships in Western romance novels but chalked it up to propaganda to get Moscow agents to let down their guard.

Then there was her affiliation with Dominique. Initially, she was following orders to engage in an intimate relationship in order to increase accessibility to intelligence. That was consistent with her advanced training as a Red Sparrow. There was to be no emotion. Instead, simply a means to an end in the game of espionage, spy-on-spy. But even then, as with her growing relationship with Yusuf, she was constantly vigilant, always looking over her shoulder. Was it love she felt for both Dominique and Yusuf? Or were her emotions driven by fear? Fear of failure? Fear of being alone? Fear of being found out by her superiors or her handler? Devotion based on love, like Alexandra and Paul had, was different, without overtones of fear and distrust. She yearned for that love, which made her both vulnerable for wanting something she did not have but sought, and secure knowing she had lived without it for all those years. Hence, she didn't need it.

Had her handler noted this change and concluded she had already gone rogue? He had set her up to be assassinated as a result. The prey had now become the predator driven by the emotion of revenge. She would now have him in her crosshairs for being a co-conspirator in the ambush that resulted in Dominique's death and her attempted assassination.

Gaining mutual trust with Alexandra and Paul, even in the company of Yusuf, would be virgin ground for her to navigate. She felt confident thus far in their burgeoning relationship. Yusuf also seemed relatively comfortable. They would exchange thoughts after this rendezvous, the sole purpose of which was to test the waters. She was certain other former colleagues would have experienced similar misgivings and apprehension during the initial stages of defection.

CHAPTER 6

"Thoughts on this first interview with Francine and the subsequent hypnosis session?" Daan enquired.

"Francine was understandably cautious when we first met," Alexandra stated. "I got the sense she was being honest with her intentions and responses to my questions. The forensic hypnosis session revealed no new facts or deviation from her earlier recollections. She seemed sincerely bothered that she did not know all the facts, why they had been ambushed, or why she had been intentionally targeted."

"And Yusuf? What is your sense of his part? Is this Armenian Turk, codename Rakici, a wild card?"

"Francine referred to him only as Yusuf. We should do the same. No doubt, Yusuf is a prominent planet in Francine's orbit. I do not believe he is her handler or controls her in a technical way. But there is a delicate influence and Francine draws on his strength. We need to be cautious with him. They certainly appear to be a team as much as Paul and I are. If we ask Francine to become the centurion, we are also inviting Yusuf. That is just a given."

"You don't seem to be completely confident," Daan commented.

"That's because I'm not. I just can't put my finger on it. Perhaps it's because I haven't known Yusuf very long. I know more about him second hand. Unlike Paul, I hadn't even met him before. So, I didn't have a sense one way or the other. I'd prefer to be careful, for now." Alexandra held Daan's gaze all the while, maintaining an introspective reflection.

"Caution taken," Daan conceded.

"And, Paul, your thoughts?" Daan followed up.

"Francine's motivation is not wholly mercenary although she ardently wants to find Dominique's killer, and to ensure that justice is served, ideally in her style. But revenge is just one of several recruiting criteria for external centurions. Ideology is another, as we have briefly discussed. I am convinced she has abandoned communism in favour of the personal lifestyle benefits of Western democracy. A third recruiting criterion is ego, which can be closely tied to revenge. Her ego is not so large that it could become a shortcoming."

Daan nodded slowly but with judicious deliberation. Extending Francine an invitation to become an external contracted centurion was a major deviation from established recruiting policy and subsequent protocol for the European Union Intelligence Unit. There was no room for error.

"The final criterion is financial," Paul added. "That is an unknown. Unless Francine had a second lucrative income source and an offshore bank account, we may assume that her previous employer was not overly generous with a compensation severance package replete with additional unspecified retirement benefits."

Daan probed for a recommendation. "So, you are in favour of recruiting her?"

"Yes, but let me cover one last very important factor," Paul replied. "The capture of Baird Durand is another crucial variable. If we can convince Francine that Baird and Dominique's killer are somehow linked, perhaps one and the same, I'm cautiously confident that she will be loyal to our mission. Caution remains an overarching factor. If we tell Francine that Baird did kill Dominique and she finds out that he did not, we run the risk of losing our credibility with her. We need to ask ourselves – is a future relationship with her important, perhaps even critical? And as for the flipside of that coin, would she turn on us and, in doing so, turn Yusuf against us if she concludes we deceived her intentionally? Our challenge will be to keep Baird Durand as her number one priority. Following that train of thought, if Francine finds Dominique's killer first, and it isn't Baird, I'm not certain we will be able to hold her as we pursue the hunt for Baird. Her strongest motivator at this juncture is revenge."

Daan probed for reassurance. "Is Yusuf a wild card?"

"Employing the same recruiting criteria, we need to find out more about his background before I can speculate with greater confidence," Paul replied. "We do know that Turkish Military Intelligence encourages Spartan habits. Yusuf is the opposite. He has a discriminating appetite for comfort and luxury, the latter including the finest French cuisine and wine that are infrequently served to the rank and file even in Ankara. That was supposedly a motivation for him to leave their employment if, in fact, he has left their employment. It would be reassuring if our intelligence could be verified by someone senior within Turkish Military Intelligence, or a confidant in Moscow."

"You seem hesitant, also," Daan commented.

"I am. Like Alexandra, I have a sense that there is more to Yusuf than meets the eye. He seems to be loyal to Francine. But his loyalty to her appears to be a bit contrived at times, maybe insincere, perhaps manipulative, as if he is using her to get at something else. Perhaps it's cultural and I have erred in this assessment. But I'm thinking we need to be wary until we have a better grasp of his personality, motivation and loyalties."

"Point taken and I acknowledge your concern about the unknown," Daan said. "We need to mitigate that as a risk-management strategy. If he does have an ulterior motive, how should we use him?"

"As long as we can keep Francine focused and content, he could be a strong ally. If anything happened to her there is a high probability that Yusuf would become a loose cannon on the deck, a definite liability. Ultimately, we need to keep Francine happy and healthy, and focused on finding Baird. We accomplish that by ensuring she believes Baird is linked directly to Dominique's death. He might not have pulled the trigger but he hired the assassin who did. That has to be the *raison d'être* of our mission."

"You seem quiet, Alexandra. Something bothering you?" Daan commented, having scrutinized her reserved reaction to Paul's assessment of Yusuf.

She paused to ponder the potential implications before responding to his baited observation.

"Why had Dominique invited Francine to accompany her and Rudolf to Moulins-lès-Metz knowing that Francine was a Russian agent? What was her motive? Dominique had hidden Rudolf in a safe house, hidden him from enemy agents who desperately wanted to learn what Rudolf knew about stolen Nazi gold and other treasures. It doesn't make sense. With Dominique now dead, we may never know. Like Herr Blosch, her knowledge has gone with her to the grave."

"Good question," Daan replied. "Dominique knew Francine was an FSB agent. She was attempting to cultivate her as a double agent."

"When I asked Francine why Dominique had invited her to accompany them to Moulins-lès-Metz, Francine said she didn't know. She added that it wasn't uncommon for Dominique to invite her on other occasions."

"Curious," Daan commented. "I had an in-depth conversation with Commandant Parent after the Moulins-lès-Metz ambush. He indicated that Dominique believed Francine was close to becoming a double agent for the French. Perhaps this was an acid test of Francine's honesty from Dominique's perspective." Daan continued to ponder before transferring his attention to Matthieu. "Comments, bearing in mind Alexandra's last point?"

With Daan's consent, Matthieu had dispatched the female members of the Delta Force to clandestinely accompany Alexandra and Paul to the café where additional members of the Delta Team had established a perimeter security. Had that heightened level of safety been necessary or had they over-reacted? Nothing had happened, perhaps because a potential assassin had become aware of the Delta Team presence and the fire power that might have been unleashed. Had this suspected shooter decided to withdraw? As Alexandra correctly assessed – *"Reculer pour mieux sauter"* – *we need to step back in order to take up a more strategic position from which we may re-engage.* Better to be safe than sorry. The consequence of any threat at this juncture outweighed the costs, monetarily and physically.

"It will be a delicate balance to maintain, as you suggest, but I'm confident Francine could be our centurion," Matthieu commented. "In response to your question, Yusuf remains the wild card. I agree with Alexandra and Paul. We need to be cautious. If we divulge information to Francine, it is a given that Yusuf will know about it, and vice versa. We need a strategy to manage the unknowns, particularly Dominique's motivation for inviting Francine to accompany her and Rudolf to Moulins-lès-Metz. It's another unknown, which could be a stepping-stone or a landmine."

"Recommendation?" Daan invited.

Matthieu replied without hesitation. "Francine and Yusuf might relate to Alexandra and Paul because of their partner loyalty, regardless of our uncertainty about Yusuf's sincerity and motivation, and Dominique's perplexing invitation to Francine to accompany her and Rudolf to Moulins-lès-Metz. My suggestion would be to have Alexandra and Paul, as a couple, engage with Francine and Yusuf, as a couple. It would be an even match, one-on-one. In the interim, we find out as much as we can about Yusuf."

Daan eyed his colleagues. "Thank you, good conversation.

We have two priorities. First and foremost is the capture of Baird Durand as the final truant member of the *Quer*. If he dies in the process, so be it. The second goal is to identify and neutralize the threat to Maria's code. Mounting intelligence suggests that this latter threat is more than likely linked to the old KGB, Moscow-related but not necessarily Moscow-directed. We cannot assume that FSB agents are completely blind to its existence. They just have new-school priorities for the simple reason some in their ranks do not want to be perceived by their superiors as old-school. As a result, they may be privately tracking ex-KGB entrepreneurs operating primarily in Western Europe with self-interest or perhaps a mercenary purpose. Else, they would have eliminated them by now."

There was a consensus.

Daan chose his words carefully. "Alexandra and Paul, contact Francine and Yusuf, as a team. Do not mention Maria's code or even acknowledge any enquiries from Francine or Yusuf, or anyone else for that matter, regarding its existence. Instead, give Francine support to find Dominique's killer. Emphasize to Francine that there is a high probability Baird and Dominique's assassin are one and the same, or at least linked. Remain vigilant for the omnipresent unknown."

Matthieu added, "While the two of you are working with Francine and Yusuf, we will be tracking the sons of the current members of the *Quer* as possible beneficiaries. Membership has passed down from father to son since its inception. Once these sons realize their fathers are missing, a new and perhaps more menacing breed of *Quer* leaders may quickly rise from the ashes like a phoenix."

"Or like Hydra out of Lake Lerna with seven new heads already in place," Paul proposed. "The eighth head being a master financial controller like Herr Blosch. As an afterthought, the eighth could be a foreign master spy, either of KGB or FSB vintage, or other foreign persuasion including Chinese."

In all the cases Daan had worked on as Director of the European Union Intelligence Unit, this one held the most unknowns with the greatest potential consequences. For these interdependent reasons, his anxiety was elevated. He had complete confidence in Matthieu, Alexandra, Paul and others on the European Union Intelligence team, to respond to intervening variables operating in their environment. It was the possibility of unknown unknowns fracturing the trajectory of their mission that posed the greatest threat.

In the past decade, there had been a noticeable increase in the means and methodology of threats to the economic and political stability in the European Union. Most traditional threats had been internal, which made intelligence gathering easier. Additional resources and budgets had been granted to its charter by the European Union Commission following the increase in the breadth and complexity of the threats and a strategic sense of other hazards perceived but not yet seen on the horizon.

With growing frequency, external threats, especially cyber, had originated primarily in rogue and otherwise emerging nation states on the African continent whose own internal stability was fragile as a result of the disruptive interventions by Russia and China. Both were vying for access to material and human intelligence resources. Today, the Chinese commanded the single largest footprint, predominantly in the eastern half of the African continent. Shipping resources to and from Chinese ports was a relatively efficient process. From east coast ports like Mogadishu, the Suez Canal provided unencumbered access to nation states bordering the Mediterranean including current members of the European Union in addition to others striving to become members, like Turkey. The purpose of the supposed Chinese trade intent was suspicious.

Since the end of the Cold War, which had not ended but had

only morphed, Russia had modified its focus of influence away from some West and North African regions to the Middle East. Their renewed funding had been directed toward terrorist groups who willingly filled the gap left by retreating Russian military forces. Covertly compensating others to do your dirty work deflected ownership and accountability. This was not a new strategy for either side in the Cold War but one often employed at that time. Old wine, new wine skin.

The motivation for funding these terrorist groups correlated with the designation by Middle East Islamic States of foreign populations to become de facto infidels. Not surprisingly, most were previous Cold War enemies of the former Soviet Bloc. Your enemy's enemy is your friend. There were increasing numbers of fast guns for hire, so to speak, many with sophisticated lethal armaments delivered via long-range highly complex unmanned aerial platforms. The two-dimensional predominantly bullet and bomb battlefield was now a multi-dimensional virtually unseen cyber battlespace. All combatants had rules ranging from no rules to flexible rules determined by everchanging circumstances. Some combatants wore uniforms. Others employed uniforms as decoys. Some traditional allies in arms had been retained while others transitioned into temporary allies of convenience. Ultimately, security was what you made for yourself.

Employing Francine and Yusuf as centurions like contractors fell within the soft definition of allies of convenience. Their motivation was to carve out a niche in this rapidly evolving and technically sophisticated New World Order. The probability of them becoming permanent members of the European Union Intelligence Unit remained infinitely remote. That reality did not preclude them from morphing from temporary allies of convenience to a more long-lasting status not yet defined. Miscalculation at any juncture could change that tenuous prospect.

CHAPTER 7

It took twenty-three minutes to run under the light of a full moon on a bearing of 267 degrees from the Desert Springs Interrogation Facility that put him at the rendezvous point. There, he signalled for the pre-arranged pickup.

By the time the security patrol found his body, the cold of the desert night was being replaced by a rapid rise in the morning mercury. A death adder quickly slid away in search of another temporary shelter from the blistering heat when the body was turned over. Part of the head and upper torso had been torn from their natural positions when a 30-calibre sniper round found its mark.

"It was a professional military-style mission," Daan advised. "A Soviet Makarov PB 9mm pistol with sound suppressor was found close by. Four rounds remained in the standard 8-round clip. A second empty clip was found in the hip pocket of the deceased's camouflaged trousers. Each of the five incarcerated members of the *Quer* was found assassinated in their respective cell, two rounds in the head of each, double tap. In addition, one guard was found sprawled at a side exit door to the facility. He too had two bullets in his head. Preliminary investigation revealed a recent twenty-thousand-dollar deposit in a second private bank account of the guard. An analysis of his cell phone records discovered recent calls linked to a throw-away cell phone with a South-East Asian service provider."

"Where is the leak?" Alexandra asked, shaking her head in mounting exasperation. "Is it the same leak that resulted in Dominique and Rudolf being murdered and Francine being seriously wounded?"

"We don't know yet," Daan confessed with equal frustration. "But Francine needs to be made aware for her protection and her motivation to find Baird Durand soonest." Daan assumed nothing. Instead, he considered all scenarios and what impact a security breach of this magnitude could have on all aspects of their current mission. If he could be confident of anything, it was that the leak did not come from within the European Union Intelligence Unit. Regardless, he would review every decision point taken since they had broken through the previously impenetrable bastions of the *Quer*.

"It begs the question," Matthew proposed, "that if Baird Durand set up this hit, why? What does he have to gain by having the other members of the *Quer* dead? By tradition, sons of the now-deceased members replace their fathers. Although Baird would be the senior member, he might not be guaranteed the luxury of what had traditionally been the senior status of a long-serving member. If I was one of the new junior members, I would suspect Baird as being responsible for my father's death and, as a result, I would rally the other junior members to vote against Baird." After a brief meditative breather, Matthieu summarized, "The silence of the deceased? If someone else is responsible, what do they have to gain? Is Baird Durand now top on their hit list for an assassin's bullet?"

Daan focused on Alexandra and Paul. "You have your marching orders. One other point. Yes, ask Francine to judiciously approach potential members of the constabulary and governance whom she believes may have been on the payroll of the *Quer*. Ask her to try to determine whether they might be willing to transfer allegiance to the European Union Intelligence Unit."

The Desert Springs Interrogation Facility was not the only location established to house those whose intent was to disrupt peaceful commerce and global stability. However, it was one of the most remote and least accessible facilities. Clearly, it was not remote enough and certainly not completely inaccessible to someone whose mission was to penetrate its bastions. Its security had been ruptured. A subsequent investigation would be undertaken immediately if for no other reason than to protect other guests.

Just as the European Union Intelligence Unit had been created to counter threats against the economic and political stability of the EU, other organizations had been tasked with similar mandates. Investigation into this breach would be undertaken starting at the executive level.

The 27 member states of the European Union accounted for an approximate population of 425 million, an economic force that, if violated, could destabilize the global economy. As the head of the European Union Intelligence Unit, Daan's operation would fall under scrutiny as an integral part of the global security network. A threat to one was a threat to all.

Matthieu had recently been seconded to lead an investigation into a similar breach of universal security in another facility. Daan had a feeling Matthieu would be called upon again to head this investigation. On that previous occasion, he had been teamed up with Davana Kaur from an Australian and New Zealand Intelligence Unit colloquially referred to as the Thin Red Line, a throwback to the British Empire because of its worldwide network like the Five Eyes, but in this instance, less the United States.

As an intelligence agent, Matthieu had nothing but praise for Davana's superior intellect. She had an uncanny investigative ability and, like Alexandra, she had a prodigious memory that allowed her to complete cognitive and mathematical gymnastics at an Olympic Gold standard. That was where the similarities ended. Although slight in stature, Davana was feisty in nature. She was an avenger who worked best alone in the Black World, off the grid to most, like a stealthy nuclear submarine. She kept in regular contact and only surfaced once she had achieved mission success.

In contrast, Matthieu operated above the surface and worked best collaboratively.

At one point, their professional status had crossed the border into a more personal relationship. Both realized that an intimate rapport adversely affected their individual strengths so they stepped back. Yet, Matthieu always remembered the perfume she wore which was derived from oil of the davana herbal plant common to Southern India and used as an antidote for an unbalanced day. The assassination of the *Quer* detainees in the Desert Springs Interrogation Facility had certainly contributed to his unbalanced days as it had done to all his EUI Unit colleagues. Matthieu surmised that Davana and Alexandra together could be a formidable force for problem solving. He would propose the option to Daan next time they spoke.

For now, Matthieu's mind was focused on any possible link between Baird Durand and his current mission to identify the source of the breach in security of the Desert Springs Interrogation Facility.

Concurrently, Baird was not aware that Claude Etien Marchand was not one of the deceased *Quer* detainees. There were only five detainees in reality. Claude Etien Marchand, the truant member of the *Quer*, was a creation of the EUI Unit. He had been impersonated by one of the EUI Unit agents responsible for the capture and incarceration of Baird's colleagues. But for the grace of God and his astute observation through the window on the port side of the yacht, Baird would have been in an unmarked desert grave with his *Quer* colleagues, the guard from the Desert Springs Interrogation Facility, and their assassin. Baird was unaware that Matthieu and Davana were only steps away from him and days away from successfully completing their mission: identifying the source of the breach in security at the Desert Springs Interrogation Facility.

The *Quer* with its seven members served as a de facto Board of

Governors for central banks in major global monetary institutions like cabals influencing from the shadows. Since its conception, the *Quer* had evaded detection by all manner of incursion, most recently the European Union Intelligence Unit and its international intelligence gathering affiliates.

As the lone evader of EUIT's ambush, Baird Durand no doubt surmised that the privilege to operate unencumbered had not yet run its course, unlike the life of the assassin whose lifeless body had been discovered at a compass bearing of 267 degrees from the Desert Springs Interrogation Facility. Baird's inability to communicate with his colleagues and the Teutonic banker in Geneva was merely an anomaly to be resolved.

CHAPTER 8

His cellphone vibrated with an incoming message. Baird smiled inwardly. *One less item on my to-do list with my fellow Quer colleagues and the Teutonic banker,* he mused. Yet access to primary bank accounts had been mysteriously denied! It was imperative he re-establish immediate access to funds.

Only a few of the Wewelsburg Castle associates returned his cryptic e-communiqués. Their responses, from obscure hunting lodges hidden from view in Bavaria and the Black Forest region, were clipped and guarded. Images of his hooded *Quer* colleagues face down on the plush carpet of the yacht stateroom and his harrowing escape had forced him into temporary hiding. For now, he would gaze out the window of his covert retreat at the Grande Île in Strasbourg's historic city centre, the de facto capital of the European Union Parliament. Ironically, that parliament had been a principal focus of the *Quer*, an easy prey with a select few key senior officials on the payroll. But they would soon be enquiring about their monthly stipends. He would need both answers and access to funds in order to retain their tenuous loyalty.

Thus far, all his efforts to contact Herr Blosch at his place of work and at his secluded residence had been unsuccessful. The bank merely stated that Herr Blosch was on a medical leave of absence. That was highly irregular. He had never taken a sick day in his working career. But it was not improbable for a man of senior years. He lived alone and told no one of his address, not even senior members of the *Quer*. No doubt Herr Blosch would re-establish contact after his period of convalescence. Baird wasn't paranoid, just very careful to protect his identity. More worrying was the absence of corroborating communication from his confidential sources in the senior ranks of the Fourth Reich.

Baird thought about his dwindling list of options. *This might mean having to travel to Geneva and to the bank. I would have to leave the protection of my ancestral lair overlooking the southern fortification tower across the Ponts Couverts that has become my secluded yet secure base of operations.*

The triple threat of having no immediate access to funds, having minimal e-communications with colleagues, and having to con-template stepping outside the sanctuary of his house caused his acid reflux to become hyperactive. He was reluctant to have his doctor call in a renewal prescription to the pharmacy because that would leave an e-trail of Hansel and Gretel crumbs. He supposed he could have his family physician write out a prescription in his daughter's name. But that deviation could, in itself, raise flags. He could just purchase over-the-counter non-prescription antacid med-ication. Not changing from his routine, especially under abnormal circumstances, had been his default mode for assuring anonymity.

He re-evaluated the worse-case scenarios. The underground tunnel connecting his Bavarian-style abode to the turreted southern tower remained intact should emergency egress by land be neces-sary. Access to the middle and north towers had since been denied due to flooding. That meant he would have to leave the south tower by the ground-level access door which would expose him to public view.

The secondary backup escape route to the river and the speed boat secured alongside the concealed miniature wharf remained an alternative. Since childhood, he suffered from aquaphobia as a result of almost drowning in a pond on his family farm. Thus, this secondary, waterborne option remained the greatest threat to his mental health.

His third escape strategy would be to remain in situ, hidden in a cellar storage room purposely constructed and provisioned should either his subterranean tower or water routes be blocked. This final hideaway had an escape hatch leading to the wine cellar of the Café Salon de Thé, adjacent to his house and only accessed by one loyal confidant, the proprietor of the restaurant. There he would change into the traditional black and white attire of a café server complete with black trousers, white shirt with black bowtie, black vest, long apron and white towel neatly ironed to exacting standards. He would then warily wend his way up the narrow wooden stairs into the café kitchen and out to the patio and freedom from surveying eyes which tended not to notice the obvious, the constant flow of ubiquitous servers.

He preferred not to have to implement any escape plan but instead to maintain normalcy in his daily routine which had become inexplicitly atypical. The scent of treachery lingered in his mind, pre-empted by duplicitous lives and double entendre.

His was a more solitary introverted existence by choice, a manifestation of circumstance, which had become a default habit. When contacted by Herr Blosch to gather on the yacht in order to meet the seventh member of the *Quer*, Claude Etien Marchand, Baird made the conscious choice not to join the others at the gangplank but instead to board the yacht from the port side and from his own speedboat. On other occasions, his prudence had paid off despite the anxiety caused by his irrational fear of water. It had assured his survival once again although he was unaware of just how perilous his persistence was. He was acutely aware that his last name, Durand was derived from the old French, *durant*, which meant to endure, to survive, to last.

CHAPTER 9

"As we are meeting again, I conclude that I have passed your forensic test of veracity," Francine responded to Alexandra's welcoming invitation. She was pleased and a bit surprised at the speed at which clearance to offer her a contractual appointment had been received. She surmised that secrecy surrounding her Moscow affiliations was not so secret or not of significant concern. Alternately, her training in the tradecraft was a sought-after asset. Or her close affiliation with Dominique may have facilitated the process. Had her misgivings about her FSB handler in Paris been correct? Had he or someone else who knew of her espionage status divulged her true identity to French Counterintelligence, or to a third party who had subcontracted to a fast gun for hire, an assassin? Who was the traitor? Where was the leak? Was it Alexandra or Paul? She was as confident as she could be that it wasn't Yusuf.

"You still buy the cappuccino for both Francine and me until such time as we receive an initial expense instalment including a sizeable confidence payment," Yusuf laughed, his expression projecting a Guy Fawkes mask. For a moment, Paul sensed that his accent seemed East German or maybe further east. Some words sounded as though they bled into others, some consonants were either too hard or not harsh enough in contrast to his occasional distant American twang.

Paul slid a book across the table. "You may find the genre and content to be to your liking. If what you see is acceptable, we can provide you with further literary references."

Yusuf scanned the title page briefly: *A Complete Anthology of Sir Arthur Conan Doyle.* "Looks like an interesting read." He opened the cover and turned the title page. "OK. The literary content is rich. We buy the cappuccino."

Alexandra announced, "Your mission is to find out who ambushed you at Moulins-lès-Metz and, equally important, why."

"You have our undivided attention," Francine confirmed. Her acquired Parisienne stare seemed to convey something more than a simple acknowledgement. In her training to become a Soviet agent, she recalled one of her trainers, an ex-NKVD warrior, citing Lenin: "The West are wishful thinkers. We will give them what they want to think." She concluded such dogma came from the lips of dinosaurs. At this juncture, her life depended upon truthfulness, not deception. There was nothing unassuming about her nuanced intent. She would not become extinct.

"What do you know for certain and who do you suspect?" Alexandra asked unequivocally. "That will provide a place to start."

Francine began with the honesty that characterized their previous meeting. "Perhaps naïvely, I had accompanied Dominique to Moulins-lès-Metz unaware of any of the facts. I trusted Dominique. I was ambushed. I now relearn hard lessons taught as part of my KGB training: Gather all the facts. Access all the intelligence. Validate all the sources of information about a case before embarking. Even then, *doveryat' i proveryat'* – trust and verify."

"We don't know much except there is, as you correctly suggested, a confederate in the French Intelligence network," Alexandra replied with a hint of exasperation. "We believe it may be Moscow-related but not necessarily Moscow-motivated or Moscow-directed. The operative expression here is: may be Moscow-related. We're not positive. As you well know, Francine, there is a perceived righteous obligation to murder in the realm of espionage. There is one too many unknowns. Your ambush had all the trappings of a professional hit. It smelled of a vendetta. As you alluded, it was perhaps a rogue KGB affiliate. There are tentacles that reach into coffers of the Fourth Reich directed to some degree by an olden third-party organization with calculating, malevolent intent. This is not a one-off incident. Instead, it has global implications."

Francine pursed her lips in pensive silence. Certainly, in the old KGB guard, murder was a righteous obligation. She had first-hand experience. Espionage, and intelligence gathering to a slightly lesser extent, were dexterous and dangerous games of chasing suspected spies and fleeting shadows. Both were renowned for their lethal outcomes in the pursuit of information within the prism of misinformation. She could not wash her hands of responsibility like Pontius Pilot.

"Interesting. Yusuf and I have reviewed the events of Moulins-lès-Metz several times and have some suspicions. Your Western perspectives will shed new light. Let us first talk about who and why, and second, the influence of an olden third-party organization, as you say."

"The Cold War was bi-polar and, as such, myopic," Yusuf conjectured. "I can fill in a few blanks from an Ottoman Empire Middle East standpoint which you may find most helpful. There are advantages to sitting on the periphery of the main ring and simply observing. A wise man will acknowledge that there have always been other seemingly suspicious players."

Paul smiled warmly. It was a matter of perspective. *Enemies yesterday. Friends today. Who tomorrow?* He was acutely aware that loyalties change that fast. Not to be glib, Paul simply could not trust those he couldn't trust. Until such time as he had a more comprehensive grasp of what motivated Yusuf, he wouldn't, couldn't, trust him completely.

"It is time to put differences aside and collaborate in earnest for mutual benefit," Yusuf proposed as an opening bid. Paul held his gaze, thus allowing Alexandra to place her undivided attention on Francine, as planned.

"The who and why are complex questions," Francine proposed. "I suspect there is more than one who, and more than one why. When the FSB was created as an incarnation of its former self, the KGB, a vetting process took place akin to Stalin's purge of the 1920s and '30s. Not all KGB agents were offered positions in the new guard. Those who were not murdered or sent to gulags to ensure compliance with silence edicts transferred allegiances mostly to the CIA, MI6, or Mossad. Still others escaped to the West and became intelligence entrepreneurs. It was a lucrative business although short-lived for the few who tried to play both sides against each other."

"Fast gun for hire as in the early 1960s American TV series *Paladin*," Yusuf suggested. "It was all about Western economics of supply and demand tempered with moral conviction, although morality took on different definitions. It was a game of intelligence and counterintelligence often with fatal consequences. The antics of Ian Fleming's quintessential 007 James Bond character spanned the reality from exacting realism to absolute fiction. On occasion, Moscow's spies engaged in tactics Fleming had described on paper, on the premise that MI6 and the CIA would disregard the manoeuvres, thinking them to be deceptions. Fleming's fiction became fact."

Francine continued, "One of these new entrepreneurs was codenamed Dmitri. I don't have too much detail on him. I will get more. We never met but his reputation preceded him. You mentioned a vendetta. Dmitri certainly had an axe to grind with the FSB hierarchy. It wouldn't be his style to actually pull the trigger. However, he is capable of contracting that out to one of his many colleagues, a strategy of ex-spy on ex-spy followed up with assassin on assassin, killing the killer to cover their tracks. If it is Dmitri, be extremely wary. He is a venomous viper."

"Could he have organized the ambush in Moulins-lès-Metz?" Alexandra asked. The purpose of her question was twofold. First, she wanted to get a sense of Francine's honesty. She would carefully observe Francine's physiological response. Second, she wanted to fish for facts not yet known that might identify tangential variables not yet considered as vital to shedding light on those responsible, both planners and doers. She would have to test for validity and reliability by comparing this intelligence with what other sources had provided.

Francine responded without pausing to reflect or hesitating to consider a contrived answer. "The thought has crossed my mind. But I don't know why, unless Dmitri was contracted by another party who paid extremely well. You simply redefine morality as I just suggested. That's a distinct possibility and may relate to your second point, your reference to an olden organization with a Fourth Reich connection."

"I get the sense you are familiar with a relationship," Alexandra probed, pressing Francine for a more detailed explanation.

"Let's go back to the last months of the Second World War. The rapidity of the Russian advance into Berlin was motivated in large part by the bombing of the Reichsbank in February 1945 which resulted in gold, other monies and treasures being squirrelled away in various abandoned mines throughout Germany, especially Bavaria, by a select few disloyal yet entrepreneurial Nazis. Some gold was quietly deposited in a few Swiss banks. The Russians desperately wanted to get their hands on it. Today, Moscow is confident that the Fourth Reich has possession of most of it, if not influence over those who do have it. Another entity is controlling some deposits that are held in Swiss and other international banks including the

Vatican bank. Additional monies and stolen treasures were moved to locations in South America."

"Does the name *Quer* ring a bell?" Paul interjected, testing their depth of knowledge of the olden organization, all the while allowing Alexandra to assess their responses.

Francine and Yusuf looked at each other with doubtful yet neutral expressions. Yusuf was the first to respond. "I recall reading something about a clandestine organization in the annals of the Ottoman Empire, among other references in my previous employer's library. I'd have to research further."

There was potential for authenticity in his response. Paul surmised that it wasn't the truth, the whole truth and nothing but the truth, but might have a vein of veracity. Yusuf had not been wholly up front when they first met at the Palermo marathon and there was no reason to believe he had adopted higher standards of integrity today.

"Francine?" Alexandra prompted. She wanted to keep the open flood gates of information flowing but did not want to take it in a direction that was not natural.

Francine complied. "Moscow had strong suspicions that there was an organization like a cabal that had powerful influences in the international banking and commerce communities. However, I don't recall hearing the name *Quer* mentioned." She held Alexandra's quizzical gaze. Like Yusuf, she sensed her reply was not being received as the whole truth. Deception was a standard operating procedure in the arcane tradecraft.

Francine looked at Paul as much to break Alexandra's stare as to create a link which she felt was slightly more comfortable. "You asked, Paul. Is that the name of the olden organization you mentioned?"

"It could be. Not sure though," he replied.

It was Paul's turn to interject a pregnant pause into the

conversation in order to re-evaluate a response that would garner an initial level of confidence at this early stage in the relationship. The hiatus allowed Alexandra to reinforce her focus on Francine.

He added, "Some people affiliated with this supposed organization could have been involved in your ambush."

Francine squinted under Paul's scrutiny. Her healing flesh wounds and the fractured radius of her right arm twitched with pain at the reference to her ambush.

Sensing intrigue, Alexandra quickly linked the baited speculation that Paul had cast into the stream. She then looked directly at Francine.

"It is certainly worthwhile following up from a combined Russian and Eastern Europe perspective. Can you also delicately find out who may be on another employer's payroll, such as those in the senior ranks of the constabulary and governance?"

Francine raised her eyebrows slightly at this request as if to suggest she knew where she would begin her enquiries. *Both Alexandra and Paul are a seasoned investigative team to a high professional standard,* she surmised. Little did she realize they were novices as an investigative duo.

"We have our homework. I'll get back to you as soon as we have some reliable intelligence or better still, verifiable evidence," Yusuf confirmed. His expression remained neutral though his tone left a hopeful thread suggesting he looked forward to the challenge and perhaps another rich literary installment. He wasn't aware of the banker backing Alexandra and Paul. But he suspected the resources were considerable. He concluded that it was not singular but had multi-national tentacles. The magnitude would correlate with the seriousness of the need for intelligence. That, in turn, would impact on the dynamics of their risk assessment.

"Be careful playing in this sandbox, folks," Alexandra

cautioned. "I don't think I need to remind you that some of these players are not very nice."

"Particularly nasty," Francine confirmed with a stiletto stare. Like Yusuf, her expression showed neither fear nor fearlessness. Instead, she responded heartily in anticipation of the challenge spurred on by the opportunity for revenge, in addition to a possible future collaboration and trusting relationship.

She rubbed her right elbow gently with her left hand while carefully flexing the fingers of her right hand. The discomfort further reminded her of her mortality. Memories of the Moulins-lès-Metz ambush were not far from her conscious mind. She recalled the searing pain emanating from her right radius that had been shattered as the bullet struck. There was a righteous obligation to avenge a wrong. Whoever it was that shot her had made a grievous error in not confirming the kill, the double tap. She would not repeat that tactical error. She could not, however, ease the gnawing headaches accompanying the relentless and agonizing memories of the ambush and worse – the thoughts of a reprehensible collegial betrayal.

CHAPTER 10

"We have some background information on Yusuf. But first, how did your initial assessment go with our centurion gladiators?" Daan enquired.

"Like bloodhounds, they are on the scent as we speak. They are motivated to identify, expose and bring to justice those responsible for the Moulins-lès-Metz ambush. Justice being their justice, their style. Francine will get back to us as soon as she has anything of substance," Alexandra advised confidently. They were one step closer to finding Baird Durand and identifying those senior governance and policing executives who had surreptitiously been on the *Quer* payroll.

With that update, Daan gave Matthieu a look to share the information he had amassed.

"Yusuf is an intriguing enigma to say the least. He is well read on the Western Enlightenment. Of possible importance is his whetted interest in eighteenth and nineteenth century philosophers – Machiavelli, Rousseau, Voltaire and Hobbes. He is also an avid reader of the myth of the American West. He sees himself as an aficionado in that genre. His favourite authors are A.B. Guthrie, Zane Grey and Louis L'Amour. He spends his leisure time also watching old black and white Western movies like Roy Rogers and the Lone Ranger. He is intrigued with the good cowboys because they wore white hats. Perhaps of interest, Al Capone also admired the white hat imagery. He wore a white fedora because he wanted to present himself to the American public as a good guy, like Robin Hood, robbing from the rich and giving to the poor. Of course, Capone wasn't good by any stretch of the imagination."

"I got a sense that Yusuf sees himself as a bit of a solitary cowboy riding the plains of the untamed West," Paul suggested. "He made a reference to Paladin whose *raison d'être* was to right the wrongs, although he dressed in black including a black hat. Paladin's calling card read: *Have Gun Will Travel*. In Turkey, military intelligence was the closest Yusuf could come to carrying a gun in the anonymous untamed Wild West of Cold War espionage. As you aptly described him, Matthieu, Yusuf is an intriguing enigma."

"That fits his emerging persona," Matthieu implied. "From his perspective, Francine appears to be his stalwart partner like Roy Rogers and Dale Evans."

"Or maybe Dale Evans and Roy Rogers, from Dale's perspective," Alexandra countered in a feminist tone. "Regardless, we can play the angle of the moral hero to test Yusuf's veracity and provisional loyalty, even if that loyalty isn't necessarily a political calling but instead a philosophical ethos like righting a wrong. I think he is as committed as Francine to catching the person who hired the assassin, in addition to the actual triggerman who killed Dominique and wounded Francine. I offer that as a suggestion because each time we spoke about Moulins-lès-Metz, he became quiet. Not so much withdrawn but contemplative, as if strategizing. Yusuf and Francine make a good pair in this regard."

Maintaining his focus on Alexandra, Daan corralled his thoughts. "I'm thinking Yusuf is the wild card in the deck as we suspected. But that isn't the issue. The question remains: Can we trust him to back you up if push comes to shove?"

It was Alexandra's turn to think carefully before responding to this scenario, which was no longer just theoretical, given the mounting death toll associated with this case. She looked over to Paul. He returned her gaze before responding.

"I believe that Yusuf would back us up, if for no other reason than he would abide by the Paladin mantra – to right the wrong, to bring to justice those who attempted to assassinate Francine. Indirectly, that is our commitment as we close in on Baird Durand. I am confident Yusuf perceives this cause to be righteous and honourable. Francine was almost killed and that is proof enough for him. The means by which he would back us up would probably be unorthodox by our standards, akin to a lone wolf acting independently as opposed to being a committed member of the wolf pack."

Daan nodded slowly yet deliberately in agreement. Reflective responses to thoughtful questions carried more weight. "Fair enough. Bear that in mind as we proceed."

Alexandra asked a question that caused Paul to stop briefly and consider a previous conversation they had engaged in.

"Do you remember when we first talked about Francine at the café on Boulevard Henri IV across from the Garde Republicaine barracks in Paris?"

"Just before we met with Dominique."

"Yes, I was suspicious of her motivation and asked for your opinion. You mentioned that Francine looked like a Parisian woman in every respect except one. She never smiled with her eyes."

"Correct. And as a result, I judged her to be Soviet in upbringing because Russians don't naturally smile in public. It's perceived to be a false façade, a weakness when they do."

"You're absolutely correct," Alexandra acknowledged. "And Yusuf doesn't smile with his eyes either. He can be charming and charismatic but even then, his eyes are a mask, as you say, a false façade. Most continental French men tend to be more astute when observing subtleties in women and vice versa."

"C'est vrai," Paul acknowledged. "Come to think of it, I've never seen him smile fully either. Is this a cultural response or a learned behaviour? The Turkish Military Intelligence organization has a very stringent vetting process. Might that suggest their training in cultural innuendos is flawed?"

"Or Turkish Military Intelligence has been compromised and foreign agents who are now at senior levels in that hierarchy are hiring other confederates, like Kim Philby did in MI6," Alexandra countered. "The Soviets cultivated the Cambridge Five prior to World War II. This was about the same time the clandestine Turkish Military Intelligence unit was officially being formed."

Her observations caused Paul to follow a parallel path of reconsideration of his own logical thought process.

Alexandra tilted her head ever so slightly. "Is Yusuf behaving in this manner in an effort to lead us astray or is he purposefully demonstrating learned responses from training in the tradecraft or from Hollywood's Silver Screen? The unfaltering Lone Ranger and Tonto, in addition to Paladin, Yusuf's mentor hero, always presented a less emotional response, often featureless as they pursued the bad guys in the black hats. The audience had an idea of how they might react emotionally, based on their reputation to remain detached. But that was not always guaranteed. It added to their persona and mystique."

One of the attributes Paul loved about Alexandra was her mysterious French nature, her own mystique. *What did others think of her, Francine and Yusuf? What was she missing, the false positives, the false negatives?* he mused. *She was constantly assessing Francine and Yusuf for truthfulness as she did with others. No doubt they were doing the same. What were they missing? Again, Paul reflected on the ancient adage: You can't completely trust people if you don't wholly trust yourself.*

Paul felt a tinge of misgiving about his qualified endorsement of Yusuf. He would absolutely trust Daan, Matthieu, and other colleagues in the EUI Unit. But. There was always a but. He recalled from his academic training in statistics that you could only be ninety-nine-point-nine-eight percent certain. Never one hundred percent because there was always an unknown factor. This mission had more than one unknown to cause him to constantly question, not least of which was Yusuf, and Francine to a lesser extent. That was simply good survival strategy.

"One more bit of news," Daan added. "I previously mentioned the possibility of Matthieu being seconded to work with another intelligence colleague, Davana Kaur. That has been confirmed. Their primary mission will be to find the source of the security breach that resulted in the assassination of the remaining members of the *Quer* in the Desert Springs Interrogation Facility. They had recently plugged a security leak in another case. Suffice it to say, Matthieu will only be available to work with us part-time. I say part-time because there is a high probability the source of the leak at the Desert Springs Interrogation Facility may be linked to recent activities of the *Quer*, and the whereabouts of Baird Durand." Looking directly at Alexandra and Paul, Daan stated, "If your travels cause you to cross paths in public, only approach Matthieu if he first acknowledges you by rubbing the bridge of his nose. Otherwise maintain your distance."

Again, Daan added, "Note that in the past several months, we have been experiencing probing of our electronic and physical security bastions by foreign sources, some traditional and others new to the playing field. We can expect this increase in incursions to continue. Let me know all suspicious activities. A worry on the electronic side is the location of the servers being employed. The largest increase in land sources is from the Middle East and North Africa, no doubt because of their respective proximity to the European Union."

"Replacing HUMINT, human intelligence, or augmenting it?" Paul uttered.

"Not either/or but both/and," Daan proposed. "Closer to home, inner and outer space satellite platforms are not new. However, the increase in drone technology has brought a new definition to VMROPs (versatile mobile remotely operated platforms) with the emphasis on versatility because they have the added capability of launching multiple missiles with pin-point laser accuracy."

Paul responded, "Everything old is new again. In the Second World War, Sir James flew Mosquitos out of airfields in southern England on missions over Nazi-occupied Europe and out of Malta on missions over North Africa. The Mosquito was initially rejected by the Air Ministry because supposed experts didn't have a vision for lightweight, high speed, low altitude aircraft. Once produced though, the Mosquitos were initially employed to conduct aerial photography, then as fighters and also as bombers because they were lightweight, high speed, low altitude aircraft. Except for the fact that drones are unmanned, they are lightweight, high speed, low altitude, multi-purpose aircraft including electronic aerial surveillance. Everything old is new again."

"Arial photography and electronic surveillance provide an indication of what is present yet camouflaged. But it doesn't always provide the truth, the whole truth and nothing but the truth like eyes-on human intelligence gathering," Alexandra suggested. "As good as I am as a forensic psychologist, I do miss some aspects of the human side of human intelligence. Hypnosis provides a deeper perspective of the mind. But even then, not everything is revealed and certainly not on the initial assessment. For that reason, I refrain from using certainties, but instead speak in terms of probabilities. Add to the mix those trained in purposeful deception like spies, and the challenge becomes even less reliable when considering a single source. Individuals are simply fickle."

"So, we have a better feel for Francine, but who is Yusuf?" Paul asked rhetorically, not expecting a definitive response. "What is your *shrew* telling you?"

Alexandra shook her head slowly as she gently massaged the amulet that hung around her next. "As Matthieu suggested, Yusuf is more of an enigma. As you surmised, he is more of a Paladin with a *raison d'être* to right a wrong. Add in the fact he is an opportunist and a romantic, a survivor, but more of a lone wolf, an unorthodox player, like Davana, and an unknown wild card in the deck. On my initial assessment, I asked whether he was an Armenian Turk or a Turkish Armenian. I now do not believe he is either. Like a chameleon, he adapts to the environment for his advantage. We have to be prepared for anything, particularly behavioural responses out of what we would perceive to be the norm." Alexandra frowned in response to her own analysis before concluding her prophetic assessment. "Most importantly, I do not see him as a lethal threat to us. Others who have crossed him or threatened Francine, like the trigger who attempted to assassinate her, yes, absolutely. But I could be wrong. There is always the fickle human factor."

Not only is she mysterious and beautiful, but my puppy love is simply the best, Paul mused with a smile of contentment.

CHAPTER 11

"Not much of a family holiday," Alexandra apologized to Collette and Jean as they sauntered toward a restaurant overlooking the caldera and the azure Aegean, painted vibrant hues of orange by the palette of the setting sun. Santorini offered tranquil vistas and cooling breezes at every turn. Apart from the milling tourists, Santorini was a placid, almost perfect retreat for weary travellers seeking refuge from their everyday hectic schedules.

The peaceful atmosphere was disrupted by a heated argument. The commotion was drawing the attention of patrons of the restaurant seated inside and on the outside patio.

"You come with me now, bitch," the man yelled as he slapped the young girl on the face.

Collette leapt forward and with a roundhouse kick, her foot connected with his head, knocking him to the ground. Blood spurted from his nose. He spat out broken teeth accompanied by a cocktail of saliva and blood. He attempted to stand and lunge at Collette but fell again as her left fist struck his throat. Dazed, he stayed down. The crowd applauded as the young girl escaped from the grasp of the belligerent man into the nucleus of their protective circle which formed spontaneously around her providing physical and, more importantly, emotional support.

Jean and Paul stood in stunned silence as Alexandra hurriedly grabbed Collette, pulling her back. *My dear daughter is not well, contrary to what she told me a few days before.*

"Take her back to the hotel and stay out of sight, Jean. We will join you in a moment," Alexandra whispered as she scanned the environment for any adverse follow-up. Paul was conducting a parallel 360-degree surveillance. Both locked eyes on Matthieu who was standing several paces behind, astutely providing cover for their tactical exodus.

Jean stared in shock at his fiancée. He then wrapped his arms around her. The intimacy of their embrace was warm yet wanting, as was their momentary awkward kiss.

"The honeymoon is over. We need to return to Paris immediately," Matthieu directed as he continued to scan the immediate environment. There was no room for debate in his statement. With Collette's swift departure, the attention of the crowd returned to the young girl who had been assaulted. A few patrons continued to provide physical protection and emotional support. The man who had assaulted her slithered away, encouraged vociferously by other patrons.

Under the cloak of Matthieu's continued surveillance, Alexandra and Paul returned to their hotel by the most direct route while hugging the shaded façade of the houses and shops in an effort to remain as inconspicuous as possible.

"What was that all about?" Alexandra asked Collette who remained as distraught as she had been immediately after her violent encounter.

Collette sat unresponsive on the bed in her room, staring at her running shoe and fist, both stained with blood.

Alexandra motioned to the others assembled to leave her alone with Collette.

Matthieu followed, ever conscious of Jean and Collette's stares.

Paul led Jean into their adjoining room.

Alexandra sat beside her daughter holding her in a consoling motherly embrace. She did not have to speak. Collette snuggled into her mother's shoulder. In the fullness of time, she admitted, "I guess I'm not OK."

"Tell me what you were thinking, feeling and sensing before you lunged at the man." Alexandra responded.

"I saw Yvon attacking me and I saw the girl needed to be protected. I was that girl for a brief moment. But she didn't have the presence of mind or the skills to fight off her attacker. I also saw the Saudi student who grabbed me on the sidewalk outside the Sorbonne. I was feeling rage. And then I thought about my miscarriage, and Jean and you and Paul. I had to react, to fight off the girl's attacker. I just had to. He was attacking me."

"You're going to have to confront these inner demons if you want to be a successful clinical counsellor."

"I know that, Maman. Can you help? I don't want to see Frederik because it might put my practicum in jeopardy."

"Understood. I can call another colleague in Cologne, Franz Schmidt. His wife is also a counsellor so you could speak with either or both of them."

Collette lowered her head as tears filled her eyes and began to flow down her cheeks.

"Right now, we need to say something to Jean and Paul. I suggest we remind them about the stress you've been under since the Saudi student attacked you. They'll understand your reaction. To soothe their concerns for your well-being, we'll explain that you will be seeing a clinical psychologist. But we say absolutely nothing about Yvon's sexual assault or the miscarriage. You can talk to Franz and his wife about it in the strictest of confidence. Are we agreed?"

"OK, Maman. Agreed. We don't have to tell anyone else, do we?"

"No, dear, no one else. I'll send Jean back in so you can speak with him alone. I'll talk with Paul." She would have a private conversation with Matthieu who, she sensed, was more attuned to the circumstances and security implications than any of the others. She assumed rightly or wrongly his knowledge of the background circumstances regarding Yvon's sexual assault would be a comfort to her beyond just the present circumstances.

⋈

"Run!" Beads of sweat formed on her upper lip. Her eyes darted as she scanned the dense thicket. She picked up her mother's gun. "That was a shot in a million," Maria praised her. "You are a natural sharpshooter, daughter. I have taught you well, but not without consequences."

"Wake up. You're having a bad dream. You're thrashing about, fighting something," Paul uttered as he embraced Alexandra.

"My mother was yelling at me to run, but I didn't."

"Run from what? Where? When?"

"It was a long time ago. I was a teenager. It was shortly after we met in Montigny-lès-Metz."

"Tell me about it."

Alexandra gathered her wits. Her mind raced, flooded by a torrent of merging images. Some she recognized. Others she did not. Her marriage to André had been fraught with dishonesty and mistruths. She needed to be completely candid with Paul, to hold nothing back. But what would he do if she revealed the details of his son Yvon's assault on Collette?

Paul was aware that ghosts from the past were haunting her but could not guess the extent. He too had his own double closet overflowing with ghosts. From her reaction, he concluded that her closet was overflowing.

This truth needed to come out but was now the right time? And then there was the truth about why her mother had yelled at her to run. It had become a repeating nightmare she had endured over the decades. She didn't run but instead picked up her mother's gun. She took the shot in a million, as her mother later congratulated her. Her mother had been pinned down, wounded. Alexandra had retrieved the gun and pulled the trigger in defence. The Sixth Commandment – *Thou Shalt Not Kill.* She had committed murder. She had not confessed her sin. She had never confessed, not even to Father Luke. Her mother had sworn her to secrecy. If she did reveal the truth, her mother might be murdered as she had murdered. She had lied to her God in not confessing. Her mother had explained that she had not lied because God already knew. Was the sin in lying or not revealing the whole truth? Was her sin now in complying with her mother's dictate never to reveal what had happened and, in doing so, protecting her mother from others who might be sent to kill her? But her mother was dead. So, was she still sworn to secrecy? Or was the sin in lying to Paul by not telling him the truth, the whole truth and nothing but the truth? Was it God's punishment to keep her from experiencing a loving relationship without guilt, without confessed remorse?

Her mind spun out of control. Should she divulge all those details to Paul? Now would be as good a time as any while they held each other. Yet her embrace was not sincere. He would understand. But it might bring up questions about Yvon's sexual assault on Collette, and his drowning and the drugs. But Paul knew about the drowning and the drugs. Why would he suspect a link to an assault he knew nothing about? *This was God's punishment,* she concluded.

André had never known the secret about her defence of her mother. Their marriage had not dissolved just because of that secret. One secret had led to another and another. André had complained on numerous occasions that his mother-in-law had a disruptive influence on her daughter, his wife. He had never enquired, though, about how his wife felt. Not like Paul. Yet she was treating Paul as she had done André. She was withdrawing, not divulging the truth. True love was physical, mental, spiritual, sensual and much more. Perhaps she was incapable of commitment. Did she need to atone to her God?

She became dizzy even lying still, incapable of halting the roller coaster ride.

"*Je t'aime*, and never ever forget it no matter what happens," she whispered in earnest as she continued to return his embrace. Could he sense that she was holding back? He would know if she asked him. Then, she would have to wear another mask, one of many she had worn with André. She had a double closet full of masks. Alternately, she could run away as she had done from André. She was now comparing Paul with André when there was absolutely no comparison. It was an insult to Paul to even suggest a similarity.

"*Je t'aime aussi,*" Paul responded as he continued to hold her close. *But why had she added the proviso, "no matter what happens?" What could happen that might compromise his deep adoration of her? What was she holding back?*

He looked at her with unconditional support but also with anticipation. *One day she might be as trusting as I am with her,* he thought. *Yet Suzette never was.* Their marriage had eroded. They never formally divorced. For all intents and purposes, they never were a couple. He had given up on their relationship and merely walked away.

"I'll tell you about it later, why my mother had told me to run, why I didn't, why I picked up her gun, and why I shot her attacker," she mumbled. *But what if later never comes?* she thought. The eternal dilemma of duality, to reveal or continue to conceal, to disclose the details or to plead no conscious knowledge. She seemed to be rambling.

"After this case is over, we need to go to Sir James's cottage in Dover for a holiday, just to relax," Paul proposed.

"Agreed. I need to sit in my mother's chair and you need to

walk in the garden. Let's not wait until then. We need to go now, even for just a few days. I need to make peace with my mother, my past."

"OK. I'll email Walter Burns to prepare the cottage for a short visit."

"I'll speak with Matthieu," Alexandra advised. "He'll understand, having witnessed Collette's outburst last evening. We can make alternate arrangements to meet with Francine and Yusuf, if need be."

Why would Matthieu understand having witnessed Collette's outburst? Would it not be more reasonable for Alexandra to want to spend more time with Collette rather than getting away? Paul pondered. *I'm not a psychologist but it doesn't seem logical. What is she running away from? What is she running away to? Or is she just running, not knowing where or why?*

Alexandra called her friend Jo to confirm that she would be available to look in on Collette. It seemed Jo had seamlessly transitioned from being her best friend and confidante to becoming the sister she never had and an aunt to Collette. Alexandra had developed a special mother-daughter relationship with Collette and they talked about most things. But daughters would chat with aunts about certain personal issues which were beyond those maternal moments. Alexandra had personal experience, having been raised under the watchful eyes of her own aunt. They had chatted about things she could not talk to her mother about, even if her mother had been a stay-at-home mom, and not away so much.

She wondered who her own mother had talked to when growing up. As a member of the French Resistance, the *Maquis,* during the latter years of the war and as a counterintelligence agent throughout the Cold War, sworn to secrecy, close friends would be few. Was Madame Deschaume the sister she never had? Together, they had helped Sir James escape from the Nazi SS across the Pyrénées.

Was Sir James the brother she never had? They had certainly engaged in many conversations regarding their work as agents when she visited his cottage in Dover. Those discussions would have crossed into the realm of very personal matters, like when she was pregnant with Alexandra.

Her mind continued to race, seemingly out of control and without a brake. As a child, she never wanted to fall asleep for fear that her mother might not return from what were referred to as her business trips. Now, she did not want to fall asleep for fear those nightmares of the deadly assault on her mother and her own intervention would return. It was apparent she needed to make peace with those ghosts. Like Arctic wolves, she could lock them up fleetingly but could not silence completely their distant haunting howls.

Who takes care of the caregivers? She asked herself. She knew the answer to that question but it was too simplistic. She had debriefed with Frederik after every horrific case she had taken on throughout her career as a forensic psychologist. Yet those formal collegial discussions never seemed to touch on, to delve into the core issues – why did she not run when her mother had told her to do so. Why had she picked up her gun and killed without second thought and later without remorse. She and her mother had never sat down and talked about it. She desperately needed to have that conversation.

CHAPTER 12

"Welcome back to Dover. It has been too long since you visited your English cottage."

"Thank you, Walter," Alexandra replied. "The cottage will forever belong to Sir James, despite his passing and bequest to us. It will always be his home, and we, his guests. We are so grateful to you for all your years of loyal service, and for staying on to take care of the property."

"You have been well, Walter?" Paul enquired. "Have there been any further enquiries regarding the sale of the property or unwanted intruders caught on surveillance videos snooping around?"

"Yes, I have been well. Thank you for asking. And I am pleased to advise that there have been no more trespassers. If you'll excuse me, I will bring tea into the sunroom for you."

"This sanctuary is so tranquil," Alexandra commented. "Each time we come to Dover, I gain a greater understanding of why Sir James bought this cottage and retired here, and why my mother visited him so often. They would have reminisced about when she helped him escape capture by the Gestapo in 1944, and their evolving personal and professional relationship after the war. What secrets would they have harboured, he as an MI6 agent and she as his counterpart with French Counterintelligence? Their respective worlds were exponentially more stressful than we have experienced."

"They would have been considerable if we just appreciate what your mother revealed in her final letter to you," Paul added. "I get the feeling that Sir James left many more hidden secrets in his cottage for us to find. We only have to reflect on the note he left for us with his Will and what he has already told us. I'm convinced he did not reveal everything, for our own protection, perhaps like your mother. We would discover the other clues when we were ready."

"And I wonder about the relationship Major Mike Murphy first had with my mother as a member of the American OSS in Normandy laying the groundwork with the French Resistance in preparation for the Allied Invasion on D-Day. And later as a CIA operative, mentoring Tom Hunt as his protégé. Sir James, Major Mike and my mother must have sat in this sunroom and exchanged harrowing stories. I would love to have been a fly on the wall."

"We all have our crosses to bear, *ma princesse*. I thought I had buried my Ebenezer Scrooge ghost from Christmas Past. Just talking about the *Quer* has dredged up some lingering issues. I need to find Baird Durand and condemn him to hell, once and for all."

Alexandra interrupted his darkening descent. She had personal experience with the depth and breadth of such a trajectory. If there was ever a time to intervene it was early in the moment before the memories gathered weight and momentum. "Not you alone but we as a team need to find him and condemn him to purgatory."

Paul knew he needed to deal with his ghosts from when he served in Sarajevo with the United Nations Protection Force, and the evidence-finding missions at scenes of war crimes. Most prominent in his own nagging nightmares was the image of the little girl lying face down in the ditch, her emaciated arms tied behind her back with barbed wire that had ripped into her wrists, and her light blue dress stained with blood that had oozed from a bullet hole in the back of her head. He had resigned himself to the fact there were different levels of justice required. The cowards who murdered the little girl without remorse needed to be doomed to purgatory along with Baird Durand. But perhaps a more fitting sentence would be to live a long life knowing each night they would face the recurring nightmares and relentless headaches without the mitigating effect that a myriad of addictive drugs and alcohol might provide. All sins would be remembered, never to be forgiven.

"You are rubbing your amulet. What is your *shrew* saying?"

A stillness filled the space between them before she broke the silence. Her stare was crowded yet vacant, serene yet anxious, hesitant yet assured.

"My mother is talking to me."

"And what is she telling you?"

"She is giving me permission to be honest with you about something that occurred years ago. It was after we first met in Montigny-lès-Metz. My mother and I had just returned to Luxembourg. We were out for a walk in one of the wooded parks when a man whom I later learned was a KGB agent attacked, bent on killing her. She was wounded in the ensuing confrontation. She yelled at me to run, but I didn't. Instead, I picked up the pistol he had knocked out of her hand. He was strangling her from behind, perhaps 20 paces away from me. Because he was much taller than her, I had an unobstructed view of his head. I knelt and took careful aim. I deliberately squeezed the trigger. The bullet struck his head, spraying blood in a wide arc across a shaft of sunlight. He died instantly. My mother told me I had taken the impossible shot and, as a result, had saved her life."

As she spoke of the chronology of events, her voice was calm, yet almost too calm. She was present, yet almost absent. Although looking at Paul, she was gazing beyond him at two others, her mother, and the KGB agent, alive one moment, dead the next as a direct result of her deadly response. There was an absence of emotion in her voice and in her behaviour. Yet, her eyes were very much alive as she considered the violence being projected on the monitor of her mind. At one moment, she was with her mother strolling calmly in the wooded copse. Next, she was in a psychotic-like state of helter-skelter, her mother threatened with imminent death. The hands of the agent were cutting off Maman's breath of life. Then, relief came as the body of the attacker fell to the ground and lay eerily still. It was quieter than any moment she could recall, save for the pistol's blast still reverberating in her ears. Her mother was with her in life but bleeding. All those absences explained as business trips were no longer mysterious. In less than a few minutes, all those days, weeks, months and years of loneliness had been compressed.

Paul leaned toward her with concern, astonished by her bravery. He had held a pistol and had stared into the evil eyes of his intended victim. He had taken aim carefully. It had been a split-second decision. But he had not pulled the trigger.

"How did you handle it all these years?" he asked, distressed. He wanted to hold her, to comfort her, perhaps as much as he wanted her to wrap her arms around him, to reassure him. That would come later. For now, he needed to provide her with support for what must have been her deepest most disquieting secret. *How could she have held it in and not displayed any overt signs of distress?* he asked himself. *Nothing she could disclose could be more harrowing.* He recalled her saying, "No matter what, never forget that I love you." In reply, he wondered why she had made such a worrying declaration. Now he knew. Or was there more?

"I had never seen a dead person before let alone someone I had killed. I remember being numb. I didn't know why he was trying to kill my mother but I soon surmised that my mother must have been a policewoman, maybe a detective. That seemed to settle things for me because I concluded I was doing something morally right. My mother arranged for me to talk with a psychologist. I was never really emotionally distraught because I had saved her life. I just knew I wanted to become a forensic psychologist when I got older.

I wanted, needed to know why people behaved the way they did – Maman, the KGB agent, me."

Paul gaped at her in stunned stillness. "In the letter your mother left for you in the safe deposit box, she alluded to it. You were yelling something about taking the impossible shot in your sleep the night after Collette assaulted that man at the restaurant in Santorini."

"It haunts me. The images were the Arctic wolves that I could lock up in the recesses of my mind but never truly silence," she admitted.

A sense of pent-up relief seemed to calm her. She reached out. Their embrace was mutual, empathetic and reassuring, then quiet and quieting. *How I missed such intimacy, such honesty, such devotedness with André,* she lamented.

How I missed such intimacy, such honesty, such devotedness with Suzette, Paul lamented.

Neither wanted to intervene in the closeness.

Paul reluctantly broke the silence of the moment. "Are the Russians after you for killing one of their own?"

"I don't think so because my mother called for backup and the body was disposed of quickly. She described these people as a house-cleaning crew. There were no witnesses that we were aware of. French Counterintelligence let it be known that it was someone else, a convenient pseudonym, who had killed the Russian agent. No name was mentioned, although the KGB would have suspected my mother being involved somehow because she had been this agent's intended target. Only recently have I connected the dots. The KGB agent I shot and killed was after her code and I suspect they are still after it. My mother never told me about the code, only that they were after a secret she knew about."

"That would explain why your apartment in Luxembourg was bugged. Daan was confident it was old KGB and not new FSB.

And then there were the two people on the Eurostar we suspected as being Russian agents. Francine talked about KGB agents who were not invited into the FSB when it was formed in 1995, and one in particular, codenamed Dmitri, whom she described as being a venomous viper."

"Do you think Dmitri may be connected to the assassinations of the incarcerated members of the *Quer* and the guard at the Desert Springs Interrogation Facility?"

"As Francine suggested, if it was him, he probably didn't pull the trigger. He would have contracted out those killings and then had the assassin assassinated by a sniper to ensure any connection to Dmitri would be speculation at best. That begs three questions. First, who was the assassin? Second, who was the assassin's assassin? Third, who was the contractor? A fourth question, perhaps, who organized it?"

"So, do you think Dmitri and Durand are in partnership? Or is Dmitri an entrepreneur and Durand is now at the top of Dmitri's hit list?"

"Or vice versa?" Paul conjectured. "Alternately, is there someone else out there? The stakes would have been high. The payoff had to have been considerable, as a result. Matthieu and Davana are confident they are very close to identifying the person responsible for killing the *Quer* members in the Desert Springs Interrogation Facility. Ideally, there will be a definitive link. The worst-case scenario would be more unknowns being heaped on the growing haystack of conundrums."

"Maman always warned me not to eliminate the unknown, the unsuspected, the obvious that is front and centre, yet not seen because we are blind to its presence, by its enduring presence, like Kim Philby and other agents who had scaled the bastions surreptitiously over decades. There could always be another reason. Francine described Dmitri as a venomous viper and a notorious strategist, never to be wholly trusted. Even exposure to his tainted reputation would dictate a period of detoxification."

"A tangential thought," Paul murmured. "The Roman legions were readily aware of the need for and benefit of cleansing the body, mind and soul after engagement with either unruly hordes or disciplined enemy forces. For this purpose, they built baths heated by natural springs like those around what is today Baden-Baden in southern Germany and Bath in Western England. There they would debrief and relax in preparation for the trauma of subsequent skirmishes or worse, blood-letting battles. We need to follow in their footsteps to cleanse, to purify our stressed souls before we advance further against the unseen yet perceived unruly hordes and enemies."

"I'm with you. Are you thinking of the hot springs at our favourite Liechtenstein retreat?" Alexandra asked gleefully. There was a lightness to her persona brought about by the revelation of a secret shared only with her mother, Maria, a French Counterintelligence agent and before that a member of the *Maquis*. That had burdened her soul for too long. Alexandra was wholly present in the moment. Her eyes were focused on her puppy love and on him alone. Her mother and the KGB agent had been relegated to the memory bank of her past as were the haunting howls of the Arctic wolves.

"Or hot baths in Zürich or Lucerne?" he countered.

"Why just either/or? Why not both/and, both Liechtenstein and Zürich and Lucerne and other hot spring locations. We have crossed the Rubicon with Caesar's Roman legions."

"A tangential thought," Paul conjectured. "Caesar had his enemies, assassins, from within the Republic – *et tu Brute*. History suggests sixty Roman senators, many his personal friends, may have been involved in the conspiracy to assassinate their leader."

"Are there enemies, assassins affiliated with the *Quer*, perhaps within their inner sanctum, like Marcus Junius Brutus?" Alexandra asked, all the while maintaining her enquiring stare.

"Those members of the constabulary and governance Herr Blosch mentioned while we were being hooded on the yacht?" Paul speculated. "It will be interesting to hear what Francine discovers. Herr Blosch can't be the only person potentially prepared to negotiate."

CHAPTER 13

While Alexandra slept in her mother's chair, Paul walked round the garden trying to recall the conversations he had had with Sir James. His attention was drawn to the monkshood and other poisonous plants in his *jardin anglais,* surrounded by the beauty of edible flora such as pansies, which could satiate the palate and nourish both body and soul. Sir James had talked about the need for balance. What was deadly for some was sustenance and protection for others. Some held healing powers while others contained fatal toxins. Co-existence was the key. Returning to the sunroom, he stared at the bookshelf where Sir James had hidden Maria's codebook in plain sight.

Alexandra stirred. "You seem deep in thought, *mon colonel.*" She seemed more relaxed, more composed than before her disclosure of the attack of the Russian agent and his subsequent death by her own hand and her mother's pistol.

Paul smiled. Maria's guidance to her daughter resonated with him – not to eliminate the unknown, the unsuspected, the obvious that can be front and centre, yet not seen because we are blind to its presence. He sensed that more intelligence was in the bookshelf, or a clue to where they could unravel more answers. Was it this obvious, front and centre? In the bookshelf, the seventh book on the seventh shelf. A bound book that looked ancient, entitled *Druid, Celtic and Wiccan Gardens.*

Walter had previously mentioned that someone had broken into the cottage shortly after Sir James's death, ruffling through the bookshelf searching for something but not finding anything.

Was this it, in plain sight? He took it from the shelf and stared at Alexandra questioningly.

"When I was a little girl, my mother told me a story about a fairy-tale character who had been taken to a secret place. She said the seven ribbons in the box she had given me were from this secret place. When I tied them on my dolls and teddy bears, I imagined they were empowered and transported to the fairy-tale land. She cautioned me that there was good and evil on the trail to this fairy-tale safe place."

"Are you thinking what I am thinking?" Paul suggested. "When Sir James gave me your amulet, he recited, 'Those that guard and those that bless share, in time, life's timelessness.' I recited those words of blessing and protection, on his direction, when I tied the amulet around your neck."

It was Alexandra's turn to stare, perplexed.

"Maman figuratively pointed to it with her fairy-tale stories. Is this the source of the code? She did not spell it out, so to speak, in order to protect me until I was old enough to decipher it and understand the severity of the consequences of such knowledge."

"I agree. Sir James knew it because he cited the words of Wicca. Likewise, he just pointed us in that direction in order to protect us until we were ready. I suspect that he and your mother colluded in their verbal clues to us, just in case something happened to either of them. Redundancy has its place. Could this book on *Druid, Celtic and Wiccan Gardens* be a clue to the source code? If so, we just have to figure it out."

"Seven of seven. The seventh of the seven," Alexandra recited. "The seventh of the seventh is reference to the seventh member of the *Quer*, also my heritage. The seventh book on the seventh shelf, *Druid, Celtic and Wiccan Gardens*. There were seven ribbons in my box that my mother blessed when I was a child. That is why she left instructions with the clerk in the jewellery store to advise me. She did everything but tell me what it meant."

"When you examined her code, what was the basis upon which it was created? What is the mathematics, the functionality of the numerical platform?"

"It's interesting because all the one-time code pad coding systems I have studied are based upon a derivative of the Fibonacci-type sequence, one way or another. That is the basis of cryptography. My mother doggedly pursued all counter-code methodologies known to Counterintelligence at the time. She knew that true randomness of numbers is a mathematical impossibility because numeric-based codes, no matter how well enciphered, could be broken. So, she based her code on a completely foreign mathematical format to any Fibonacci model. Its strength is that it is not sequentially predictable. Instead, it is based on clear code, so clear that it is unclear to those who cannot recognize it for what it is."

"Not known because it's not looked for," Paul proposed. "T.S. Eliot wrote that in his poem, *Little Gidding*."

"A good analysis. Perhaps T.S. Eliot was a latent cryptographer or spy."

"He wouldn't be the first or last author or poet to have dabbled in the cryptic halls of espionage."

"My mother used other numeric-based formats when transmitting non-secret logistic information and saved her code for the most top secret and highly sensitive. Thus, there was less code available for hacking. Coders, like artists, like to sign their masterpieces. My mother was very careful not to leave a signature. For some who were none the wiser, the absence was a presence. You could say that anonymity was her monogram. In addition, she did not give her code a name because she didn't want to make it noteworthy. Ironically, it became noteworthy for its anonymity."

"It's based on clear code, but so clear that it is unclear,"

Paul commented. "That's how you just described her code, her methodology."

"What are you thinking?" Alexandra asked.

"Walter said that the intruder thumbed through the bookshelf but didn't seem to find what he was looking for. Perhaps he didn't find what he was looking for because there was nothing there, nothing hidden. We have been hunting for a Fibonacci-style code. But you said that your mother purposely did not use a numeric platform. What if there is no code source? What if the non-sequential deciphering model Sir James gave us in the other books is all there is? It's that simple. What if Sir James and your mother left all these supposed clues as nothing but red herrings? Thon did the same when he created *le fantôme*, the fictional character to mislead the Nazis to allocate and waste resources chasing after nothing. Unfortunately, along the way, innocent people were tortured and left to suffer a gruelling death or simply killed outright."

Alexandra stared out of the window, searching, imagining what her mother would have seen. "My mother lived a very complex life yet always sought simplicity. That was how she achieved balance in our own life. Perhaps you are correct. She and I played word games when I was a child. Her words were always simple. It was so clear to me. I can see how it would be unclear to anyone else who did not know her, who did not understand her culture, who sought complexity in her intent because they saw her work life as complex, which it was in some respects. But she was not. She was the enigma, being an unknown unknown. That was her key to survival as a young member of the *Maquis* during the war. Her code was the manifestation of this duality, that cryptic perplexity."

"Like her daughter in many respects!" Paul added, "Such is the mystique of mystery. And I love you all the more for it." He concentrated for a moment before summarizing. "I'm thinking that simplicity is her source code. Only you knew her and, as a result, only you are able to figure this out."

"What Sir James and my mother are saying is continue the ruse, continue to leave false clues, red herrings, but do so in balance with some truths, mixed with meaningless redundant rhetoric. Sir James achieved balance with his garden and my mother came here to experience the balance."

Paul rubbed the stubble on his chin as he stared at Alexandra. "Sir James's garden is my kryptonite and your mother's chair is yours."

Their thought process was interrupted when their cell phones vibrated simultaneously with a message from Daan. The subject line read: BAIRD'S IDENTITY. "He uses aliases, Brennus or Brennos or Banona, which are ancient Gallic Celtic names. One of his distant relatives married into French royalty of the Louis XII era. Baird inherited property in Alsace, around Strasbourg. We have set up surveillance on a yacht he owns, currently anchored in Heraklion harbour on the island of Crete. As an aside, a French battleship was commissioned *Brennus* in 1896. I would like you to proceed to Strasbourg to follow up."

"Brennus. Interesting," Alexandra muttered. "If I remember correctly from my Continental History courses, there was a Celtic leader of the Senones clan by the name of Brennus. He conquered Rome around 390 BC. Another Celtic leader of the same name laid siege to Delphi about ninety years later. Geographically, the Senones occupied what is today the Alsace Vosges region, and the area south-west of Strasbourg. The probability of Baird's association being just a coincidence has to be very small. Our Baird, or whatever his aliases, has an elite professional warrior caste lineage, an aristocracy, akin to the bygone Knights of Rhodes and Malta, not to be underestimated. To his advantage, if he is in Strasbourg, he is on his home turf, which he probably knows better than the back of his hand."

"Dover will have to wait," Paul muttered. "Back into the fray, *ma princesse*. We engage the battleship *Brennus* or the Gallic Celtic warrior, better informed. I'll ask Daan for Delta Team support. Like Roman legionnaires, we stop to bathe in hot springs along the way in order to rejuvenate and strategize with clearer minds."

Alexandra lingered in deep concentration without confirming Paul's commentary to re-engage.

He gazed at her lowered head. "Talk to me. What are you thinking?"

"Truths of those times are masked in the mists of the Moselle. My mother often whispered that caveat to me when I enquired about the work that took her to Alsace on business trips. She would remind me that my roots are those of Charlemagne and my dynasty Merovingian. In them, I would unearth the truths. I am sensing there is destiny on our horizon, and I am about to unearth some truths as we go to Strasbourg."

"Baird's supposed military prowess and wisdom is no match for Charlemagne's princess, Alexandra Vanessa of the Merovingian dynasty," Paul predicted. "The mists of the Moselle, with their source in the Vosges Mountains, retreat in her presence. And she is advancing. Baird would be naïve to assume that he has home-turf advantage."

Alexandra concentrated in earnest on the prophecy informing her of Charlemagne and her Merovingian dynasty. Never before had she understood her mother's words for what they were – not so much a premonition but a divine blessing of her mantle, her calling if she accepted it, like a knight accepting a benediction from his sovereign and investiture by the priest into the caste of the knighthood. Sir James spoke of it, her duty, her obligation. Her strength would come from her partnership with Paul. Trust was at the core of that union as was faith in her own ability to succeed. Not to doubt. She was her mother's daughter – *de l'audace, encore de l'audace, et toujours de l'audace* – audacity, more audacity, and always audacity.

"We advance on multiple fronts seeking inter-relationships," Paul suggested. "That has been a limiting operational modus operandi for us thus far. On the Thon case, we had just one focus – Thon. With the assistance of Frederik, you accurately identified Thon's Achilles Heel. Perhaps because it was successful, we employed the same linear methodology with the *Quer*. Both Sir James and your mother left us the answers. Yes, be simple, but not simplistic. If we are to dismantle the *Quer*, we must think as Baird Durand was trained to do by his father and his father's father and others in his lineage. We strategize within the context of ancient Celtic and Druid cultural paradigms. You are the forensic psychologist, *ma princess*. What is Baird's psychological profile? Therein, you will unearth the truth."

CHAPTER 14

Daan texted Alexandra and Paul again. Marcel Cousteau would meet them in Strasbourg. He was the best Delta Team surveillance man Paul was aware of. Marcel had served with Paul as his driver with the United Nations Protection Force in the Former Republic of Yugoslavia a decade earlier. They were comrades in arms in the truest sense. Paul had saved his life when Marcel had been wounded on a mission in Bosnia. Most recently, Marcel had come to Paul's rescue when his life was in imminent danger on an EUI Unit mission which culminated at the Hotchkiss factory in Saint-Denis and Compiègne, north of Paris. Alexandra was indebted to him for saving Paul's life and bringing him back to her.

"Marcel just texted that he will meet us at the Brasserie Au Petit Bois Vert on the Quai de la Bruche, but he will be a bit late."

Alexandra scanned other incoming messages. "Our newest centurions are making progress. Francine heard from one of her contacts who was once loyal to the *Quer*. He asked her whether his loyalty reward points are transferable. She suggests that I call her for further details on this, and on another matter."

"Make the call. Daan will be anxious for some progress."

Alexandra tapped her phone keypad.

"Francine, good news I hope."

"Making headway. Apparently, the stipend well has dried up for those members of the constabulary and governance to whom Herr Blosch referred. One loyalty cardholder would like to discuss options for himself. He indicated he would be in a position to negotiate with other constabulary and governance colleagues who have reported that payments from their previous associate have also unexpectedly disappeared. A few have financial commitments that cannot be met as a result of the stipend well drying up. They are looking for another source of income. My contact didn't identify his former employer but would be prepared to disclose such information for a sizeable confidence payment."

"Well, isn't that interesting," Alexandra confirmed. "Good news indeed. I will get back to you soonest. You mentioned a second matter."

"We talked about an olden organization. Word has it there have been multiple shooting deaths in a warm climate, which may be related. The person who pulled the trigger in that case was assassinated. The assassin's assassin is female and now in Switzerland, possibly living in Lucerne in a luxurious condo overlooking the lake. My source doesn't know who hired her, but she recently returned from Valencia. Yusuf and I are en route to follow up on a lead regarding Dmitri, who is living in Valencia and may have been involved in the ambush at Moulins-lès-Metz."

"Thank you for this update. As always, play safe in the sandbox."

"And you too," Francine replied. "As we previously discussed, there are multiple players involved, none of whom have a cordial reputation."

⊣ ⊢

"Daan, this is Commandant Parent. Do you have a moment?"

"Always have time for you, Benoit. What is the Police nationale Anti-Terrorist Unit up to these days?"

"We have identified a mole in the French General Directorate for Internal Security who may have been involved in the fatal shooting of Capitaine Dominique Roland. Can't confirm right now but I'm confident he is related, as in familial relations, to

Baird Durand, the member of the *Quer* whom you are looking for. I should soon know if he is Baird's son. Thought that you might want to know he is currently at la Gare de l'Est in Paris en route to Strasbourg. Your man, Marcel Cousteau, is also here and headed for Strasbourg. He doesn't appear to know the target, so I surmise it is coincidence they are both at la Gare de l'Est. I don't want to be on a collision course with your investigation. Can you contact Marcel and advise? I'll make myself known to him thereafter."

"Thanks for this, Benoit. I'm texting Marcel as we speak. Do contact him and, when appropriate, point out your target. Use the code word 'Peacekeeping' when you approach Marcel. For your information, Alexandra and Paul are presently in Strasbourg and scheduled to meet up with Marcel. We suspect that Baird Durand is hiding out there. I'll let them know, also."

⚔ ⚔

MARCEL FOLLOWED COMMANDANT PARENT OFF the TGV and under the sign proclaiming *Bienvenue à Place de la Gare de Strasbourg.* Other members of the Anti-Terrorist Unit fanned out just as a woman in a black chauffeur's coat and hat approached the target and quickly escorted him to a waiting taxi.

"Something is going down," Benoit announced as the target slumped into the back seat. The taxi driver jumped out of the vehicle, ran south across the median choked with bicycles, and into another vehicle, which sped away unencumbered by one-way traffic congestion. The woman rapidly removed her chauffeur attire, and threw them into the back seat of the taxi. She then darted north on foot with Benoit and his team in pursuit, and Marcel following. As they approached rue Moll, the woman turned and fired her pistol with silencer protruding from the barrel, unbeknown to bystanders. One of Benoit's agents returned fire from his un-muffled pistol. It was clearly heard by pedestrians on the sidewalk who immediately scrambled for cover.

The incident was reported to the media as a thwarted terrorist attack on the European Union Parliament. Two terrorists were killed. Their names were not released for security reasons. The Police nationale Anti-Terrorist Unit and local gendarmes were given full credit for a successful response without civilian casualties or collateral damage.

⊣ ⊢

"WHAT HAPPENED WITH BAIRD'S SON? Why was Commandant Parent part of the Police nationale surveillance team?" Paul asked his comrade in arms. "It is rare to have the most senior officer in the field. Daan directs our work at a strategic level but rarely gets directly involved operationally."

"Good question," Marcel replied. "I don't know but I agree it is a deviation from what could be the procedural norm. Perhaps the Anti-Terrorist Unit has different modus operandi. "

"If the target was Baird's son, as Commandant Parent suggested, then that bolsters our suspicions that Baird may be here in Strasbourg or very close by."

"Any indication where his son was going?" Alexandra followed up.

"As we speak, the techies are working on his cell phone recovered at the scene. He did have a tourist flyer in his pocket with the name Salon de Thé Café on it. That may be the Kaffee Struebel at the south end of the Ponts Couverts, a three-minute walk from us."

"*Carpe diem* – have a nice day. Let's go for a stroll," Paul suggested.

As they crossed the bridge and passed by the third fortification tower on the right, Marcel pointed and said, "It's just to the left off rue Finkwiller."

"Another coincidence?" Alexandra looked at the street sign that read Place Henri Dunant. "Dunant, Durant, Durand. Baird, Brennus, Brennos, Banona. How many names might this seventh member of the *Quer* have? How many does he need? What is he hiding? Better still, who is he hiding from?"

"Henri Dunant was Swiss by nationality, the founder of the Red Cross and first recipient of the Nobel Peace Prize. It is ironic that a social activist and a member of the infamous *Quer* possibly share the same name," Marcel speculated. "There is also a rue Henri Dunant in Colmar."

"All too close to the olden Senones neighbourhood of Brennus, the conqueror of Rome," Alexandra conjectured. *If Strasbourg is the epicentre of Baird Durand's empire, his home turf, as Paul described it, Charlemagne's princess is prepared to engage,* she mused. *This would be the point in the Hollywood Western black and white movie where the good guy in the white hat would draw his revolver from its holster, open the cylinder, ensure that each of the six chambers was carrying a bullet, flip the cylinder back into place and return the pistol to its holster, all while the camera panned in close to capture the drama of the scene. This real-life scene would be boring in contrast,* Alexandra reflected. She was inching closer to the standoff, all the while hoping the final scene would end without the shoot-out on Main Street in front of the saloon at high noon.

"And maybe too convenient," Paul added. "As your mother suggested, do not be too quick to eliminate the unknown, the un-suspected, the obvious that can be front and centre. Colmar is just a little over an hour's drive from here."

"If the two of you want to snoop around this neighbourhood," Marcel proposed, "I'll drive to Colmar and be back in time for dinner. How about 7:30 at the Restaurant Corbeau on Quai

Saint-Nicolas? It's very popular but I know the owner. I'll make reservations."

"*Jusqu'à ce soir, mon ami* – until this evening," Paul replied. "For now, we will sample the *petit déjeuner* at the Kaffee Struebel. This is too picturesque and tranquil a locale to pass up on a little R&R opportunity, however brief."

CHAPTER 15

They sat around the corner table at the Restaurant Corbeau on Quai Saint-Nicolas, facing the window and with their backs to the wall. Their surveillance of the restaurant from this strategic location, including the entrance, was unencumbered. Marcel's familiarity with the configuration of the seating plan and influence with the owner had its advantage. The normal din of the dining activity masked their conversation.

"Anything turn up in Colmar?" Alexandra asked Marcel.

"Nothing. The rue Henri Dunant in Colmar is a short street in a semi-residential district with garages and yards backing onto it. Nothing as auspicious as its namesake here in Strasbourg. I sense the street names are just coincidental. Having said that, if we are to attribute any credibility to the name as a clue to Baird's whereabouts, it would be here in Strasbourg. And how was your *petit déjeuner?*"

"The croissants and cappuccino were lovely but Alexandra wasn't feeling comfortable. Her intuition was calling for caution, yet the ambience couldn't have been more tranquil and relaxing. So, we walked around like inquisitive tourists and finally ended up at Au Petit Bois Vert Brasserie at the north end of the bridge."

"Just as well," Alexandra remarked. "Daan called regarding the male who had been killed and the female chauffeur who fatally shot him outside the Gare de Strasbourg. He asked that we pass this intel along to you. The deceased's identity has been confirmed. He is Baird Durand's son, Joseph Brennus Durand."

"The Brennus lineage continues," Marcel interjected. "But it was troubling that he had been working at such a high level in the General

Directorate for Internal Security. The question to be answered is: Did Joseph Brennus Durand rise to that position through his own talents or is there another Russian spy senior to him in the French Intelligence hierarchy who helped him to advance? He was estimated to be in his late-forties, early-fifties. So, either scenario is possible."

"*C'est vrai.*" Alexandra acknowledged. "He was spying for the Russians and at least one other unknown party. Moscow or the other employer may have become upset with his dual loyalty and levelled the playing field. His FSB handler in Paris has been tentatively identified, but there is no further ID on the other employer, if there is one."

Marcel smiled. "It's good news for us in the search for Baird Durand because the death of his son may flush him out of hiding and cause him to make more emotionally subjective decisions."

A text message from Daan appeared on all three cellphones simultaneously. "Commandant Parent advised that the government did not have a valid next of kin recorded on Joseph Brennus Durand's personnel file."

"So, Baird Durand may not know his son is dead," Paul conjectured. "I will ask Daan if Commandant Parent can quietly release the details of his death through back channels, as I doubt further information will be made public, given the fact the media has recorded the incident as a botched terrorist attack on the EU Parliament. They would not want conflicting information out of concern for losing face with their readership which is diminishing with the popularity of electronic media."

"Not so good news regarding the female chauffeur," Alexandra noted with minimal enthusiasm. "She had no ID and was just carrying a throwaway cellphone from which she had neither sent nor received any calls or texts. Daan suspects she would have used it to confirm the kill and then thrown it away. Her fingerprints are not on file with Interpol. The only characteristic that Commandant Parent can confirm is her approximate age as late twenties to early thirties, and her ethnicity. Her complexion and facial features appear to be a mix of Caucasian and Asian. Whoever she was working for has taken considerable trouble to hide her identity. No prints suggest Chinese or Russian and definitely off the grid, yet professionally trained in assassination or related tradecraft."

It was Marcel's turn to frown while analyzing the mounting intelligence and speculative evidence. "When agents go so black that they are not even unofficially listed as missing, we can safely assume that the classification of the mission was well above top secret in the department. There would be no record of the mission or who ordered the hit. There are two possible explanations. First, if it's within an agency, more likely only one person tasked the agent. Second, it was contracted out to a third party."

Marcel thought for a moment, then added, "There is actually a third possible scenario. It could be a rogue agent no longer on anyone's espionage payroll but with an axe to grind, a vendetta. The flip side of that coin is that it was a newbie attempting to raise their own profile in the ever-increasing marketplace for assassins. I suggest that is a much lower probability but still a possibility."

"One final point," Alexandra added, "there may be another Moscow connection. The pistol she was carrying was a Soviet Makarov PB 9mm with silencer. Given what you have described, Marcel, this could either muddy the waters or bring some clarity to our future direction. We have witnessed it before where another entity tries to deflect their own national interests by leaving Russian hardware, like weapons, in the wake of their actions. Here, I am thinking Beijing. Not to be outdone, Moscow is known to leave a trail of Chinese fortune cookies also in a deceptive strategy to deviate attention away from the Kremlin."

"A Soviet Makarov PB 9mm with silencer is the same make and model used by the assassin who killed the other members of the

Quer in the Desert Springs Interrogation Facility," Marcel conceded. "The nationality of that assassin is estimated to be Caucasian/Asian also. The fingerprints were not on any Western police or intelligence database either. This agent again was also late twenties/early thirties."

Was it mere speculation, or coincidence once again? Alexandra pondered. "The Makarov PB had been used by the KGB and is the weapon of choice of the FSB. Perhaps of interest, the Russian special forces, the Spetsnaz, use it. It is also popular with spies of different colours. Moscow-related but not necessarily Moscow-directed?" Alexandra again reflected. *The female chauffeur's fingerprints may have come up negative, but Dmitri's covert signature seemed to be popping up all too often. Time for a tête-à-tête with Francine.*

"If you wanted to leave a trail of bread crumbs away from you leading everywhere and nowhere in order to cause confusion, how would you best accomplish that?" Marcel asked.

His question left Paul and Alexandra pondering the question and his motivation for posing it.

Marcel replied to his own question before his colleagues. "You leave the exact same crumbs. In this case, the same make and model handgun with the same brand of silencer. Whoever is behind these shootings has access to a good supply of Makarov PB pistols. In order of priority, I would say Moscow-related first with easy access to FSB armouries. Both weapons would qualify – the male assassin at the Desert Springs Interrogation Facility, and the female assassin who killed Baird Durand's son, Joseph Brennus Durand. Thinking back to previous cases the European Union Intelligence Unit has investigated where there were fatalities, the Makarov PB was involved. All pistols showed signs of use. None was new. A coincidence? Perhaps." Marcel slowly shook his head. "I would not be surprised if the Makarov PB was and remains the personal weapon of choice for Francine and Yusuf, and Dmitri."

CHAPTER 16

As they approached a three-storey, low-rental apartment block on a beachfront property in Valencia, Yusuf said, "We have no idea what Dmitri looks like, only that he lives alone on the top floor of this apartment building facing both the street and the side lane. There's a fire escape ladder at the back. It is a classic KGB abode selected with an operational eye for maximum surveillance and hasty escape if need be. My source tells me the other apartment on the third floor adjacent to Dmitri's is vacant as is the apartment immediately below his. The landlord lives on the bottom floor."

Francine acknowledged the information with a subtle nod and whispered to Yusuf, "You sit here and sip your beer like a tourist. I'll enter the other apartment and listen for Dmitri to climb the stairs. Then I'll step into the hall and get a good look at him as he is about to enter his apartment. Text if anything untoward catches your attention."

"I suggest we reverse roles," Yusuf responded.

"In this neighbourhood, men sitting in cafés are the norm. Look around. The only women sitting sipping wine are prostitutes, attracting the attention of every man, like bees to the honeypot, so to speak. I am not a Red Sparrow and have no intention of adopting that role at my mature age."

She had undergone training to become a Red Sparrow as part of her indoctrination into the tradecraft many years ago. In her youth, she had been exceptionally attractive with her blonde hair, blue eyes, shapely physique, intellect and quick wit. Few targets, mostly male but also female, could resist her charms. With finely-tuned seduction skills, she had also been trained in advanced hand-to-hand self-defence which she had employed on occasion with the unruliest clients who mistakenly assumed she was a quick and naïve pickup. Some had to be carried out of the temporary accommodation while others limped away to lick their wounds.

Yusuf's response to her reference to Red Sparrows was reserved although he tried not to express any overt emotions. He knew of their reputation for giving all for the Kremlin. Physical and sexual abuse was a common occurrence. Revenge was sweet once the intelligence had been acquired. From Yusuf's perspective, it was OK for others but not Francine.

"I don't like it but I see your point," he replied. "Be careful. As you say, Dmitri has the reputation of a venomous viper."

Francine followed up with a confident reply. "Who's the ex-KGB and ex-FSB agent here with years of clandestine experience, and who's the ex-Turkish Military Intelligence officer with limited field proficiency?"

In retrospect, he couldn't recall an occasion when he had won these objective arguments with her because she was invariably correct, and she knew it. Instead, he preferred pillow talk as a means of détente. Between the sheets, he won more debates but only because she allowed him to win, and he knew it.

Yusuf hesitated, then acquiesced. "Point taken. But be careful because he will more than likely be armed. You know KGB and FSB procedures when contacted by unknown foreign agents. Add to these suspicions his current status as a disgruntled ex-KGB agent, now private-sector intelligence entrepreneur, and you will be facing a short-fused aggressor. So, don't be alarmed."

Francine's cell buzzed. The text message read: "The confederate from Paris you mentioned is no longer available. Call when convenient."

Yusuf held her attention. After a brief moment, he glanced down at her cellphone with a quizzical expression. Clearly, the text was not merely social. Averting his stare, he prompted, "All OK?"

Francine nodded with a tic of a reply as she deleted the text. Her facial expression gave nothing away that might suggest anything to the contrary. He concluded the source was known to her and, more than likely, related to Dmitri.

Francine knew how to be sensually seductive with her choice of words. Her training as a Red Sparrow had taught her how to avoid the need to formulate an awkward response. To do so would transfer control of the conversation from her to the other party. She knew how to be neutral or cold and calculating in order to avert the need for a more detailed response and, in doing so, retain control. She was always the predator. His was a close-ended question with a hint asking for elaboration. Hers was a close-ended non-verbal reply with a strong indication the conversation had ended. He was good and she knew it. She was better and he knew it. Together, they were superior and they both knew it.

"I'll meet with Dmitri alone. I don't want to spook him," she confirmed.

Yusuf squinted and slowly shook his head from side to side. "I'm not comfortable with that."

Francine suspected his concern was motivated by more than unease, a manifestation of the heightened potential of the venomous viper to strike. "It's an initial contact so I suspect he will be cautious and not interested in talking too long. He will correctly assume that I have backup. That is standard operating procedure for first contact. If I was still a KGB agent in the throes of a mission, he might shoot first and ask questions later. But he is an espionage entrepreneur seeking sources of income. As a result, he will want time to check me out. As long as I do not give him reason to feel threatened, he should remain relatively unruffled, at least as calm as an ex-KGB agent can be, given the circumstances. I know that you are concerned," she conceded. "We can relax this evening over dinner with Spanish wine and Portuguese Port thereafter."

While Yusuf enjoyed a cool beer in the shade of the café, Francine suffered in the suffocating heat of the apartment with no breeze from closed windows or the luxury of air conditioning known only to the affluent rather than the poorer residents of the spartan barrio. On occasion, she stood back from the window watching Yusuf sipping his beer under the shaded canopy and estimating the time of arrival of her target based on the extended reach of shadows over the streets as the sun set. She was ever conscious of her movement not wanting to alert those who occupied the apartment below with the potential squeak of a loose floor board. She regretted her decision not to accept Yusuf's offer to reverse roles.

Such was the balance of the nimble and the perilous in the arcane game of espionage surveillance.

CHAPTER 17

The sound of creaking stairs attracted her attention. Francine rose from her makeshift seat on the floor of the apartment devoid of even the most basic furnishings. The arthritis in her hip reminded her of her mortality and a hard landing she had taken while undergoing parachute training with the Russian Special Forces, the Spetsnaz, when temporarily attached to the GRU, the Main Intelligence Directorate. She was getting too old for this line of work. At least as a Red Sparrow, the accommodation and ambiance tended to be more luxurious, even if a few of the clients were not.

Feet scuffed across the landing. She opened the door slowly and glanced over at the commanding presence of a seasoned, physically fit man silhouetted against the light from a single window illuminating the hallway. He had the advantage of the sunlight at his back that impaired her vision of his otherwise unremarkable features and equally obscure persona. At first blush, he did not appear to be the tragic abandoned figure his previous employer had portrayed him to be. She concluded he could be rented by anyone for a price beyond the meager budgets of all but the most influential. He may have mellowed slightly since the heyday of the Cold War but, when startled, adopted the stance of the venomous viper ready to strike. A mangy feline drew her attention as it followed him up the stairs in quickstep announcing its approach with a raspy snarl while rubbing figure-eight circuits around his ankles. The malign defiance of one complemented the other.

"Do I know you?" His voice was as composed as it was cold yet compelling. He scanned her features and mentally frisked her for any threats. These were honed tactics of a tradecraft she knew all too well. *Vesgda na strazhe* – always on guard.

"I don't think we ever met," Francine replied nonchalantly as her eyes adjusted to the diffused sunrays in the corridor.

He replaced his keys in his pocket and kept his left hand hidden between the door jam and his side. His elbow bent momentarily and straightened again still remaining out of sight along his side. "Do we share similar alumni?" he enquired cautiously, all the while evaluating her intent. She had positioned herself close enough to assess his response but not too distant so as to be at a disadvantage if she needed to react to a threat. He surmised that she had been trained in the art and science of offensive and defensive engagement by professionals.

"Perhaps a different cohort in a different institution immersed in a similar discipline," Francine replied with both hands exposed in an overt attempt to reduce his heightened alertness.

With his right hand, Dmitri slowly pulled out a packet of Belomorkanals from his breast pocket and offered her one. "Care to join me?"

"I prefer North American brands with filters when I do smoke." The recollection of vile Soviet cigarettes was akin to the acid reflux experienced from consuming greasy British cookery too often.

"I too have developed a preference for Western brands but thought that you might be homesick."

Francine's response gave nothing away. A neutral demeanour defined her intention. She sensed his tension wasn't increasing. Ideally, he would relax. To smile openly would elicit aggression from him. Only with fellow Russians and then only with close friends in private would it be appropriate to smile. Having lived in France for several years, she had had to learn how to let her guard down, to smile but not with her handler who would frown in contempt of liberal Parisiennes.

As he tucked in the flap and replaced the pack of cigarettes in his pocket, he probed further for her intentions. "How can I help you?" His question was as much provocative as cautious. With his ongoing assessment, he interpreted her impersonal façade as anything but neutral. She had an agenda that dictated respect for its potential.

"It is I who may be in a position to assist you," Francine replied in a tone that bordered on seduction, which he recognized not so much from local ladies but from an earlier time in his career. The details of that previous encounter remained elusive. Not knowing was always dangerous. Not remembering could be fatal.

Francine could still hold the high ground in any game of seductive ploy for male prey who, she surmised, wanted to extend an interaction with a mature female who was not a novice. She had not only not lost her skill but had augmented the lessons learned from observing the quintessential mysterious Parisienne women as equal partners in the early evening *cinq à sept*, the occasion for a mutual tryst, a metonym. She was acutely aware of the adage – Paris's greatest gift to the world was its beautiful women. She had accredited herself as one of those greatest gifts to the world. The gaze she consistently garnered from admiring French men, *flâneurs* among other gentlemen of purpose, as she frequented the myriad cafés and strolled the boulevards of the City of Lights. It was in stark contrast to the abrupt unsophisticated Muscovite men ignorant of the basics of etiquette and the *courtoise* – the courteous.

"Let's walk along the beach," Dmitri said after a pensive interlude. "I find the sound of the waves soothing after a day at the office. Meet me downstairs in five minutes. I need to feed the cat."

⇥ ⇤

SHE CONFIRMED YUSUF'S ENQUIRING GAZE as he looked at her from his table at the café. From her vantage point in the doorway, she nodded with an indifferent yet slim smile. Her demeanour was relaxed. His remained calm yet still wary as a result.

The stairs creaked in reverse order announcing his descent to the foyer and the entrance to the aging apartment block. His feline friend trailed at a discrete distance as if also trained in the discipline of surveillance and counterespionage.

Yusuf tipped his bottle to sip his cerveza and to obscure his appearance as Dmitri joined her and led the way to the beach. He sensed no immediate threat to her.

The sound of the waves will mask any conversation being recorded, Francine mused. *He wants to walk so he shouldn't be wearing a wire. He must think I am because his DNA is KGB, homo-shpion – homo-spy.*

"Do you require a résumé, without letters of reference from previous supervisors or employers?" Francine enquired nonchalantly in anticipation of an equally vague response. She let the enquiry hang. His reply would provide further indications as to his underlying intention, however veiled.

"A résumé only describes imagined or exaggerated competencies with a suggestion of inflated capabilities. In the absence of a résumé and letters of reference, I would need to confirm demonstrated proven abilities and potential capabilities. It is just good human resource management hiring practices. вы бы согласились? *– Would you agree?*"

The new and the old worlds seemed to meet in him like the turbulence of weather systems, each with its own desire for supremacy. Francine needed to respond simultaneously to both, to be terse without being abrupt, yet conciliatory without seeming appeasing, provocative and evocative. "I found you and your apartment which I might add has a commanding view of the beach from the top floor."

He smiled wryly. "Fair enough." His demeanour remained

wary but marginally less offensive. Rome wasn't built in a day. She was constructing the foundation of a relationship that she knew would allow her to elicit the needed intelligence regarding the ambush in Moulins-lès-Metz: who had ordered the assassination of Dominique and Rudolf, and the attempted assassination of herself. Most importantly, she wanted to know who had pulled the trigger. She would retaliate accordingly once she had amassed all the intelligence and confirmed its accuracy.

"I understand that one of your associates currently residing in Lucerne recently visited you here?" Francine was on a fishing expedition offering traces of bait without feeding the prey.

"Perhaps you were vacationing in Valencia and saw me with someone. It is a popular holiday location, especially the old city and the beach. I have many acquaintances who visit." Dimitri was careful to distance himself from any connotation of operational association.

"And perhaps I maintain a condo in Switzerland overlooking Lake Lucerne," Francine countered.

As their gazes met, neither seemed to alter their response – the parry and the riposte. "Fair enough." He fell back a half pace to gauge her verbal expression and body language from a peripheral perspective.

It was Francine's turn to take the initiative. She shortened the length of her own stride to get a more encompassing view of his response without being obvious.

"And perhaps you were paid in full for the Moulins-lès-Metz contract?" she commented. She sensed he would have looked surprised had he not been involved. Yet she noted an involuntary twitch in his eyelid. She concluded that he was aware of the contract and the identity of the assassin.

A spasm of pain in her elbow reminded her of her recent duel with the grim reaper once again. With the sudden spike, she smiled inwardly anticipating the satisfaction she would get from the final checkmate move. He was in her net gasping for water. He just hadn't realized it, *yet*.

They walked in silence, Cold War warriors, impeccably camouflaged among the unenlightened and indifferent tourists.

"Are you suggesting that someone may have been overpaid?" he countered with a slight shrug implying indifference rather than inquisitiveness.

"I merely ask the question." Francine saw an opportunity to advance her relationship, albeit tenuous. "Do I sense some doubt, perhaps?"

"Sometimes it's hard to get good, hired help. But the contractor seemed to believe an independent third-party witness who verified that all goods and services had been delivered."

"Perhaps you need a better independent third party," she suggested. "You may wish to confirm that your source in the General Directorate for Internal Security in Paris is still available. My informant suggests that he has taken early and permanent retirement."

Dmitri regarded Francine with a shadow of wariness yet remained intrigued by how she had gained this knowledge, unbeknown to him. The suspicion in his contrived smile deepened. He mused, *she seems to be comfortable and proficient in the murky world of intelligence gathering. Yet there are too many pedlars of misinformation engaged in fraud. Their wares were partial truths laced with courteous deceit.*

"Allow me to confirm your credentials. How can I contact you?"

"There is a café across from your apartment."

"I know the waiter. I'll have him deliver an invitation for you to join me there should I wish to continue our conversation. To whom should I address the invitation?"

"*Côtes du Rhône*. It is my preferred wine."

"And a trademark wine it is for a lady with a discriminating palate for exquisite fruits of the vine," Dmitri said while masking his aloofness. He had more affection for his feline friend who seemed to know when to approach and when to keep her distance.

"*À bient*ôt, Dmitri," Francine responded pertly as if addressing an acquaintance of many years.

It was his turn to give an expressionless response.

"*Hasta pronto*, Côtes du Rhône."

"Скоро увидимся – *See you soon*," Francine confirmed.

Dmitri watched her stroll toward the paved beach promenade all the while scanning his mental Rolodex file. He had once prided himself on his prodigious memory but lately found it necessary to allow his intuition to play a greater role, especially on occasions like this when his recollection proved elusive. Memory was the hallmark of the tradecraft. His cell vibrated.

"What did she ask?" The enquiry was neutral.

"Routine. Would I like to discuss business?" Dmitri replied in an equally bland tone.

"What did you say?"

"I would leave an invitation for her to join me later."

"Anything else?"

"*Nyet* – No."

CHAPTER 18

Francine sauntered back to her pre-arranged rendezvous with Yusuf. She had not anticipated this level of success after just the first encounter with Dmitri. She felt energized as a result but always cautious. *Had this first encounter been too successful, too quickly?* she wondered. The Red Sparrow would preen her feathers in anticipation of fine dining and sampling of some exquisite Spanish libations in celebration. That would be followed by an evening rendezvous with her chosen feathered mate and not a Moscow-arranged assignation.

"You asked me to call. *J'écoute*," Francine said quietly.

"I'll be brief," Alexandra spoke. "The confederate from the General Directorate for Internal Security was killed at *La Gare de Strasbourg* by a female assassin. His name is or was Joseph Brennus Durand. The word Durand in old French means to survive. I can only conclude that Joseph has not inherited this aspect of his family heritage."

Alexandra listened carefully for Francine's response not just to the disclosure of the information but, more telling, the emotional inflection. She surmised that Francine would express some level of Parisienne empathy if she wanted to convince Alexandra of her commitment to sever ties with her former employer. On the other hand, her current circumstances might dictate otherwise in order to maintain her cover, which was more transparent than opaque.

"And the assassin?" Francine enquired, devoid of compassion.

"Are you free to speak at this time?" Alexandra followed up.

"I'm free to listen for a minute but no longer as I am about to meet someone."

106

"I'll be brief then," Alexandra replied. "The assassin was killed by the police who had Joseph Brennus Durand under surveillance. The media reported the incident as a foiled terrorist attack on the EU Parliament."

"That's plausible," Francine replied, again in a pragmatic unemotional manner. She anticipated that Alexandra would pass along additional details because she had asked if Francine was alone. In response, Francine slowed her pace to allow more time to hear what Alexandra had to say.

"We have no confirmed identification of the assassin, though. Can you find out who she might have been and, more importantly, who was paying her?"

"I'm not surprised she remains anonymous. As I mentioned before, there are many players in the sandbox. An increasing number are new and ardently vying for primacy in the pecking order within their own organizations, in addition to freelancing entrepreneurs. I'll see what I can find out. Any other details to help me narrow down the search?"

"She was Caucasian/Asian and used a Soviet Makarov PB 9mm pistol equipped with a silencer. It had all the trappings of a professional operation."

"I'll make a few enquiries but can't guarantee immediate results. In the fullness of time, however, the details should emerge as a direct result of there being one less competing gladiator in the arena."

"Understood," Alexandra confirmed.

"The Makarov PB was the weapon of issue for the KGB and remains the weapon of choice for many FSB agents. It is also a weapon favoured by agents of other nationalities," Francine confirmed. "Any other information on the confederate?"

"Joseph Brennus Durand was on Moscow's payroll and was

possibly working for another employer as yet unknown, but I can't confirm the latter," Alexandra added.

Francine knew that Joseph Brennus Durand was an FSB informant. She had followed him one day in Paris when he met with his handler who turned out to be her own handler. Francine also knew who his father was and that the olden organization Paul had referred to was the *Quer*. But there were still too many unknown variables. She wasn't aware how much her handler knew and how much he had passed on to Moscow. Neither did she know the identity of the other party to whom Joseph Brennus Durand was supposed to be providing information.

"Are you still free to talk?" Alexandra asked, conscious of the fact a minute had passed since she first enquired.

"Yes, but make it quick."

Not knowing who Joseph Brennus Durand's second contact was, beyond Moscow, caused Francine concern. Was there a connection between this yet unknown other party and Dominique's murder and her own attempted murder? Had Joseph Brennus Durand been involved, co-opted by Dmitri? Of lesser concern at the moment but of equal importance was the composition of her previous cell. FSB handlers routinely supervised four operatives. If Joseph Brennus Durand was one and she was a second, who were the other two agents? Were they active or sleepers? And to whom did her handler report? For security reasons, no one in the hierarchy of a cell knew the identity of others laterally or vertically, beyond supervisors. All routine messages were communicated via anonymous drop boxes.

"One final point," Alexandra queried. "Have you made contact with Dmitri?"

"*Yeshche nyet* – Not yet," Francine lied. "Thank you for this information. I will be in contact."

Alexandra sensed an increase in Francine's tension, so she

ended the call. She did not want to misinterpret any pertinent detail due to a rush.

Yusuf had been monitoring Francine's return to their beachfront café rendezvous. His disciplined stare as a Cold War warrior monitored her steps for any indication of covert surveillance she might have picked up while speaking with Dmitri. More than likely, it would be one of his associates, possibly an assassin summoned to establish positive ID in the event Francine was to be eliminated. It was the relentless, perverse game of cat and mouse. But who was playing which role, and who was entering and exiting the stage from different portals? Had different stage directors cast them in more than one role, simultaneously? Who were the predators and who were the prey at any given point in time that could change at a moment's notice?

Francine smiled as she sat down.

"And?" Yusuf probed.

"It went as I expected. Dmitri will leave an invitation with the waiter at the café across the street from his apartment where you were sipping your drink if he wants to meet again."

The past had not been fully exorcised so the lingering paranoia of treachery left her suspicious of everyone, courtesy of the profession. The real and the psychosomatic pain of the bullet wound from the Moulins-lès-Metz ambush reminded her that when momentary carelessness and resilient courage collide, the outcome could be anyone's guess but rarely good. That hard-learned lesson not to lower her guard would remain with her. Yusuf had reminded her on more than one occasion that the best-laid plans often go awry the moment they are activated. He remembered it from one of the references he had read on Western philosophy. Francine sighed slightly as she gently massaged her elbow – a collision with fate she regretted. The corporeal emotions for revenge would be her final *coup de grâce* though.

She was confident there would be a return match with Dmitri. He could not resist the enticing charms of the Red Sparrow. She was equally sure she would get more information regarding the identity of who had pulled the trigger. At that juncture, the seductive Red Sparrow would shed its soft feathers and transform into the lethal black hawk.

By the time they meet again, Dmitri will have learned that Joseph Brennus Durand, his contact from the French General Directorate for Internal Security, had taken permanent retirement. Alexandra had described his assassin as female Caucasian/Asian. Francine was not only aware of Moscow's penchant for employing Asians, she had worked closely with a few. To describe them as ruthless and without remorse would be a serious understatement. Francine was also aware that Beijing employed Caucasians on similar missions. For both, it was a convenient method of muddying the waters to cover the tracks. Francine would subtly enquire with Dmitri in an effort to ascertain if he was also employing such mixed cultural resources. In the same conversation, she would attempt to confirm the national lineage of the Lucerne assassin.

CHAPTER 19

"**M**ight I conclude that my credentials meet with your approval?"

Dmitri stood and greeted Francine in a ritual embrace with disciplined fingers conducting a cursory search for a wire or other electronic surveillance device. His mannerism was patently Slavic Rus' devoid of explicit emotion, not Iberian with ritual displays of expressive affection. *Vsegda na strazhe* – Always on guard. He nodded, seemingly unconcerned. His eyes conveyed no telltale message of intent.

The waiter lifted a glass of wine from his serving tray and placed it in front of Francine with a practised gesture. It seemed like a pale prelude to what could be the ensemble and final movement of a predestined symphony with the details of the finale yet to be scripted. Francine benignly adopted the role of second fiddle without a bow. She saw no reason to challenge his jousting innuendoes at this time.

At their first meeting, she sensed contempt for her gender. At this meeting, her perception was confirmed. It was a common chauvinist attitude among the old KGB guard within the bastions of the Kremlin. She smiled inwardly – *One more defining tidbit of intelligence to strengthen my assessment of a potential vulnerability in his profile.* That was the preliminary mission of a Red Sparrow, to identify strengths and most importantly, weaknesses.

"A Côtes du Rhône especially ordered for the lady with timely and accurate information. It appears that I do in fact have an opening in my organization for an independent third-party verifier due to an early unannounced retirement."

"I deal only in cash," Francine announced matter-of-factly. His oblique greeting was yet another weakness. It left room for her to take charge of the conversation as she had done when they first met and when they parted company on the beach. She deduced that Dmitri's analytical skills had become clouded like cataracts darkening and dampening clarity of vision from too much time sketching naïve tourists in his outdoor seaside studio. This impairment had been marginally mitigated with Siberian vodka.

"Cash is my preferred method of remuneration, also. But first, introductions. You seem to know more about me. If we are to conduct business, I should know who I am dealing with, at least."

She had anticipated this opening serve and rehearsed her return volley.

"At this juncture, it is best to maintain confidentiality for security purposes. Côtes du Rhône will do for now. Certainly, I do not want to retire prematurely." Her nod was tentative, her expression impartial, her tone provisional. His greeting had been Slavic Rus'. Her mannerism would be equally terse and dispassionate.

It was all about business, obtaining crucial intelligence regarding the Moulins-lès-Metz ambush – her priority. A bonus would be information relating to the whereabouts of Baird Durand – Alexandra's mission. Both guaranteed considerable compensation which she could invest offshore in a self-administered unregistered retirement pension plan, at least in the short term.

"Fair enough, for now. Nor do I," Dmitri acknowledged, not wanting to appear too insistent at this preliminary stage of their fledgling business relationship. His frustration was mildly palpable. He was accustomed to getting what he wanted. Instead, he was aggravated having to concede once again to someone younger and female. He gained a sense of solace knowing that he would win gold in the final round of the tournament. No informal contract had been agreed upon and no money had yet changed hands as a stipend of good faith or down payment provided for goods and services yet to be received. *The final payment may never have to be paid,* he mused.

Francine raised her wine glass. With a slight bow of her head but not her eyes, she uttered, "To a mutually beneficial business relationship."

Dmitri reciprocated with a nod, all the while noting that she delicately but deliberately drew her fingers down the length of the stem of the wine glass, erasing any fingerprints.

As a young agent climbing the ladder in the KGB hierarchy, he had consumed too much too often in a feeble attempt to impress his superiors with his stamina. That level of alcohol consumption had only temporarily dulled his cognitive abilities. Today, it was readily apparent that the fogging of his memory was increasingly becoming a problem.

Unlike the Asian chauffeur, her prints could be verified in FSB and, more than likely, Interpol files. She would not leave any physical traces. The deliberate smudging of her identity merely communicated her desire to remain anonymous at this point in their wary relationship.

These characteristic behaviours were two more clues that Dmitri noted as he added to the mental profile he was building. He was close to unmasking the mystery persona that sat at the table with him. He was confident they had crossed paths somewhere. He had a fuzzy recollection she was good at what she did. Once, he had been better. No doubt she was a professional, schooled by the best in the arcane tradecraft, which seemed a little less secret by virtue of familiarity.

Francine sat patiently confident that Dmitri would make the next move. Her stillness was more of a purposeful manoeuvre and less a falsely baited tactic, which he could employ to pinpoint her identity and *raison d'être.*

His reputation had preceded him as a strategic Rodina agent constantly seeking alliances for his own advantage. He was known for speaking less and pondering more. Backhanding the ball into his court, thus interpreting his analysis, put him at a slight disadvantage.

She watched him cock his head in an attempt to discern whether an unheard sound was in fact a warning of an approaching predator stalking its prey from the cover of seemingly benign verbal camouflage. He weighed the mix of subtle coquettish signals of the Red Sparrow. He would continue to allow her to take the lead. Time was on his side yet caution would continue to be in order.

"As you have surmised, I am an entrepreneur," he explained. "My business is my business. I contract my services as do you. In this regard, we could be competitors or collaborators."

"I prefer the latter." Francine grinned faintly. Public displays of emotion were a sign of weakness in today's Russian federation and, more importantly, it was interpreted as a need for wariness. Yet she wanted to extend a tentative invitation to explore mutually beneficial options, actually less mutual but more for her benefit. It was a fine line between Soviet and Western cultures that she had walked before with growing success, learning as she strolled along the Champs Élysée and other grand pedestrian boulevards in the City of Lights. Her challenge at the moment was that Dmitri was neither East nor West but both and neither at the same time. There was no fine line to walk. Instead, there was just mist-shrouded no man's land renowned for its erratic unmapped mine fields laid with no apparent logic.

"You mentioned Moulins-lès-Metz. Were you vying for that contract?" Dmitri enquired nonchalantly as if her response was not the true intent of his question.

He sensed that her motivation in referencing the incident was somehow linked to the fatal outcome. He doubted it was financial.

She didn't seem the type for it to be political. It could be personal. If so, was it for personal gain or personal loss? The latter would be more passionate and, as such, more dangerous. The greatest inducement was vengeance, but he didn't detect retaliation in her demeanour. It had to be something else, something detached.

The ball was back in her court. The longer it took for her to compose her response, the more time he had to assess her identity and prepare his reply.

She was prepared. She replied immediately. "I heard about it recently from a source in the French General Directorate of Internal Security who seemed to be working for more than one employer."

She was as curious about the motivation of his response as he was about hers. She waited.

"Greed abrogates integrity, it seems," Dmitri proposed. "If accurate, this begs the question. Did the person who awarded me the contract know of this duplicity?"

His reply added little she did not already know or suspect to be true.

Francine gazed at him over the rim of her wine glass as she took a sip of her Côtes du Rhône. She savoured the taste. She relished the upper-hand she held at the moment, but would relinquish it in favour of verifiable intelligence.

"Perhaps I was not awarded the contract because I asked too many questions. It's just how I operate. I need to know details when planning such operations. I did find out there was a connection to wealth acquired through less than ethical means. It had been hidden by the Nazis during the final weeks of the war as they hurriedly prepared to vacate Paris. It remains to be recovered."

Dmitri inhaled slowly as he considered her words, which he interpreted to be more speculative than informative. It was widely known that Reichsmarschall Göring had stolen vast amounts of gold and other unrecorded treasures. He had hidden what he was unable to transport back to Germany and his private Bavarian estate.

"Perhaps it is not wise to ask too many questions," he replied in a tone more speculative than informative.

"Perhaps so. I just like to do my homework thoroughly. This differentiates me from people like your third-party verifier who has retired prematurely yet permanently."

"Point well made. You mentioned wealth taken and hidden. Am I correct in concluding that you have some first-hand knowledge of its theft and its approximate whereabouts? I say approximate as I doubt you would be here if you were certain of it."

He has taken my bait, Francine grinned inwardly. *Time to gently reel in the line and observe his response. Will he dive deep in an attempt to throw off the hook or surface to feign defeat. More than likely, he will merely swim so as not to give any indication of his status.*

"I only know of its theft." Francine paused to assess his reaction and bait another hook. "Was your trigger in cahoots with someone else, maybe your third-party verifier? Did they find some of the wealth and decide not to share? With you?" *How intent was he on acquiring treasures of value?* she pondered. *Was this just one of his motivations or his sole raison d'être?*

"Perhaps I need to invite my associate from Lucerne for another Valencia vacation as my third-party verifier for the Moulins-lès-Metz contract is no longer available," Dmitri proposed. He gave away nothing. Instead, he watched for her response.

The mention of gold seemed to manoeuvre him away from his comfort zone to following her lead. *His Achilles heel*, she surmised. She would continue along this track.

He held her gaze without responding.

"My source suggested that the retirement of your third-party verifier might have been Moscow-related but not necessarily

Moscow-directed or allied with another yet unknown international employer further east. It would be interesting to find out what your Lucerne associate knows about that. Perhaps early retirements are his speciality and he has kept all the stolen wealth from the Moulins-lès-Metz contract as a bonus payment."

Dmitri gleaned nothing from her response. Either there was nothing there or she was not prepared to disclose her intent. He allowed the silence to hang.

"I am assuming rightly or wrongly that your trigger is a 'he' and not a 'she.'" Francine tilted her head and shrugged her shoulders. She waited for his response, as interested in what he had to say as much as how he said it.

Dmitri squinted, maintaining his stare without comment. His increasing uneasiness became evident. She seemed to know a great deal regarding this aspect of his business. He needed to fly fish without being fished himself.

He broke his silence. "It is appropriate that I have a discussion with someone else." His response was blunt. This meeting was over. "But before we adjourn, you should know that Moscow finds it beneficial in this post-Cold War era to diversify its contracts with a myriad of operatives each with their own speciality. This keeps them at arm's-length. There is one senior contract administrator for the Western European Union. There are supplementary contract administrators in other geographical jurisdictions. This network is in addition to spies and their spymasters. You may be more familiar with the latter."

He awaited her response. There was none. "I liaise mostly with the Western EU administrator, among others." Again, his comment was finite. It was to inform, not to elicit further discussion.

"Reduces the paperwork," Francine remarked with a customary brief nod. The ball was in his court again.

"That it does. In addition, I have one personal project and would be prepared to employ you as a researcher. It relates to wealth management. We can chat when next we meet."

"*À bientôt*," Francine replied, as she bid him adieu. She sipped the last of her wine and drew her fingers methodically down the length of the stem one final time. Her communication was also clear. Hers was the last word in the meeting without a set agenda or time and date confirmed for the next rendezvous.

CHAPTER 20

"Alexandra, you asked me to call with any updates."

"Progress, I hope, Francine?"

"Yes. I had a preliminary discussion with Dmitri and can confirm he was involved in the Moulins-lès-Metz ambush. Moscow has administrators who award contracts. I'm not certain who that is but can suggest that the Moulins-lès-Metz ambush could have been Moscow-related somehow. More perplexing is that I do not know why Dominique and Rudolf were ambushed, how the assassin knew. Equally confounding, why I was also in the crosshairs. I think I may have been a target of convenience. Or I just happened to be in the wrong place at the wrong time, but that is doubtful. If the assassin was that professional, that good..." Francine interrupted her own analysis.

"What are you thinking?" Alexandra prompted.

"If the assassin was professional, that good ... they would not have made a mistake." She reconsidered her logic but just briefly. "I was an intended target."

Alexandra sensed a deeper emotional issue. "Hold that thought, Francine. You were talking about Dmitri and the Moulins-lès-Metz contract."

"In this case, the administrator contracted Dmitri and hired the assassin who currently lives in Lucerne, Switzerland. I'm confident that this was not the first time Dmitri and this Asian shooter collaborated on an assassination, arranged by a Moscow administrator."

"Do you have a name?" Alexandra enquired.

"Not yet. In the fullness of time, though, it should be easy enough to find her, and it is a female by the way. I can confirm she is Asian. Clearly, Moscow wants to establish and maintain a distance in such matters. I can say from personal experience that they are not averse to dispatching their own people as circumstances dictate."

"And the killing of Joseph Brennus Durand?" Alexandra asked.

"He may have been one of Dmitri's informants but was on at least one other payroll, in addition to Moscow. Dmitri indicated that he was not directly involved in the killing of Joseph Brennus Durand. At least, he is not admitting to it. Indirectly may be another matter. Reality is more prosaic. But, in this tradecraft, there is more truth in story than detail in fact. Too many mistruths and partial truths exist. Dmitri has his fingers in many pies."

"Was Dmitri aware that Joseph was dead?"

"He wasn't and seemed genuinely surprised when I told him."

"I can imagine. And the Asian assassin?"

"I don't think Dmitri knows anything about her or why she was awarded the contract, if it was a contract as opposed to a personal mission, a vendetta. Perhaps Moscow knew that Joseph Brennus Durand was an informant for Dmitri. If so, perhaps Moscow's contract administrator was controlling both, or playing the field with Joseph, Dmitri and Moscow, and possibly another party. I'm not sure though."

"Having now met Dmitri, what is your opinion of him? Is he still the venomous viper?"

"Dmitri sees himself as the Child of Sputnik, removed from the din of the day-to-day rattling of Cold War sabres and debating of ideologies. His childhood hero was Yuri Gagarin."

"Old school?" Alexandra responded.

"Yes and no. The new guard of the FSB saw him as the bastard child, not modern and, as such, ineligible for any inherent rites of passage with lineage as privilege. Yet they seem to be contracting work to him, like the Moulins-lès-Metz ambush. Although he wasn't there, he supposedly organized it. We need to remain open to the possibility that Moscow may not have ordered it. I'm just not certain at this juncture. As we suggested, it's somehow Moscow-related but not Moscow-directed."

"So, if Moscow continues to contract Dmitri, there must be another reason. What useful purpose does he serve?" Alexandra prompted.

"One of my sources from KGB days suggested that Dmitri was convinced the Allies had developed a super code. The hierarchy of the FSB told him he was wrong, that this supposed super code was just a phantom, a ruse circulated by the Americans so the Russians would waste resources chasing a ghost. That was one of the reasons he wasn't invited to join the new FSB. In reality, there were a few in the hierarchy of the FSB who were convinced a super code did exist and thought Dmitri was close to finding it. They wanted Dmitri to lead them to it. They could deny culpability if there wasn't a code. Conversely, they could dispose of Dmitri and take credit if there was."

"And if Moscow finds this supposed ghost code first?" Alexandra queried.

"Good chance Dmitri will be retired permanently like Joseph Brennus Durand," Francine speculated. "Either way, the Lucerne assassin profits."

"There are shades and shadows entwined among motivations that conceal threats. The art of navigating a conundrum," Alexandra conjectured.

Francine quietly exhaled. She then prophesied: "You never want to come between an operative and their unremitting mission." She purposely did not mention how Dmitri's interest was piqued when she alluded to hidden Nazi wealth.

"What's your next step?"

"Dmitri wants to speak with someone else, I suspect his contract administrator. He will get hold of me thereafter and may offer me some work as a researcher, an innocuous enough job title. I need to be very careful and proceed slowly. In response to your earlier question, yes, he remains a venomous viper."

"And you are the mongoose, the dreaded snake killer," Alexandra reminded her.

"*Da, ty prav, tovarishch* – Yes, you are correct, comrade. The mongoose will attend to the viper in the fullness of time."

And with relentless vengeance, Francine ruminated. She knew once she crossed the Rubicon on that trajectory, there would be no turning back. She had made that commitment after the Moulins-lès-Metz ambush, while convalescing in the safe houses which the West had initially provided her on the south coast of England and later on the west coast of Canada.

Alexandra listened judiciously. The EUI Unit would follow the mongoose to the viper, and follow the viper to his contract administrator. Along the way, they would pay a visit to the Lucerne assassin.

Alexandra noted that Francine's demeanour had taken a dramatic change after she mentioned the assassin being professional and not making a mistake. It had triggered something. She needed to follow up if for no other reason than to provide a level of emotional support.

"Let's get back to your comment that the assassin was professional and would not have made a mistake. You paused as if that thought had triggered something."

"It was nothing. I was just speculating." Francine attempted to downplay her previous comment but without success.

Alexandra gave her space to consider. "You were speculating," she reiterated as a prompt for her to continue. Alexandra waited for Francine to re-engage.

"Since the Moulins-lès-Metz ambush, I have not been able to

figure out how the details of the shooting were known and communicated to the Lucerne assassin in advance. It was less than twenty-four hours between the planning and execution of the trip from Paris to Moulins-lès-Metz." Francine continued to reflect on the events, some hazy, some clear. "That is barely enough time for the assassin to get to the intersection, survey the scene and get set up."

"What are you thinking?" Alexandra prompted, not wanting to disturb her train of thought which seemed to be trailing off. At the same time, she wanted Francine to continue to think out loud.

"There had to have been someone very close to Dominique. When I say very close, I mean working with her on this case or someone who was being briefed by Capitaine Dominique Roland on a minute-by-minute basis. I say this because time was of the essence. That person would have known that Rudolf was in our custody and would have been in direct communications with the Lucerne assassin who would have been on standby. In Dominique's department that could only have been Commandant Parent or his immediate superior, Commissionaire Poulin. Commandant Parent was with Dominique in all the interviews. He briefed Commissionaire Poulin after every session. Dominique told me that Commissionaire Poulin had insisted on being briefed. I'm confident that Commissionaire Poulin is your mole."

It was Alexandra's turn to thoroughly consider the ramifications of this scenario. She needed to have a highest-security conversation with Daan.

"A second issue that has been in my craw," Francine proposed, "was that Dominique had asked me to accompany her the evening before we drove to Moulins-lès-Metz. She informed Commandant Parent the next morning, well, asked his permission. He didn't seem to object for whatever reason. He made one call just before we departed Paris. I overheard the brief conversation with

Commissionaire Poulin. She would have had time to notify the assassin."

"How long after that call did you leave?" Alexandra asked.

"Shortly thereafter, within twenty minutes. That begs the question again: Was I an intended target or a victim of circumstance, in the wrong place at the wrong time? The assassin would have known that Commandant Parent was in a second car following us. Yet the assassin didn't take a shot at him. Yes, he would have been pressed for time. But a professional shooter could have pulled it off without any difficulty. A shot at Commandant Parent's car would have assured the assassin more time to get away while Commandant Parent was momentarily pinned down," Francine concluded.

Alexandra sensed that Francine was reviewing the facts of her analysis.

"And?" Alexandra prompted.

"And I conclude that I was an intended target, not a victim of circumstance. The assassin had a second contract to kill me. It was two birds with one stone. I just don't yet know why I was a target. I now know that it was unrelated to the Moulins-lès-Metz mission for Rudolf to show Dominique the location of the stash of gold and documents. That has been the conundrum all along. I thought they were the same. They were not. It smells of Dmitri, the venomous viper."

"Strategy summit needed," Daan's text from Alexandra read.

CHAPTER 21

"Our centurions have been busy," Daan said with a complimentary tone. "Concerns? Recommendations?"

"How well do you know Commandant Parent and Commissionaire Poulin?" Alexandra asked with a hint of foreboding in her composure.

Daan pursed his lips as he stared at her. "I know Commandant Parent well. We have worked closely together on several cases over the years. Commissionaire Poulin less so. I only know of her. We have never worked together."

Alexandra reiterated her conversation with Francine.

Daan sat stunned by the revelation. Alexandra had never witnessed this side of his personality but was not surprised. If even a few of the details were true, the implications would be horrific.

"What I say here, stays here," Daan responded. He stared at Alexandra, Paul and Matthieu individually holding their focus until all nodded in confirmation. "The probability of Benoit Parent being dirty is so infinitely small, I would say it was virtually impossible. Commissionaire Poulin, yes. I have suspected her for a long time. I just had no proof, no irrefutable evidence."

Alexandra's objectivity dissolved. She maintained direct eye contact with Daan and thought, *Sometimes you wish you were wrong. This was one of those occasions.*

Daan continued, "Although Commissionaire Poulin is junior to Commandant Parent, she advanced faster despite not having the breadth and depth of experience. Word had it she had been promoted quickly for politically correct reasons. There was pressure to have visible-minority females in executive positions. That still could be correct. Of greater concern, there may be a confederate, another foreign operative above her at the political level. If we are lucky, it may have been Joseph Brennus Durand. I'm thinking we are unlucky and there is a more-senior infiltrator, a Russian spy above him." Daan suggested. "I'll need to call Yolina Lambert at the EU Commission due to the international implications."

Alexandra opened her mouth slightly, about to pose a question. Daan's response would take the conversation in one of two directions neither of which she had anticipated. She would need to ponder carefully, not only the details but also her reply and the wording.

"Before you ask," Daan pre-empted her, "I have not expressed my concerns with Commandant Parent because prior to this discussion I had insufficient evidence to do so. As I mentioned, I have known Commandant Parent a long time and I know how he thinks. He does not respond well to speculation without a thread of hard evidence or at least strongly suggestive intelligence. With Francine's disclosure, I need to have that conversation with him, perhaps with Yolina present." He stared at Alexandra. "Yolina may want you to participate in that discussion, too."

Alexandra acknowledged his thought with a tic of a nod. Relating the facts would be easy. Options for a strategic response would require greater depth of analysis. She would need Paul's input. She and Paul had talked briefly about potential implications. With Daan wanting to speak with Yolina first, Alexandra would take advantage of the hiatus to talk in-depth with Paul. He would have had similar conversations with Daan when they served together in the Former Republic of Yugoslavia. As a result, he would know better how to proceed. Strategy was his strength, especially the weighing of options.

"What else did Francine reveal? Hopefully, nothing as grave," Daan followed up with a tentative grin.

He was still considering operational and tactical implications. Of particular concern was the immediate threat to any of the EUI unit personnel. He would need Matthieu to brief all Delta Force leaders on this intelligence without revealing critical details.

"Nothing as earth-shattering but still relevant to our hunt for Baird Durand. Francine didn't mention Yusuf once in any of our conversations," Alexandra replied, accentuating her observation with raised eyebrows and a slight tilt of her head. She maintained her fixed stare. "A curious response. He may just be playing the support role. I'm not sure. It just seems odd. That could be both good and bad. I am confident Francine was being truthful with me, for the most part. On occasion she holds back, not revealing everything. No doubt she has her own agenda and wants revenge for Dominique's merciless murder. But I am convinced that that is not her sole *raison d'être*. There is an ideological factor that seems to be anti-communist. She has an axe to grind with her previous employer and now with Dmitri."

Daan conceded, "We were aware of that variable when we made the decision to take her on as the contracted centurion mongoose. You just need to keep reminding her that Baird Durand is involved in Dominique's death," he stressed.

"My other concern relates to the Lucerne assassin," Alexandra said. "If Francine becomes convinced the assassin pulled the trigger in this case, she may alter her compass bearing and try to kill her. She may or may not resume the hunt for Baird Durand thereafter."

"I agree," Daan validated her concern.

"There is a tangential risk," Alexandra stated. "The Lucerne assassin is a professionally trained mercenary, psychopathically efficient and lethal. We lose our centurion mongoose if she gets to Francine first. I recommend we find the Lucerne assassin before Francine does and take her into custody for a protracted period of interrogation, thereby keeping her out of circulation."

"I recognize your concern but it would stretch our resources," Daan replied. "Finding Baird Durand remains our highest priority. We need all boots on the ground."

Daan turned to Matthieu. "Assign the Delta Surveillance Team to follow Francine to Dmitri and Dmitri to his Russian contract administrator. We are dealing with seasoned professionals trained by Moscow's best. Dmitri will be on guard, Francine and Yusuf less so, perhaps beyond their normal proficiency. So, be very careful not to spook them. Take all the time you need. The contract administrator may lead us to others in Baird Durand's network and the Moscow agent assigned to track down the code."

Matthieu acknowledged the directive with a brief bow and asked, "On the media-reported pretext that Commandant Parent and his anti-terrorist team foiled a terrorist attack on the EU Parliament, can you ask him to return to Strasbourg to assist Alexandra, Paul and Marcel? Joseph Brennus Durand was going from Paris to Strasbourg for a reason when he was killed, either to visit his father or re-establish contact with another agent not yet on our radar, or both. He had formally submitted a vacation request to his employer for one week. So, my guess is he was planning on spending at least part of that time with his father. I'm convinced more than ever that Strasbourg holds the key."

"Good strategy," Daan replied. "I'll make the request with Commandant Parent. In the interim, Alexandra and Paul remain in Strasbourg with Marcel looking for Baird Durand. Matthieu and I will follow up with the constabulary and governance loyalty reward points contact that Francine mentioned."

"As long as Francine and Yusuf stay in Valencia following up on her initial meeting with Dmitri, the Lucerne assassin is safe from them," Alexandra speculated. "But she could be contracted by others to address early retirements elsewhere. It would be interesting to find out if the Lucerne assassin and the Caucasian/Asian female assassin who killed Joseph Brennus Durand were knowingly or unknowingly contracted by the same person, possibly Dmitri. One unknown has been bothering me. Was this female assassin who murdered Joseph Brennus Durand and was subsequently killed by Commandant Parent's team, a protégé of the Lucerne assassin? I say protégé because she is deceased, so obviously wasn't at the top of her game. Commandant Parent may be in a better position to assist us."

Matthieu looked at Alexandra and Paul and quietly asked, "Are you OK working with Commandant Parent in Strasbourg? I apologize for not asking before I suggested that option to Daan."

"Absolutely," both replied in unison. "We have developed a close relationship with him since the Thon case."

"In addition," Paul added, "had it not been for his assistance, the outcome of my abduction to the Saint-Denis Hotchkiss factory and Compiègne would have been very different. I owe him a debt of gratitude along with Marcel for my rescue."

"I second that, as do Jean and Collette," Alexandra added with sincere gratitude.

"OK. Just wanted to confirm." Matthieu held Alexandra's gaze. "Speaking of Collette, no doubt you have spoken with her since the incident in Santorini? How is she?"

"We have been in constant contact. She successfully completed her practicum but decided not to follow in my footsteps as a forensic psychologist. Instead, she is pursuing a post-graduate diploma in kinesiology and will be helping Jean to develop a program on body-mind forensic analysis. Apparently, the algorithm would predict higher probabilities in criminality not only based on facial expressions but also on how the criminal mind influences posture and body movement."

"I sense you're happy with her decision," Matthieu remarked.

Alexandra's grin spoke spades. "She has baggage that has not been resolved. She is now acutely aware of that and resigned to the fact that a career as a forensic psychologist is not in the cards. She is receiving ongoing counselling from one of my other colleagues. Time will tell."

Daan rejoined the conversation. "Commandant Parent has declined the request to assist in Strasbourg. He has been seconded to the General Directorate Internal Security to assist with follow up enquiries to Joseph Brennus Durand's death. They need to determine whether there were any terrorist links while he was working as a Moscow agent."

"That's unfortunate," Matthieu muttered in resignation.

"They are scouring Joseph's department and following up on all his formal and informal associates. Apparently, the supervisor of the filing room who reports solely to him has no security clearance. Even more curious, she supervises no one despite her title, unverified qualifications and minimal experience."

"Possibly good news for us," Paul commented. "His death might spook this supervisor to adjust her position and reveal some collaborators in her own network."

"You are in step with GDIS," Daan added. "She has been put under surveillance and her activities have caused immediate suspicion to say the least. Yesterday, she took an evening sight-seeing cruise on the Seine where she left an envelope under a bench. An unidentified male picked it up and is currently being shadowed. This morning, she purchased a book from a *bouquiniste* on Quai de Montebello west of rue des Bernardins. GDIS suspects she may be receiving messages through the owner of this *bouquiniste* and communicating with other operatives via the Seine cruise ships, and possibly at other drop boxes in high tourist traffic areas. GDIS plans on keeping her under surveillance while gathering intelligence, including photos of all her contacts directly and at the drop boxes. For now, they are holding off on any arrests."

"It's the first break we've had since opening this file. Identifying those in the spy ring could shed light on their efforts to locate the code seekers and possibly lead us to Baird Durand," Matthieu speculated, guardedly optimistic.

"What is the link to the Moulins-lès-Metz ambush and the assassination of the five members of the *Quer*?" Paul prompted. "What is the status of these operations?"

Matthieu replied, "Davana and I are close to answering your questions. Not surprisingly, the guard at the Desert Springs Interrogation Facility who was also murdered is the strongest of two links. The other question relates to the assassin himself. You may recall that President John F. Kennedy was assassinated in 1963 by Lee Harvey Oswald, a former member of the United States Marine Corps. There was a Russian connection to Lee Harvey Oswald that was downplayed for political reasons. Fallout from the 1962 Cuban Missile Crisis was still too delicate. Some argued that it had been covered up. The murdered guard at the Desert Springs Interrogation Facility was also a former member of the United States Marine Corps. Lee Harvey Oswald was himself assassinated by Jack Ruby in the basement of the Dallas Police Headquarters building. The assassin's assassin, Jack Ruby, died in jail without disclosing further details. Subsequent investigations supposedly never proved a conspiracy connection. The operative word here is 'supposedly'. I submit that that was because they did not have Davana Kaur conducting the unfettered investigation into the security breach that allowed Jack Ruby to get so close to Lee Harvey Oswald. I can guarantee you that had Davana been given a free rein, the truth, the whole truth, and nothing but the truth would have been revealed. There would have been no need for Chief Justice Warren to conduct his enquiry."

With a single, deliberate nod Matthieu made direct eye contact with each of his colleagues from the European Union Intelligence Unit. "She is that good," he emphasized. "Guaranteed."

One final point," Daan added. "Regarding Commissionaire Poulin, Yolina has advised that she will follow up due to the sensitivity of the matter. So, Alexandra, no need to meet to discuss strategies. If the opportunity presents itself, continue to discuss with Francine."

CHAPTER 22

The EUI Surveillance Team tracked Dmitri as he went about his daily routine. He spent most of his time sketching caricatures of tourists on the sandy beach of the Spanish Riviera. His only other activity was talking at length with the waiter in the café adjacent to his apartment. The waiter was absent on one occasion for a three-day period. During his absence, Dmitri spoke to no one else and no one else attempted to interrupt his self-imposed solitude. Dmitri seemed to hold court over coffee on Saturday morning with a group of older men who, on other occasions, randomly strolled along the beachfront seemingly unperturbed by the throngs of tourists who were busily organizing their sun-tanning paraphernalia. On these Saturday morning gatherings of *les paysans countian,* the conversation centred mostly on local politics. Thursday evenings were dedicated to a lengthy relaxed dinner usually alone, occasionally with amateur artists with whom he seemed to have developed a quasi-professional relationship. By their dress, deportment and demeanour, all seemed to be native to the Valencia region. Innocent enough, the surveillance team surmised, mildly sceptical.

The surveillance team's interest was piqued when a street urchin handed Dmitri a note which he read immediately. He reached into his pocket and paid for the personal courier service with a handful of change. Dmitri immediately packed up his sketching pad, charcoal pencils and easel, and returned to the café where he turned them over to the waiter. The waiter then called a taxi and Dmitri departed promptly for an unknown destination. The surveillance team was caught off-guard by the speed of his reaction to the note and, as a result, lost the tail. They would be better prepared the next time the street urchin approached. Dmitri was spotted back at the café several hours later speaking to the waiter. The waiter departed from the Valencia airport that evening. His only luggage was a weathered backpack.

"I recognize the Valencia waiter from the photo the surveillance team has circulated," Alexandra acknowledged. "He was in the Café Salon de Thé in Strasbourg on the morning we had our *petit déjeuner*. That may have been why I felt uncomfortable."

"Your *shrew* is correct once again," Paul complimented her. "The surveillance team followed him from Valencia to Paris where he met with a waiter at the Brasserie Le Soleil d'Or on the Île de la Cité. A third surveillance team tailed him to the Café Salon de Thé in Strasbourg. There he exchanged envelopes with yet another waiter. He subsequently returned to Valencia where he was observed giving an envelope to Dmitri. No one seemed to have met with the Café Salon de Thé waiter, though."

"It is safe to conclude that waiters seem to be an integral part of a courier service network," Alexandra suggested. "Some remain stationary in their respective cafés while others are mobile."

"Different Paris waiters have been subsequently observed delivering envelopes to and from Danielle Caron, the file room supervisor who reported solely to Joseph Brennus Durand, in addition to other unknown individuals in Paris," Daan advised. "Do we have reason to believe they are a sub-set of this espionage network?"

"Possibly. But why did Dmitri's Valencia waiter go to Paris and then to the Café Salon de Thé in Strasbourg?" Alexandra asked. "Why not just travel between Dmitri and Danielle Caron, the file room supervisor, if there is a connection? Why take the circuitous route to Strasbourg?"

"It would be logical to assume a third important cog in the wheel is in Strasbourg at the Café Salon de Thé. Maybe Baird Durand?" Paul proposed.

"Unless Baird and the Café Salon de Thé waiter are one and the same," Alexandra speculated.

"No one has seen Baird so we can't confirm one way or the other," Paul muttered.

Alexandra replied after a lengthy pause. "When we were debating whether we should approach Francine to be the mongoose, Daan said you either want to be only seen or never be seen. What if Baird Durand wants to only be seen as a waiter to the point that he becomes unseen? Waiters are seldom noticed and rarely remembered because they all dress the same and meld into the background. They are only seen yet never seen."

"How frustrating to be so close to Baird, if he was that waiter at the Café Salon de Thé in Strasbourg! We could see the whites of his eyes, yet not know it," Paul gasped, sharing her frustration.

"If we ever get that close again and I recognize his scent, I will pounce before he can count to one," Alexandra promised.

Paul slowly shook his head. "There were tourists, a man and a woman in their late fifties or early sixties, taking photos when we were having our *petit dejeuner.* It is possible they may have photographed him. We just have to find them."

"I can't help you there," Marcel piped up.

"I recall some tourists but I didn't take any notice," Alexandra added.

"OK. So, I'm alone searching for two needles in a mobile haystack," Paul concluded.

"That's twice the probability than one needle in the haystack," Alexandra joked. "What can you remember about them?"

"They were wearing matching dark and light blue rain jackets if that's any help."

"Is that them?" Marcel asked.

"Who? Where?" Paul reacted.

"Standing by the south tower. The two in the two-tone blue jackets."

"The luck of the Irish, which I am not, and the role of the dice, which I don't throw. That's them!" Paul exclaimed.

Alexandra approached the couple tentatively. "Excuse me. You were taking pictures in front of the Café Salon de Thé across the street the other morning. We are newlyweds and this is our honeymoon. We lost our cellphone with all our photos. Would it be too much to ask you to review your photos of the café? If we are in the photos, could you email them to us? We live in Luxembourg and I doubt we will come back here."

"Yes, I guess so. I haven't really reviewed them so I'm not sure if we can help," the man replied.

They began scrolling through the myriad of photos. "The digital world has made life easier in some respects. But now I take many more photos so it is a longer process to vet them for the best shots."

"There! That's the one. Can you email it to us?" Paul asked.

"Sure, no problem."

"Wonderful. This is our email address. Thank you so much. We would be deeply indebted to you. We would be honoured to take you to our favourite restaurant if you are ever in Luxembourg City," Alexandra offered.

"Damn," Paul muttered as the tourists walked away. "The photo does show the waiter we assume to be Baird Durand, but only his back, not his face. It's as if the waiter was suspicious and purposely kept his back to the camera."

"If not Baird, then who and more importantly what might this person be hiding and why?" Marcel countered in a hypothetical response.

Alexandra muttered, "Back to square one." How many times had she experienced this frustration when working on other cases? It was like walking on a pebble beach with two steps forward and one step back, or worse. *Reculer pour mieux sauter – we need to step back, then take up a more strategic position and re-engage.*

"Maybe just square one and a half if we believe the waiter is Baird. We just have to track him down," Paul suggested, equally irritated.

"Not a complete dead end," Marcel offered. "Let me follow up with the management at the Café Salon de Thé. I'll say I want to thank the waiter in person for his excellent service. Wait here while I go back to the Café and enquire."

"We will meander to the north end of the Ponts Couverts. If it is Baird, and he is skittish after the death of his son, we won't want to be seen together more than we already have. He might have the café and surrounding area under closed circuit TV surveillance. He is a survivor, after all, as the French derivative of his name translates."

"That was quick. Marcel is on his way," Alexandra whispered.

"Good and bad news," Marcel accounted. "The owner said the waiter works part-time and infrequently to fill in for other staff or on other occasions when they need an extra pair of hands. He hasn't worked since that morning."

"That sounds plausible. Cafés do have many part-time waiters," Alexandra commented.

"I left my phone number with the owner and asked him to give me a call when the waiter is next scheduled to work. I explained I would be staying in Strasbourg for a few weeks. It's a long shot but the best we have for now," Marcel concluded.

CHAPTER 23

Dmitri greeted Francine, "It is good to see you, Côtes du Rhône. Welcome to my beachfront studio with a view. It's an advantageous location to meet prospective clients. I apologize for the delay in contacting you but my waiter friend has been away attending to family matters. After we discuss our own business, we can retire to our café for cappuccino or wine if you so desire."

There were other waiters with whom he could have left a message to rendezvous. What's so special about this one in particular? Francine pondered as she watched Dmitri sketching on a pad.

"I wasn't aware you were a caricature artist and very talented with charcoal it seems."

"It's how I make a living to support my meagre lifestyle, sketching tourists on the beach in satirical poses. They pay handsomely for renditions of their inflated egos. Most are females well past their best-before due dates. They add a generous gratuity when the charcoal returns their youthful physiques."

"Is this a retirement hobby?" Francine asked innocently yet fishing for any fry of information.

"I sketched in my youth, often my schoolteachers. My inflated grades mirrored my artistic talent more than my scholastic prowess. For my former employer, I would sketch American and Canadian military officers in their NATO messes in northern France and southern Germany where they gathered for social events. It was an ideal opportunity to interview them in a more relaxed ambience. I would then report back to Moscow on their professional affiliations. A brigadier general meant there was a brigade in the region. Infantry, Armoured and Artillery colonels identified the composition of the battalions and regiments in the brigades. It was a very simple means of gathering military intelligence. If the officers didn't identify their trade, their narcissistic wives certainly did when I sketched them in complimentary poses. You can learn a great deal by stroking female egos with enhanced physical attributes and necklines with southward trajectories, the latter with the tacit approval of their husbands."

"Such techniques are lost to those who have replaced the old guard," Francine acknowledged. "*Eto neudachno* – it is unfortunate."

Red Sparrows of both and all sexual orientations frequented *pigeonnieres* and *dovecotes,* some directly plying their perfected skills to secure intelligence while others gleaned the insight indirectly through intellect and fulfilling the unmet desires of their target, not always limited to the physical. Both were variations of the oldest profession. Francine inwardly gloated. Abraham Maslow, the American psychologist, may have authored the hierarchy of needs theory, but Ivan Pavlov, the Russian physiologist, perfected the understanding of classical conditioning. He received the Nobel Prize for his work. Maslow did not. Dmitri had his methods of gathering intelligence. Francine had hers.

"*Da* – yes. Unfortunate for them but fortunate for me," Dmitri agreed. "I can still garner industrial intelligence from mostly American and British tourists, some of whom are on vacation from their technology-related jobs. There is always a price to be paid for accurate information, as you have demonstrated. Perhaps I could sketch you?"

"Perhaps, but without the surreptitious interrogation," Francine winked.

She admired the contribution her female Red Sparrow colleagues made to the world of espionage and intelligence, less so the male counterparts whom she perceived as perverse self-satisfying gluttons of the carnal gutter. Dmitri's method of employing the arts to achieve the objective was intellectual, even scholarly. She admired that.

Once a professional gatherer of intelligence, always a professional gatherer, but always with finesse, she surmised with pride.

"And you have other sources working for you in your current profession as intelligence entrepreneur?" Dmitri suggested.

She too could maintain a façade of composure replete with pleasantries while conspiring to murder her former Cold War *tovarish* – comrade in arms, now her adversary and target of her own revenge, like Shakespeare's Prince Hamlet.

Dmitri bowed. "And you have been busy learning about my business, Côtes du Rhône." He too had done his homework and learned more about her. "When last we met, I mentioned I might have need for a researcher and verifier. Have you given it any thought?"

"Always interested in honing my skills with appropriate compensation," Francine replied nonchalantly so as to appear interested but not overeager. "You briefly mentioned financial management. What might the job duties entail? As I previously mentioned, I like to have all the facts before I agree to the terms and conditions of the contract."

"Suffice it to say, there would be a confidentiality clause in any contract linked to early retirement for non-compliance."

"*Ochevidno* – obviously," she replied.

Dmitri hesitated warily, deliberately holding her stare as if his consequential retirement codicil needed further emphasis. He too was fishing for fry or, perhaps, with fry as bait for larger intelligence prey. She sought more facts regarding the essence of the contract. He sought more facts regarding the extent of her experience since last they met. He wasn't seeking a long-term working relationship. None of his associates were. He sensed she was not interested in a long-term comprehensive compensation package. He didn't know what her long-term plans were and that bothered him enough to remain guarded. He was confident he wasn't in the preliminary stages of a business merger, nor a hostile takeover.

Francine maintained his glare without emotion as if her reply needed repeating. "Does your job offer as a financial management consultant have anything to do with the enterprise you and your mentor, Uri Popov, had? I seem to recall hearing that the two of you were colluding in a sideline enterprise, not completely unknown to your, our, former employer."

It was Dmitri's turn to raise his eyebrows. "I commend you, again. You have done your homework."

Since leaving the salaried position with his former employer, he had engaged in discussions with several ex-colleagues, some, like himself, who had departed for lusher pastures, and others who had transferred to the FSB, the reincarnation of its former self, the KGB. He had never before entered into negotiations with anyone like Côtes du Rhône. *She obviously knows the tradecraft but where had she gained the advanced competencies? Had she clandestinely climbed the ramparts and infiltrated its bastions, an agent of the West, a double agent of either or both? Or is she solely Russian but now running with a price on her head like Leon Trotsky? If she is that good, she might be useful. Keep your friends close but your enemies closer.* He considered his options carefully.

Francine relaxed into the chair beside him. Banter was cheap. *He was not an immediate threat at this moment,* she concluded. Neither was she an immediate threat to him.

"Your dossier is not complete. Key entries seem to have been conveniently vetted. Why don't you fill in a few details? And yes, I am conscious of the confidentiality clause as are you, I am sure," she said.

"I wasn't aware you had met Uri. I don't recall him mentioning you. You don't seem to be his type."

"We never met face-to-face but his reputation was well known by a select few of our mutual colleagues."

Dmitri looked at her. How much truth should he reveal and how much bogus bait needed to be provided to test her level of knowledge. He concluded that her heritage was Russian although she had been immersed in Western culture. She was an alumnus of the SVR Academy, the Russian School of Espionage, but was not a current agent of Moscow. Loyalty was another matter.

"Uri was aware the Wehrmacht had hidden stolen Nazi gold and other treasures in mines throughout Germany, mostly in Bavaria, and some within a stone's throw of the Austrian border, after the Allies had bombed the Reichsbank in February 1945. On his death, Uri provided me with the locations of two of these hidden sites, later located behind the Iron Curtain. They remained hidden until the USSR started to collapse and the Berlin Wall became less secure. I found one small mine and spent several years quietly moving the gold to a Swiss bank in Zürich."

"And you sketch on this beach in order to maintain your meagre lifestyle, you say? Hardly meagre if you have Swiss bank accounts replete with gold deposits."

"Some of the gold bars were assessed at 24 karats. The only large source of 24k gold was from fillings in the teeth of concentration camp victims. It was too hot to handle, even by some Swiss bankers. So, I had it melted down and diluted with other metals to 20k or 18k in order to conceal the tainted dental source. That takes time. There is still more beyond these two mines and I would like to find it. Of course, your remuneration would mirror the quantity and karat."

"Of course," Francine acknowledged with a discrete bow.

"You asked about the Moulins-lès-Metz shooting." Dmitri

deferred to a specific topic. "Whoever was in the car had information relating to additional covert locations of Nazi repositories, in addition to other caches of monies and redeemable certificates. A third party who knew the locations of these caches of gold wanted to keep that information a secret. So, they ordered the ambush. I was awarded the contract. One occupant may have escaped, as you suggested, but the person who knew the locations was killed. I verified that."

Dmitri hesitated as he gazed out over the azure Mediterranean. His summary of the events confirmed the motivation of the third party but not the specific identity of the assassin.

"Who is this mysterious party?"

"I don't know but it has deep pockets. I was under the impression my contact in the French General Directorate for Internal Security, the GDIS, knew but wasn't saying. He has taken that information with him to the great retirement villa in the sky."

"And locations?" Francine pressed. "Possible urban centres in addition to abandoned mines in Bavaria and other former Prussian locales?"

"Word has it that Reichsmarschall Göring hid in the Saint-Denis region some of the loot the Nazi SS stole during their occupation and subsequent hasty retreat from Paris. All has not yet been recovered. In fact, very little has been repossessed according to estimates from other sources."

"And you would like me to find it," Francine responded.

"He who has all the gold has all the power."

"You want the power?" Francine paraphrased.

"Not power for the sake of power. That's greed. Greed is dangerous because it makes you take unnecessary risks. I want the power that gold will provide to show the FSB hierarchy I was correct on another matter for which they caustically criticized me."

Francine thought about the context of their initial encounter and concluded Dmitri was both a mirror and a mirage of a bygone era defined by the bipolar lens of the Cold War. He did not possess conventional wisdom that was the plumb of natural gravity. Hence, he was not one of the meek who would inherit the earth. She baited the hook correspondingly.

"The other matter to which you refer. Would that be the mysterious, elusive code?"

Without hesitation, he blurted out deliberately, motivated by ego and hatred that exposed him to risk greater than greed.

"Yes! It is not elusive as some suggest. It does exist," he replied with a confident yet deliberate tone. "I have associates like my Lucerne colleague who, for the right price, will kill whoever they deem expendable in order to find the code and deliver it to me. That's where the gold comes into the transaction as payment for goods and services received. The revelation of the existence of the code will prove I was correct in my convictions."

His glare intensified as he leaned back in his chair. He desperately wanted pride and honour but was blinded by false bravado. He could buy it with the gold.

"That's what it's all about," he concluded. "I'd be content just to live out my days sketching caricatures of naïve tourists on this beach knowing I was right and they were forced to admit their error."

CHAPTER 24

A shiver ran the length of Francine's spine. A searing pain caused her vision to become blurred as if a jagged, barbed spike had been driven into her head penetrating her left temple and eye, and running through to her sinus. A twinging ache in her elbow caused it to stiffen. She resisted the overwhelming urge to massage the joint. The ominous echo of howling wolves brought to the forefront of her mind the culmination of countless sleepless nights plagued with unrelenting violent dreams. The moment of revenge was at the precipice. She took a series of slow deep breaths.

The viper was coiled and prepared to unleash its venomous revenge. Dmitri had orchestrated the ambush that resulted in Dominique's death. The Lucerne assassin had coldheartedly pulled the trigger. But there was a third party involved and she wanted the triple crown. It took all of her intestinal fortitude not to kill Dmitri at this moment while his fingers were pre-occupied following the droplets of condensation running down the sides of his bottle of beer like beads of perspiration following the furrows on his forehead.

On reflection, he seemed too relaxed, too confident for his tradecraft. There were truths, partial truths and make-believe truths in the tactical manoeuvring of intelligence gathering. This was his turf. Francine surmised he was not alone in his seaside studio. She slowly took another quietening breath. She regained her composure. The centurion mongoose would be victorious. For now, she had one outstanding question that might reveal the identity of the third party.

"And what will you do when you have possession of the illusive code?"

"Probably nothing. Technology has surpassed these Cold War means of enigmatic communication. I suppose academics who teach about code breaking would be delighted to get their sweaty little fingers on it to advance their pathetic scholastic careers, but that is about all it would be worth."

Technology hasn't surpassed the need for all codes, Francine, concluded. *In fact, it has reinforced it. The FSB hierarchy was correct in their assessment of him. He was cut from a dinosaurian cloth in his thinking.* She would entice him further.

"This will be a rather extensive research project. I have a colleague who can assist me."

"Hire anyone you want. I only negotiate one contract, and only pay the negotiated price and only after the goods and services have been received and verified, regardless of how many people you employ."

Dmitri seemed a bit perturbed by her comment that she needed someone to assist her. *It is highly irregular to introduce potential partners in early stages of contract negotiation. Rarer still for one agent to introduce another agent. Such actions are completely contrary to operational procedures taught in any Soviet espionage academy. What is she up to?* he pondered. Again, he became defensive, not leaning back but sitting slightly more erect in his chair.

"May I introduce you to my colleague? He could be a contractor for you. I can text him now."

Dmitri would play her game, call her bluff. If this other person was a colleague, he could find out facts about Côtes du Rhône to add to her file, which, at the moment, was still slim on some specifics. At a minimum, he would learn her name or an alias. If the details were false or purposefully misleading, he would discover more about how she operated. He remained cautious.

"As you wish. I like your style and if you recommend him, I will consider the veracity of your introduction."

Yusuf's cell boogied across the table with the vibration of the incoming text message. He rose and walked toward his partner.

"This is my colleague," Francine announced as Yusuf approached from an adjacent table.

Dmitri was surprised to see Yusuf in such close proximity. He twisted around in his chair. The muscles in his jaw tightened. *Of course, she would have backup nearby,* he thought. *The difference is, she has played her cards. I have not. Or has she? She has played something; doubtful it is her strong suit.*

Such was the game of having to second-guess the malice of invisible shadows, of having to stare at nothing while being wary of everything. In the duplicitous currency of intelligence, nothing exists in the absence of context. *Vsegda na strazhe* – Always on guard.

Dmitri's agitated testosterone reaction was palpable, less so for Yusuf. Banter was equally terse. They jousted for neutral ground like two cobras not wanting to expose their strategy, which masked their respective intentions. All the while, she scrutinized their cautious cavorting with a stiletto-like stare, adjusting her stratagem to their reactions. It was all about the final act in her theatrical production.

When she had been ordered to report for Red Sparrow training, Francine had no choice. The option was simple – die or become a sparrow. She was not a naïve schoolgirl with minimal life experience. However, the thought never crossed her mind that the State would turn her into a cold and violent prostitute. She was intelligent and sophisticated, disciplined and ambitious. She would learn to become scheming and ruthless, seductive and manipulative, to lie to herself and others until lying became the truth, while retaining her warmth and passion. She had compromised her soul in order to push beyond the limitations of her religious upbringing, including her morality. At a subconscious level, she teetered on the fulcrum, between psychopathy and sanity. The training cadre were correct. Once you become a sparrow, your former self ceases to exist. Unbeknown to all those who had taken away her freedom of choice, the moment she graduated as a Red Sparrow was the moment when she regained her power to seek revenge.

She soon realized that advanced training in psychological manipulation constituted a major part of her field training, especially the study of male motivation. This provided her with knowledge she would transform into skills that few of her colleagues who were not undergoing sparrow training would have available to them. It was about manipulation, which she soon came to realize defined the game of espionage for sparrows – survival. Fitness was not limited to muscular and skeletal. It was instead mental and emotional. She could use her astute intellect to compensate for her petite body. It was all about mind over matter.

People are conundrums. If you are going to seduce them, you are going to have to figure out how to become the missing component of their psyche. You then become that deficiency in such a way that it becomes irrefutable, second nature. It was about meeting the unmet needs of the other person. Only then would they start to tell you what you want to know. In Dimitri's case, Francine had accurately deduced what he was missing and how she could fulfil that need. He had already identified his role in the Moulins-lès-Metz ambush. He would reveal the identities of the others who had been involved including Baird Durand, if he was associated.

The sparrow sat on her perch observing the target's reactions. Dmitri was at a disadvantage. He was clearly not happy. She would have to plan carefully for their next meeting and manoeuvre with even greater vigilance around the venomous viper. She would debrief Yusuf later this evening.

She gazed at Yusuf as she remembered the first time they had met. As a Red Sparrow, she attended the University of Rostov. Yusuf had been her target. Her mission was to learn all there was to know about Turkish Military Intelligence. It had been different, though. She had allowed herself to fall in love with him. She never fell out of love. They had learned to trust each other as he was manipulating her and she was manipulating him. She had mastered the ability to switch from being cold and crass one moment to warm and passionate the next, all the while detached and objective.

She remembered further back. At the start of her sparrow journey, there had been Dmitri who had been one of those who had taken away her freedom of choice. Today, he did not seem to remember ordering her to become a Red Sparrow or die, but she certainly did. He had orchestrated the Moulins-lès-Metz ambush that took Dominique away from her. At this moment, she felt utter contempt for him, absolute hatred. Inwardly, she seethed with the desire for revenge. The day would be dawning soon when she would take his ultimate choice of freedom away from him. She would pull the trigger and witness life as he knew it reunite in hell with his evil Satanic soul. Until that moment came, she would skilfully play the game within the fabricated context of truths, partial truths and make-believe truths.

CHAPTER 25

"Be careful," Francine's text read.

"And the same to you," Alexandra replied. She sensed a concerted wariness in Francine's caveat, which prompted her to follow up with a second text response.

"With your advice for caution, I sense that the threat level has increased since last we spoke. Anything in particular?"

"Just be careful," Francine repeated for emphasis. Dmitri's prediction that the Lucerne assassin would summarily execute whoever he deems expendable to get the code stayed with her. "He is a cold-blooded serpent who has not earned the reputation of a venomous viper by accident. When he mentioned the Lucerne assassin, he did so devoid of any emotion. I crossed paths with others cut from the same insensitive Cold War cloth when working with my previous employer. Some of them had literally turned in their mothers whom they suspected as being enemies of the Soviet Union. Such was the mandate of the Stalinist regime. If you reneged, you were either sent to a gulag yourself or summarily executed. Perhaps, some day, I may tell you about one aspect of my training that left me forever scarred like a facial smallpox disfigurement."

Alexandra showed Paul the message.

"In the brief time we have worked together, this is the first occasion Francine has taken the initiative to warn me, us. She doesn't adopt a defensive response for no apparent reason. I can only conclude that the danger level has been raised exponentially."

Before they could consider the context, an urgent message popped up simultaneously on their screens from Daan with a full EUI unit distribution: "Tomorrow 0830, European Union Parliament in Strasbourg. Ask for Yolina Lambert."

"It must be high priority to merit calling a full gathering of the clan. It's not an invitation to a *petit déjeuner*," Paul commented lightheartedly, but he was concerned. As director of the Crime Lab in Paris, he had recalled high-priority messages that demanded his immediate attention. They were all related to urgent matters pertaining to police investigations and delicate evidence usually being presented in high-profile politically sensitive court cases. None related to his personal security. The ominous tone of Daan's summons caused him to become more aware of the immediate environment in which he and Alexandra found themselves.

"Just received a brief cryptic email from Jean. He said he would see us tomorrow at the European Union Parliament. Details to follow."

"Curiouser and curiouser, cried Alice," Alexandra remarked. "Lewis Carroll must have been wearing his Sherlock Holmes deerstalker detective hat and had us in mind when he wrote these words in *Alice's Adventures in Wonderland*."

⇥ ⇤

"THANK YOU FOR ATTENDING AT such short notice," Daan announced. "You all know Yolina Lambert, our lead at the EU Commission in Brussels, and Commandant Benoit Parent from the Police nationale Anti-Terrorist Unit. Accompanying Benoit is Jean Bernard, the newly appointed director of the European Union Anti-Terrorist Cyber Unit."

Paul and Alexandra exchanged quizzical stares.

"I will get directly to the purpose of this meeting," Yolina announced without fanfare. "Commandant Parent has brought intelligence to my attention that will change the course of our investigation regarding the *Quer*. It has reinforced preliminary findings from

Matthieu and Davana regarding the security breach at the Desert Springs Interrogation Facility. Benoit, the floor is yours."

"We have reason to believe that Beijing was behind the assassination of the five members of the *Quer* held for questioning in the Desert Springs Interrogation Facility. Accolades to Matthieu Richard and Davana Kaur for their expedient efforts. We do not know yet who the actual assassin is or, more perplexingly, the assassin's assassin. Beijing orchestrated the assassination to make it look like a Moscow initiative, even supplying the assassin with a Russian Makarov PB pistol and silencer. The Chinese Communist Party motivation is to directly disrupt financial stability in the European Union and, in doing so, Western economies. As you may be aware, China either owns or has control over the greatest share of U.S. Treasury Bills and Bonds, second only to the American Federal Bank. With these acquisitions, they have the ability to bankrupt the U.S. if they dump them into the financial market all at once. Jean Bernard will elaborate further after I have completed my briefing."

A hush filled the room at that pronouncement. The extent of the *Quer*'s influence regarding the economic implications for the European Union had become apparent when Paul, disguised as Claude Etien Marchand, the truant seventh member, duped Herr Blosch into revealing the preliminary financial dealings of the *Quer*. The global implications, as Commandant Parent outlined, constituted an entirely different scenario.

Benoit elaborated, "Since its inception in the Gallic era, the *Quer* has grown tentacles reaching into financial institutions and political capitals of major nation states, most notably the European Union. Beijing has been positioning itself to take over control of the *Quer* and its considerable financial assets, having first stealthily positioned itself to secure the lion's share of U.S. financial assets. In brief, this incursion amounts to financial terrorism with global implications. They would also gain considerable influence over the Fourth Reich as their reluctant yet brutally efficient enforcement arm. I will now ask Jean to elaborate on the cyber link."

"With the exponential increase in technology, it should be no surprise to learn that the criminal element has not only kept pace but has overtaken the capabilities of most cyber law enforcement efforts. Within the global community, China and Russia and a host of rogue players operating out of India and numerous undisclosed African dictatorships have unofficially declared war. The battle space is global cyber, including but not limited to cyber-war, cyber-terrorism, cyber-technology and cyber-crime. The consequences make any known virus seem feeble. Germane to Benoit's revelation, the *Quer* has a cyber cell from which they have moved large amounts of their financial assets. Yes, the EUI unit has been able to freeze a considerable amount of their known bank assets via a cooperative third party, primarily in Switzerland. Effective yesterday, other stolen assets have been moved into new *Quer* accounts in other financial institutions, including Liechtenstein and Luxembourg in addition to offshore banks in locations such as the Cayman Islands, unbeknown to the bankers."

"That is not the worst news," Benoit interjected. "Jean, please provide a brief description of the Dark Web."

"The Dark Web is where cyber criminals conduct their business. Some of their cyber cells create software that can break into the databases of virtually all major corporations and governments. It is not a crime to write the software. As a result, they do not use the software themselves. So, if caught, they cannot be prosecuted. Instead, they sell it via the Dark Web to players in a growing cyber-criminal community. Welcome to the e-world of Bonnie and Clyde."

An equally dark veil like a burial shroud left all attendees with a sense of foreboding. Alexandra's *shrew* became clouded momentarily. Her normal ability to analyze the facts and recommend viable options for expedient resolution in order of priority appeared stymied as if paralyzed in a *marais* – a swamp. At this moment, the pathway to the truth was also obscured behind the opaque dark veil. Even Paul's presence seemed distant, beyond her reach.

She lowered her chin to her steepled fingers and closed her eyes. Her mother's prophecy echoed in her consciousness: "Your roots are those of Charlemagne and your dynasty Merovingian. In them, you will unearth the truths." She perceived herself facing off against Baird Durand, one-on-one, his inexact image partially obscured in an encroaching mist. There was no technology, no Dark Web. No big data. Instead, just the forensic psychologist poised for combat, like Joan of Arc, the Maid of Lorraine – defending Charlemagne's Realm.

CHAPTER 26

"Thank you, Jean." Daan responded with a renewed mandate. "It's not a preferred scenario, ladies and gentlemen. Our mission to-date has been ideally to capture Baird Durand in order to neutralize the menace the *Quer* has posed. If he died in the process, so be it. The EU could eventually take control of its financial holdings, but it would take time. With Benoit's revelation of an imminent Beijing incursion, we do not have the luxury of time." He glanced at Yolina.

"Our mission has changed from eliminating Baird Durand to keeping him alive in order to use him and his knowledge to counter the Beijing threat," Yolina confirmed. "His knowledge of the *Quer's* extensive network is integral to our revised mission for financial stability in the EU. Based on Jean's briefing, we need to identify and disengage the *Quer* cyber cell. Once we have that information, any nefarious influence by Beijing or rogue states will be more easily mitigated. Time is of the essence."

Daan reiterated, "We must conclude that Beijing wants Baird Durand dead and will do everything in its power to achieve that objective. They falsely assumed he was incarcerated in the Desert Springs Interrogation Facility with his colleagues. Although we had not realized it at the time, his escape was to our advantage. We need to keep Baird Durand alive at all costs and convince him that cooperation with us is his only option if he wants to stay alive."

"But that may be easier said than done," Yolina added. "From all indications, Baird is fiercely independent and proudly loyal to the *Quer* and its heritage, his heritage. He may play along but at an opportune moment, return to his role as the *de facto* leader of the *Quer*."

Daan laid out the agenda. "We need to have a strategy before we adjourn today. All options need to be considered."

"Including the resurrection of Claude Etien Marchand?" Paul proposed immediately on the heels of Daan's declaration.

All eyes focused on him.

"Only asking," Paul responded. "You invited all options."

"And so I did," Daan conceded. "I wouldn't have even thought about that as a primary possibility."

"Daan mentioned that, among other quintessential attributes, you have a reputation for devising the most audacious plans," Yolina prompted. "And I say that with the greatest admiration, Paul. What are your initial thoughts?"

"There is only one person who might draw Baird Durand out of hiding in the short term and that is the truant seventh member of the *Quer*, Claude Etien Marchand. Baird has never met him, to our knowledge, so would not be able to recognize him. He would only know of his name through the late Herr Rafael Blosch."

"For those of you unaware of who Claude Etien Marchand is, I will elaborate in summary," Daan explained. "There were seven original families in the Gallic *Quer*. The Marchand family was one. Louis Marchand was a descendent who chose not to continue his direct involvement with his *Quer* colleagues approximately eighty years ago, for reasons unknown to us. We created the character of Claude Etien Marchand, the apparent grandson of Louis Marchand, in order to infiltrate the *Quer* organization. Claude Etien Marchand's first contact with the *Quer* was through Herr Rafael Blosch, the manager of the bank in Geneva where Louis Marchand had an account. Herr Blosch summoned the other members of the *Quer* to convene on a yacht on Lake Geneva in order to introduce their long-lost corporate colleague, Claude Etien Marchand.

We raided the yacht and took into custody all members except Baird Durand, who escaped. Our teammate sitting at this table, Paul Bernard, played the role of Claude Etien Marchand in that charade. And the rest is history."

Alexandra broke the silence that consumed everyone as they processed Daan's brief exposé of the background. "From a motivational perspective, Abraham Maslow, the social psychologist, asserts that all humans respond to a hierarchy of needs. The first three are physiological, safety and social. My sense is that Baird Durand is meeting the first and partially the second on his own but is in the greatest need of social collegial reinforcement in a safe environment. The mysterious Claude Etien Marchand may be the ideal candidate to meet these social needs, in addition to some safety."

"Especially with the recent assassination of his son, Joseph Brennus Durand," Benoit added. "We surmise that he is emotionally vulnerable at this time, a weakness on his part that we can exploit."

"Our IT folks have recently broken into Joseph Brennus Durand's cell phone. Although a few entries remain cryptic, we can narrow them down to the most probable being his father. Our fictitious Claude Etien Marchand could send Baird a less enigmatic invitation to meet," Matthieu suggested.

"Other options?" Yolina asked.

No one responded.

"Let's continue to consider a Plan B. In the interim, work out the details and identify additional resources needed. I will authorize. Although Commandant Parent has been seconded to GDIS, he will remain available to assist. His addition will offset Matthieu part-time as he works with Davana to identify other evidence regarding the breach of security at the Desert Springs Interrogation Facility.

We anticipate there being an overlap in intelligence. Hence, some economies of scale can be achieved."

Daan focused his attention on Alexandra. "Contact Francine and advise her that new information has surfaced. Do what you have to do in order to convince her that Baird Durand was not directly involved in Dominique's murder. In fact, he has information that is integral to a matter related to the Moulins-lès-Metz ambush, specifically identifying the assassin. Francine needs to capture Baird Durand alive. It is imperative that she understands the importance of this proviso – alive."

"Francine and Yusuf are currently en route to Strasbourg," Alexandra confirmed. "She is now on Dmitri's payroll and wants to brief me on the details. I can ask her to meet me."

"Yes, but do not introduce her to anyone else," Daan insisted.

"Understood."

Yolina added, "it would be interesting to ascertain whether Francine suspects Beijing or Dmitri perhaps being on Beijing's payroll in addition to Moscow. Among the financial motivations, how desperate might Beijing be to breaking up the *Quer*'s centuries old *patres familias* tradition in favour of the 1917 Marxist–Leninist doctrine?"

Alexandra mulled over the knowns and unknowns. The proportionate balance had not changed appreciably since Claude Etien Marchand had first made his cameo appearance at Herr Blosch's bank in Geneva. Francine's warning resonated. As they were gaining traction, the need for increased vigilance was also rising.

"The Fourth Reich took Claude Etien Marchand hostage and almost killed him at the Hotchkiss factory in Saint-Denis on the outskirts of Paris, and again in Compiègne because they supposedly wanted the financial resources over which the *Quer* had control in Herr Blosch's Geneva bank. In the process, they killed two of our colleagues. We know that the two men who took Paul hostage were Fourth Reich affiliates. But were they acting on Beijing's direction?" she speculated. "We know that they have no qualms about killing in order to get what they want, much like the Lucerne assassin, according to Dmitri."

"Interesting scenario with ominous implications from both an operational and a strategic perspective," Daan acknowledged.

Alexandra looked directly at Paul. There was no second-guessing the depth of her concern. "Will the resurrected Claude Etien Marchand be dodging bullets from a Nazi Luger, a Russian Makarov PB or a Chinese QSZ-92, or all three, and possibly others?"

"Claude Etien Marchand's wardrobe may need to include a designer Yves Saint Laurent bulletproof vest," Matthieu added with equal solemnness.

"Perhaps we need another to act the part of Claude Etien Marchand for this re-run sequel," Yolina suggested. "Let's consider that as we flush out our strategy."

Benoit and Jean approached Paul and Alexandra at the recess.

Benoit apologized. "We just received approval yesterday late afternoon to create the Anti-Terrorist Cyber Unit and promote Jean as its initial director. So, no chance to let you know. The existence of this organization is on the same security level as your EUI unit."

"Congratulations, son." Paul responded as he extended his hand in sincere acknowledgement of his well-deserved promotion. He recalled how proud his father had been when he was promoted director of the Crime Lab.

"Ditto," replied Alexandra. "Will you and Collette be moving?"

"No move. I will be working out of the same building, just a different but non-descript office. I will be working for Benoit but reporting indirectly to Daan as the operational head of the EUI unit once the paperwork is signed, which should be today."

"We need to get back to Paris," Benoit announced. "We can chat more later."

Paul and Alexandra exchanged perplexed glances again. The speed of technology was exponential as was the impact on operational matters.

"The New World Order is affecting our family," Alexandra lamented. "Hopefully Jean's and Collette's lives will remain relatively stable, especially if they are considering a family."

Daan stared down at an incoming email. "Before you all leave, be advised that Matthieu and Davana confirmed the Lucerne assassin pulled the trigger on the individual who had murdered the five members of the *Quer* in the Desert Springs Interrogation Facility, in addition to the guard. We can also confirm that Beijing issued the contract to the Lucerne assassin and paid the guard to leave the side door to the facility open."

౿ ౾

"Have you considered my offer?" Matthieu asked, as they relaxed their mutual embrace.

"I have. And have you considered my counteroffer?" Davana replied as she folded her arms around him once again.

"We were here last time."

"Yes, we were," she replied.

"What is it about living in Europe, anywhere you would like, that is so upsetting?" Matthieu asked.

"It's not so much about Europe as it is about not being in Australia." Davana looked at him. "It's for the same reason that you do not want to live Down Under, because it isn't Europe. I am as much in love with the outback of New South Wales as you are with the Île-de-France region."

Matthieu recalled the deeply emotional conversations that followed the equally passionate *rencontre romantique* – romantic encounter, on the heels of solving their previous case. That had involved a similar breach of security in an intelligence system. That was why they separated both as professional partners and as lovers. Both knew they were too different. They could work but not live together. Separate but together. Yet they both desperately missed being together after the inevitable parting at the end of each mission they worked on together. At best, they arranged a *rendezvous intime* – an intimate meeting, occasionally on their own respective turf but mostly elsewhere. The last time was on the Indonesian island of Bali soothed by the sound of the ocean surf and the balmy evening breeze.

"I don't like goodbyes," Matthieu whispered as he rested his head on her shoulder.

"Neither do I," Davana purred as she held him close.

"*Jus'qu prochaine cas* – until the next case or a rendezvous at the St. Regis Bali Resort, whichever comes first."

Matthieu had thrown himself into his work after each previous parting in order to ease the pain of separation from Davana who occupied his mind and heart. He would do the same now but not with the added ambience of his other love, Paris. Daan would assure that with the hunt for Baird Durand, now the highest priority for the European Union Intelligence Unit, Matthieu would be kept busy.

The EUI Unit would be in a race with Beijing. The Chinese wanted Baird dead, in addition to the truant and elusive seventh member of the Quer, Claude Etien Marchand, who they were convinced had not been killed at Compiègne. The obituary announcing his death and cremation had been a ruse.

Matthieu and Davana had learned that a lucrative sub-contract had already been awarded to place Baird Durand and Claude Etien Marchand in the crosshairs. The identity of the sub-contractor had not been identified but was experienced in such transactions.

CHAPTER 27

"Have your travels brought you to Strasbourg and the European Union Parliament before?" Alexandra asked warmly. Given their employment histories, it would be suspicious, if they had been. It would be even more doubtful they would comment on specifics.

"First time. I like the venue," Francine replied politely.

Alexandra looked at Yusuf.

"First time for me also."

As they walked to the conference room, Francine's attention was drawn to an adjacent office that was empty. She poked her head in briefly. Her surveillance and stare did not escape Alexandra's notice. Such detailed scrutiny would be uncommon for any agent but to be so blatant as to look inside seemed out of the ordinary.

"Something of interest?" Alexandra enquired quietly.

"Whose office?"

"Not sure but I can find out. Why do you ask?"

Francine delayed her response until the door to the conference room had been closed, assuring greater privacy and confidentiality. After a further silence, she breathed her response.

"Please do find out who occupies the office."

Alexandra held her gaze, which was more cautious than curious, more simmering than spontaneous.

Francine's eyes were those of a haunted traveller who had recently been transported from a distant world, now displaying contempt for the peril of the journey. The destination brought with it guarded inquisitiveness undeterred by the jetlag. Whatever had aroused her curiosity in the adjacent office was not mere novelty. It needed to be followed up by her hosts.

Paul stepped outside and re-entered momentarily. He slid a note to Alexandra for her perusal. "The name of the person working in the office next to the conference room," he murmured.

Alexandra stared with a blank expression at the name, Alana Savoy. She passed the note to Francine who read in silence. Her expression was equally reserved. The imbalance between Francine's pressing interest and her featureless response continued to hold Alexandra's interest. *A déjà vu,* Alexandra reflected. *Perhaps my greeting remark was appropriate and she has been at the EU Parliament before.*

"Do you recognize the name?" Alexandra asked.

Her response was terse. "No."

"And?" Yusuf prompted curiously, unable to read what was on the notepaper.

"Alana Savoy," Francine advised.

Yusuf's response was also devoid of any obvious emotion.

Again, the disparity between Francine's evident concern and the absence of a reaction prompted Alexandra to press for clarification.

"What drew your attention to the office?" Alexandra asked.

"There is a charcoal caricature of a man in the office. If you look carefully at the bottom right corner of the sketch, you will see Dmitri's signature. He is an accomplished caricaturist. That's one of the things I wanted to talk with you about."

Sometimes fate just deals you a fitting poker hand, hopefully not aces and eights, Paul mused as he left the conference room again. On this occasion, he held up his cell phone and took a photo of the caricature and a second close-up of the signature. He subsequently returned to the conference room.

"Were you able to find out what position Alana holds at the EU Parliament?" Alexandra asked.

"The title on the door says Economic and Financial Advisor. Other office doors display the nameplate of the occupant. Interesting. Alana's office door has none."

"We have people in high places including governance and policing," Paul whispered. "Herr Blosch had recited those words as they were being taken hostage on the yacht. Would Alana be one of the elite senior members of the governance who had been loyal to Herr Blosch and the *Quer* and perhaps Dmitri, or others?"

And whose payroll might she be on, beside the EU Parliament? Alexandra considered. *The plot thickens.*

"What other nuggets do you have to report?" Alexandra prompted, transferring her full attention to Francine.

"Nuggets, literally and figuratively. Dmitri has asked, contracted me, to look for caches of stolen Nazi gold supposedly hidden in secret Bavarian mines and elsewhere. He also mentioned the old Hotchkiss factory in the Paris suburb of Saint-Denis. He wants to use the wealth to hire the assassin in Lucerne to find a mysterious code he is convinced was created during the early days of the Cold War. It's a personal mission, a vendetta. There were some in the hierarchy of the KGB who believed that this secret code was nothing more than a ruse, used by the West to consume KGB resources in a futile search for cryptic ghosts. But there were a select few who privately believed that Dmitri was correct. The existence of the code was far from folly."

"What do you believe?" Paul queried.

"I don't know one way or another," Francine admitted bluntly. "So, until proven otherwise, I conclude that there may be some truth in his assertion. But what I think isn't important. What is important is what Dmitri believes. He will amass the deadliest resources gold can buy to prove he is correct, even if he isn't. He has given the Lucerne assassin *carte blanche* to kill anyone who, in her psychopathic mind, she believes may be holding back. When excessive amounts of money become the motivator, truth takes a back seat. The intelligence remains: Reichsmarschall Göring had hidden an undisclosed amount of wealth in the Saint-Denis region, still unaccounted for. Now, that is sufficient incentive for the unscrupulous."

Alexandra acknowledged Francine's updated assessment of Dmitri's motivation and the Lucerne assassin's murderous potential.

"Francine, I need to update you on Baird Durand," Alexandra announced. "We have new information that confirms he was not directly involved in Dominique's murder. But we need to speak with him quickly because he has vital information that is linked to the Moulins-lès-Metz ambush and to another matter. As a result, there is a high probability that he is in the crosshairs of a trigger, possibly the Lucerne assassin or one of her associates. It is imperative that he be captured alive. I emphasize, alive."

Francine tilted her head slightly at this request as if in doubt. *Doveryat' i proverit – trust and verify*, she reflected inwardly.

"A contract for his death may have already been issued by Beijing," Alexandra added. "The Asian female who shot Baird Durand's son, Joseph Brennus Durand, here in Strasbourg may have been awarded a more encompassing contract to kill both son and father. So, I repeat, it is essential that we find Baird Durand and keep him alive. That remains our number one priority."

Francine appeared perplexed momentarily with the updated intelligence. Modifying the mandate of a mission while in progress was not uncommon. But to change from killing a target to keeping the person alive as an imperative was rare. She had never experienced such a deviation in all her career. She trusted Alexandra as much as she could trust anyone. *Where was this directive coming from? Am I being set up once again?* She pondered. *Perhaps what*

Alexandra was passing along wasn't the whole truth. That was the most dangerous, mixing fact with fiction.

"Is there something you are not telling me?" Francine asked pointedly as she stared at Alexandra.

"Nothing," Alexandra replied without hesitation. "You know what I know. Why do you ask?"

"Just a feeling," Francine replied.

"Intuition is healthy. Our relationship is growing and it is natural to question, given our respective backgrounds. Please ask if in doubt," Alexandra invited.

Francine kept her stare for an extended moment before responding with a tinge of hesitancy, "Fair enough."

CHAPTER 28

"Beijing?" Francine speculated. "That adds a different dimension. The FSB is aware that the Chinese have been meddling in their backyard, but now they're more active on the front doorstep."

Paul watched warily for Yusuf's reaction to Alexandra's announcement of the change in plan in the quest to find Baird Durand, alive.

Francine added, "That jives with what Dmitri shared with me. He had the contract, which resulted in Dominique's death, issued from whom I'm not sure. Either way, Dmitri contacted the Lucerne assassin to pull the trigger. I previously warned you that Dmitri was a venomous viper. I will modify my assessment. He is a pussy cat, albeit feral, in comparison to the Lucerne assassin."

"And your next step?" Alexandra enquired.

"Bavaria and the Black Forest are too large to stumble around looking for forgotten mines that might hold stolen Nazi gold and other treasures. My best strategy is to go to Paris and the old Hotchkiss factory in Saint-Denis. If Dmitri has suspicious eyes on me, I want him to think that I am on the trail of stolen Nazi gold."

"Can we help?" Alexandra enquired.

"Not at this time. My KGB contact has confirmed that Reichsmarschall Göring did use the Hotchkiss factory as a staging point to temporarily hold stolen property that he was shipping back to his private cache in Bavaria closer to his family home in Rosenheim. The speed of the Blitzkrieg in 1939 was a strength of the Wehrmacht. But the non-existence of a strategically organized Blitzkrieg out of Paris in the winter of 1945 was a weakness because it was too hasty and disorganized to permit all the stolen gold and treasures to be shipped to Germany. Herr Göring supposedly sealed up storage rooms in the Hotchkiss factory to be accessed after the war. He may have hidden maps and other information in his suite at the Ritz Hotel on Place Vendôme, which he had appropriated as his personal headquarters during the German occupation of Paris."

"*Très bien fait* – well done," Alexandra complimented Francine as they walked through security at the front door to the EU Parliament. "Take care, my friend, and keep in contact."

"*Je vous souhaite la même chose* – the same to you," Francine replied.

"I noticed you were watching Yusuf. Thoughts, *mon colonel*?" Alexandra quietly enquired as she and Paul returned to the privacy of the conference room.

"I was watching him when you mentioned the need to find Baird Durand and keep him alive. Yusuf didn't so much as blink an eye. It was as if he already knew or was completely disinterested. I very much doubt the latter."

"Perhaps he is sufficiently well trained not to express any indication of emotion," Alexandra suggested.

"That's a possibility. But where would he have received that level of training? I doubt Turkish Military Intelligence, as they are not so sophisticated." He raised his eyebrows questioningly. "Russian?"

"Or Chinese?" Alexandra conjectured with an equally questioning expression.

Paul stared at reflections in his mind trying to remember something that vaguely gnawed at him but continued to evade precise recall.

After a contemplative hiatus, he commented, "I'm thinking Bosnia, Sarajevo. We may have crossed paths there or somewhere related to the UN tour. I need to reminisce over cognac with Daan and Marcel. Perhaps that will prompt my memory." He stared at nothing as he riffled through the memories that remained, overlain by the images of the little girl laying face-down in the ditch with her tiny arms tied behind her back with barbed wire that had ripped into her wrists, and blood oozing from a bullet hole in the back of her head staining the back of her light blue dress.... That haunting image tended to blank out all other recollections.

Conscious of his disassociated stare, Alexandra reached for his now cold, clammy hand. With a gentle kiss, she whispered, "I can think of other things to do after a snifter of Remy Martin or a flute of Dom Pérignon."

Paul held her glance and reciprocated with a subtle but distant smile. Although he would prefer to be with her, his mind was being held hostage elsewhere.

Their thoughts were disturbed by a knock on the door. The Head of Security for the EU Parliament approached. "You asked about the occupant of the office next to the conference room, Alana Savoy."

"Yes."

"She joined the EU Parliament several weeks ago. She had previously been employed by the United Nations in Geneva. She recently divorced and changed her name back to her maiden name, Durand. That's why the nameplate on the door into her office is temporarily absent. A new one is being made."

"Can you get me her address?" Paul asked nonchalantly, not wanting to raise any alarms.

"Certainly. I'll email it to you."

Paul murmured to Alexandra, "We have people in high places including governance and policing."

"If she is related to Baird Durand and Joseph Brennus Durand, how useful would her inside knowledge of the UN and especially the EU Parliament be to them?" Alexandra asked.

Alana Savoy, née Durand, was back in her office when Paul and Alexandra left the conference room. Alexandra knocked on the door as she motioned to Paul to wait in the hallway, out of sight.

"Hello Alana, I'm Alexandra. As I passed by your office, I couldn't help but notice the delightful caricature. It's a relative I suspect as I can see a resemblance."

"It's of my father. He would occasionally vacation in Valencia, on the Spanish Riviera. That is where it was done. He knows the artist."

"How absolutely wonderful," Alexandra replied with a warm smile. She held Alana's gaze and adeptly steered the conversation in another direction. "I understand that you worked for the UN in Geneva. Did your ex work there also?"

"No. He was the City Administrator in Geneva, at least until he got fired for financial improprieties, in addition to incurring big gambling debts." She hesitated momentarily. "And infidelity," she brusquely muttered in a tone of irritated contempt. She had been raised in an extended family that instilled loyalty as a principal value, never to be violated. Somehow, she had been conned by her ex, which left her questioning her ability to make decisions based on ancestral integrity above all. Some of her friends had made ethical choices in their relationship. Others had not understood the precept of loyalty.

"Why do you ask?"

"I also look for interesting places to take holidays. Getting a caricature done would be an added bonus."

"No. Why are you interested in my ex?" Alana seemed perturbed by Alexandra's intrusive approach.

Alexandra knew that she needed to calm Alana's agitation and refocus her attention. "I lived in Geneva. Loved the city. After a while, you get to know most people." She held the thought before whispering, "Congratulations on your divorce. I was there not so long ago. Life does get better."

Alana smiled as she relaxed. Alexandra's personal connection quelled her agitation. "Thank you for your commiseration. I'm surprised at how quickly news of my divorce travels. You are the first person I have spoken to about it, except my father."

"I'm a retired psychologist," Alexandra explained.

"Ah, that would explain why you are so easy to talk to."

"Do you live with your father in Strasbourg?" Alexandra queried subtly.

"Yes, in the old city. I'm looking for a place of my own closer to the EU Parliament, but good single accommodation is hard to find. High demand and low supply," she conceded with a sigh.

"If you would like to meet for coffee and chat more, divorcée to divorcée, here is my email."

She lowered her eyes to read the card. "Thank you. You are very kind. I may do that."

Alexandra surmised that she broke eye contact in response to her lowered confidence resulting from her change in marital status and transition in employment. She recalled how she herself had felt when she decided to separate from André and what had been her life in his house. She commiserated on a personal level with Alana's visceral and emotional response. Although each person's experiences are individual, the psychological response to separation and ultimate divorce, especially when infidelity was involved, had similar attributes. The most common were a sense of utter betrayal and abandonment merged with eroding confidence and trust in self and others.

Alexandra would meet those immediate needs with a balance of personal compassion from one who had walked that thorny path and professional consultation as a forensic psychologist, all the while gathering intelligence. It didn't sound as though Alana had a true friend, one who was not narcissistic or self-absorbed. Alexandra would fill that role. She would not abandon Alana. Not violating the boundary of perceived betrayal when so vulnerable would be a delicate balance. The two were not mutually exclusive.

"Where would be convenient to meet?" Alexandra followed up.

Alana re-established eye contact. "Do you know the Kaffee Struebel? We could meet there," she suggested. A slight smile returned to her lips then quickly expanded to encompass her entire face.

"At the south end of the Ponts Couverts?" Alexandra replied as if confirming. She had tentatively established a new friendship and confidante.

"Yes," Alana replied quickly. She rose from her chair and clutched Alexandra's extended hand with a double grasp, only reserved for her few special friends.

"I very much look forward to chatting with you, Alana."

"*Moi aussi, jusque là* – I also, until then. I'll text you with a confirmed time and date."

"Just in case we get our wires crossed, what is your father's name – who you are staying with?"

"Bary. Bary Durand. He uses the traditional Celtic spelling, B-a-r-y."

On hearing that pronouncement from his post in the hall, Paul's heart skipped a beat. *Could Bary Durand be Baird Durand? The family roots went back to early Gaul, settled by the Celts and Druids. He uses several aliases – Brennus, Brennos and Banona, which are also ancient Gallic Celtic names. Is Bary one more? Could they be this close to finding Baird Durand yet inadvertently heading down an uncharted path?*

As Alexandra and Paul left the EU Parliament, they exchanged frustrated expressions of provenance perhaps lost, and exhilaration at perhaps finding the final elusive member of the *Quer*.

"Daan and Matthieu may be as anxious and as reserved as we were when we present this information," Alexandra uttered.

"On the off chance that Bary Durand could be Baird Durand, and Alana now knows you, and may recognize me, we will need to plan our approach very carefully. We definitely need someone else to act the part of Claude Etien Marchand, the long-lost truant member of the *Quer*."

CHAPTER 29

"How confident are you that Alana's father is Baird Durand?" Daan asked poignantly.

"High probability," Alexandra replied.

"And you, Paul?"

"There aren't many people with the last name of Durand in Strasbourg. His heritage is Celtic. Alana is a Celtic name. We know that he uses at least three aliases. One more, Bary, also of Celtic culture, would not be out of character. I agree with Alexandra, high probability. In addition, Alana identified the caricature to be that of her father, Bary Durand. She essentially confirmed that Dmitri was the artist, whom her father had befriended. That is consistent with other intelligence. I have a photo of the artist's signature to attest to the drawing being Dmitri's work, and we now have a likeness of her father, albeit a somewhat exaggerated caricature that might reveal important aspects of Bary's character."

"OK. We proceed on the belief that Bary Durand is Baird Durand. Matthieu, brief the Delta Team," Daan directed. He looked across at Paul. "Send me the pic you took of the caricature of Bary Durand that was hanging in Alana's office. I will forward it to all members of the team."

"We will stage some of the team in Colmar so as not to raise any suspicions with the movement of many unknown resources in Strasbourg," Matthieu confirmed. "We will assign a few here to pose as tourists and then rotate with the Colmar team. Once we confirm an address for Baird, we will have the team leaders clandestinely conduct a reconnaissance."

Pointing to Matthieu, Daan completed the introduction.

"Alexandra and Paul, I would like to introduce you to the new truant member of the *Quer*, Claude Etien Marchand."

"Pleased to make your acquaintance," Alexandra responded with a bow, a smile, a cordial handshake and a sigh of relief that Paul was not being called upon for a repeat Academy Performance.

Daan continued his introduction. "Paul, you need to brief Matthieu on every aspect of Herr Rafael Blosch that you can recall. Every minute detail, including nuances. They will be crucial in the event that Baird Durand peppers Matthieu with questions, which I suspect he will. Alexandra, provide Matthieu with a psychological profile of Herr Blosch and how Baird might react. We must assume that Herr Blosch provided Baird and the other members of the *Quer* with an initial assessment of Claude Etien Marchand to prepare them for the rendezvous on the yacht. We must also assume that Baird is aware that his son, Joseph, is dead, and the other members of the *Quer* are missing in action and possibly deceased. So, we can expect Baird to be skittish and distrustful of everyone even more than he might normally be."

Looking at Matthieu, Daan added, "Research Gallic Celtic culture because that was Claude Etien Marchand's heritage and that of other members of the *Quer*. Baird may challenge you with questions regarding Celtic traditions."

"I will contact Alana and set up a meeting to counsel her on her divorce. I won't enquire further about her father at this initial meeting," Alexandra added.

"The head of the EU Parliament security emailed me Alana's address. Can you have Marcel follow up?" Paul suggested. "I think that Alexandra, Matthieu and I should maintain a low profile. It would be best if we moved to Colmar. There, we can easily coordinate with the other Delta Team members. But first Alexandra and I need to return to Paris to retrieve the ring that Matthieu will need to wear for his initial rendezvous with Baird."

Daan agreed and added, "Marcel and the Delta Surveillance Team will provide Alexandra with backup for her coffee meeting with Alana."

Paul immediately started his briefing with Matthieu. "My overall impression of Herr Blosch is that he was fastidious to the extreme in everything he did. His office was pristine down to the polished mahogany nameplate centred with regimental exactness on his desk. He was neither Rafael nor Mr. Blosch. In another lifetime, he could have been Herr Blosch of an international corporation or more likely *Oberst Colonel* Blosch of the Third and now the Fourth Reich. His draconian behaviour was both cunning and ruthless."

"It seems to come with the turf," Matthieu responded.

"No more so than the decor of his office. The crassness of this polished, panelled inner sanctum mirrored the cold indifferent monstrosity of the betrayal of so many depositors and ostensibly anonymous deposits that fell afoul of Adolf Hitler. On the day we met, Herr Blosch was an apparently unemotional executive mandarin of his own making. Yet he appeared momentarily overwhelmed by my authority and the plethora of official documents that I presented with the finest of Swiss-watch precision. In response to his adroitness, I adopted the role of a colonel and commanding officer of a military battalion, which he tacitly respected."

"Should I be bringing the same documents with me?" Matthieu asked.

"I think just the ring," Paul replied. "Herr Blosch looked warily at all the credentials as if in disbelief. But the ring commanded the greatest attention like a magnet solely oriented on the north pole. He ceremoniously removed a key from the breast pocket of his vest and unlocked the left-hand top drawer of his desk. With diplomatic deference, he gently retrieved a felt jeweller's box. What transpired next caused my heart to jump. Herr Blosch removed what appeared to be a duplicate ring from the box and judiciously inspected both

my ring and his. He directed his secretary to summon two professionals, one to compare the signature on my documents with the
signature on file with the bank, and the other to compare the rings.
These experts verified the authenticity of both. After promptly dis-
missing them with a wave of his hand, he then returned his ring to
the felt box and placed it back in the drawer. He then re-locked the
drawer with equal precision and veneration. Finely, he replaced
the key in his breast pocket and patted his chest gently to confirm
its presence."

"I agree with your assessment," Matthieu confirmed. "Herr
Blosch, manager of the Swiss bank, was more likely *Oberst
Colonel* Blosch of the Third and now Fourth Reich. I get the sense
that I need to adopt the presence of a colonel, commanding officer
of a battalion when I meet Baird Durand, one of seven directors
of the *Quer*."

Paul agreed.

"One last point," Paul emphasized. "After I had been taken
hostage by members of the Fourth Reich in the Pont de l'Alma
tunnel and driven to Compiègne where Marcel rescued me, the
death of Claude Etien Marchand was reported in the newspaper.
The obituary announced that the memorial service for Claude Etien
Marchand was private. The remains were cremated and the ashes
scattered in the Moselle River in the Province of Alsace. If by
chance, Baird Durand became aware, you should explain that the
reporting of the death of Claude Etien Marchand was a ruse to
cover bureaucratic embarrassment about your escape."

Matthieu acknowledged the importance of this point.

"With the disappearance of the other members of the Quer and
their suspected deaths, in addition to the death of his son, Baird
could easily become overly suspicious, but calm down enough after you show him the ring." Paul emphasized, "The ring is key.
So, keep him focused on the ring. The only two people who could

positively identify Claude Etien Marchand other than Herr Blosch were the two members of the Fourth Reich who took me hostage. They were shot dead by Marcel in Compiègne. The police reported that one person of interest had escaped from the scene in Compiègne. Stress with Baird that this fugitive was yourself, Claude Etien Marchand. The two experts who verified the authenticity of the signature and the ring remained solely focused on Herr Blosch. I do not recall either looking at me. So, I doubt they could identify me as Claude Etien Marchand."

⚞ ⚟

"PAPA," ALANA CALLED OUT. "WOULD you like to join us for coffee?"

Baird cautiously looked at his daughter and her companion seated in the Kaffee Struebel's outside seating area. He then scanned the immediate environment like a hawk surveying for potential prey and predator.

"Alexandra, I would like to introduce you to my father, Bary Durand."

Alexandra rose from her seat. "I am pleased to meet you, Monsieur Durand." She extended her right hand and simultaneously reached for her amulet with her left. Her *shrew* sounded the alarm for extreme caution. *This is him,* she reassured herself.

"The pleasure is all mine. Thank you for being so welcoming to my daughter and for offering to assist her with the divorce transition. In return for your kindness, please call me Bary, as do my close colleagues."

Baird, Brennus, Brennos and Banona, now one more, Bary. Is he so paranoid or completely distrustful and suspicious of everyone? Alexandra pondered. There was no mistaking the uncanny resemblance between the caricature that hung in Alana's office and the man standing in front of her.

"A divorce process may not be pleasant but there is light at the end of that tunnel," Alexandra reassured Alana's father.

"Please excuse me," Baird responded. "I won't join you for coffee. I have a sore throat coming on so must immediately return home to the healing warmth of the hearth. Thank you again, Alexandra. Perhaps we will meet again."

Meet again we undoubtedly will but under very different circumstances, Alexandra smiled with guarded confidence.

"I had best attend to my father," Alana explained to Alexandra. "Can we meet again soon?"

"Of course," Alexandra replied with a sense of care and concern. "I will contact you."

"Bary is Baird Durand," Alexandra's text message to Daan confirmed.

"Bravo Zulu – well done," Daan's reply appeared on her screen. "Paul and I are going to Paris to retrieve the ring."

CHAPTER 30

Yusuf's text message was clear, "Francine down. *Déjà vu* Moulins-lès-Metz. Taking her to safe house 18e Arrondissement."

"Currently in 2nd Arrondissement. On our way. Text or call with address," Alexandra replied immediately.

Daan's cell vibrated. "Centurion is down in Paris. En route. ETA 25 minutes. Will advise."

YUSUF WHISPERED TO FRANCINE, "*POMOSH ujec zdes*" – help is here."

"What happened?" Paul asked Yusuf as Alexandra tended to Francine.

"We had just arrived at the Hotchkiss factory when Francine was shot by someone in a car that came up from behind us. I didn't get a licence number or an accurate ID of the shooter. The car was a black Mercedes Benz C-class with tinted windows."

"Take care of her, Alexandra," Yusuf pleaded. "I have business to attend to."

"She is in good hands," Alexandra replied calmly.

"I won't be more than a couple of days. Please keep me updated."

"Will do, Yusuf," Alexandra assured him as she reached forward and caringly placed her hand on his shoulder. She surmised from his manner that whoever it was Yusuf was travelling to see would not be in receipt of the same level of passionate concern he felt for Francine. The lyrics of A.E. Housman's poem floated through her mind: *Ask me no more for fear I should reply.*

Alexandra smiled at Francine as the cobwebs gradually started to clear from the wounded woman's mind like the morning mist dissipating in the warming summer sun. She started to regain a sense of awareness.

"You have used up two of your nine feline lives, perhaps others I am not aware of but would not be surprised to hear about."

"Much appreciate your good-humoured prognosis," Francine whispered. "That means I have seven remaining. I will just rest here a bit if you don't mind."

※ ※

THE STILLNESS OF THE EVENING echoed the squeaking stairs as Dmitri guardedly ascended to the third floor and his apartment. His slinky companion was curiously absent. *Where is the cat?* he wondered. A familiar yet uncharacteristic atmosphere brought with it an increased wariness. The upper landing seemed dark with one light bulb insufficient to illuminate the way. No light showed through the window. A familiar image greeted him as he reached into his pocket with his right hand for the keys to his apartment. He extended his left hand behind his back.

"Ah, Rakici, the Armenian Turk," Dmitri said quietly. "I should have known it was you. The cat always greets me in the lobby. You are the only other person I know who it has befriended enough to approach. Perhaps it is because you feed it treats and pat it with affection, attention it does not receive from strangers."

Yusuf's impassive expression made Dmitri suspicious. Despite his formal departure from the tradecraft, his default mode to mistrust even familiar faces had not left him.

"What brings you to Valencia once again? Are you personally delivering another communiqué from Moscow?" Dmitri enquired guardedly. He was grasping for time in order to re-evaluate the circumstances in which he found himself. He had learned long ago that a neutral response from even a former colleague was neither a signal that all was well in the Kremlin nor in his abode.

"The thought had crossed my mind that I might have you sketch a caricature of me after all these years," Yusuf replied.

"A sketch of you alone or is Tatyana here also?"

"She is in Saint-Denis tending to your business."

Ah… that is where I had seen her before, a young Red Sparrow reporting for training, he suddenly recollected. He had told her the first time they met that she had no choice. Die or become a Red Sparrow.

Meeting Yusuf's stare, he stated arrogantly, "She always had a reputation for being obedient, if not foolishly so." He slowly slid his left hand to his side.

"Nyet, nyet – no, no. Keep your hands where I can see them," Yusuf directed with finality to his tone. His complexion became sombre with those words of warning.

Dmitri stood motionless as the cat walked figure eights round his ankles. Its allegiance had switched from new friend and provider of occasional treats and pats to longer-term companion and provider of nourishment and occasional swats. Loyalty was that fleeting, that cheap.

"Bros'pistolet – drop the gun," Yusuf ordered, without breaking eye contact.

The cat jumped to the staircase as Dmitri's pistol fell from his grip and he awkwardly slumped against the hallway wall, now splattered with blood. He came to rest against the door jam.

"Eto za Tanyu – That is for Tatyana. You will never harm her again, *tovarish* – comrade," Yusuf uttered as he stared down.

"Lucerne," Dmitri gasped, barely audible. "The Chinese prefer the Swiss climate but occasionally visit Paris and other French tourist locations."

Yusuf squeezed the trigger one more time. The silencer puffed.

Double tap. The faint sarcastic smile faded from Dimitri's face. Blood puddled into the recesses of his slightly bulging eye sockets, then onto his face from the entry wound between his eyebrows, and simultaneously onto the floor from the exit wound. "I looked and I looked but I didn't see God," Yusuf muttered in a mocking voice. "Your childhood hero, Yuri Gagarin, is purported to have uttered these words as the first man to fly in space and orbit the world. More likely, it was his political boss, Nikita Khrushchev, who said it, motivated for political gain. Regardless, I doubt you will see God where you are going."

Yusuf reached down, retrieved the keys from Dmitri's pocket and opened the apartment door. As he stepped over the body, he dropped his Chinese QSZ-92 pistol beside Dmitri's disfigured head after removing all finger prints. He then retrieved Dmitri's Makarov PB from the floor. *The Chinese make poor quality pistols but it does the job at short range,* he mused. *I much prefer the Russian Makarov PB.* After filling the cat's bowl with food, he departed with the satchel containing Dmitri's charcoal pencils and the keys.

The cat and Yusuf passed each other. "Farewell, friend. I have left your final dinner at this restaurant."

⌐ ⌐

"How is my Tanya?" Yusuf enquired with deep concern.

Alexandra inquisitively returned his gaze. She had not heard this name before in any conversation.

"Tatyana is her Russian name; Francine is her French. From the first time we met at the University of Rostov, I have called her Tanya."

"She will survive to fight another day," Alexandra replied. "A doctor has attended to her wounds and has left some medication and fresh bandages. When she has regained her strength, we will be able to move her to a location where neither of you are known, and she will be able to convalesce with the best of long-term medical care."

"There is no need for her, for us, to return to Valencia again," Yusuf nonchalantly announced. "We all need to be very cautious of a Chinese tourist temporarily living in Lucerne but visiting here in Paris as we speak."

Paul acknowledged the warning. In his own mind, he stared at imprecise reflections while trying to remember something about Yusuf that gnawed at him but continued to evade his full recollection.

"I will be forever grateful to the two of you for all you have done for my Tanya," Yusuf whispered.

Yusuf may be a Paladin. He certainly has a past that influences his present, Paul surmised. His past remained a mystery though. There was honour to be defended, to right the wrong – the ethos of Paladin and other solitary mythical heroes of the American West.

Daan monitored his text message: "Centurion continues to recover. Beijing threat high and imminent. Will remain with the centurion. Have Claude Etien Marchand pick up ring from us."

"Love goes a long way to assure survival. Those whom we love, we will protect," Alexandra remarked. "Yusuf has demonstrated that."

"Perhaps so," Paul added.

"Perhaps?" Alexandra questioned.

"As you say, those we are passionate about, we will protect. Yes. But also, that which we are passionate about, we will protect. Is Yusuf's passion solely for Francine or for a philosophy, one he gleaned from reading all those Western novels written by A.B. Guthrie, Louis Lamour and Zane Grey?"

After a silence during which Alexandra held his gaze, she

proposed, "Perhaps not either/or, but both/and. Both Francine and a philosophy."

Paul nodded. As long as he and Alexandra wore white hats, the symbol of the honourable good guys in the black and white Western movies, they would not have to meet Yusuf on Main Street at high noon.

"There is something about Yusuf that is worrying you," Alexandra commented.

"There is something about him that has been puzzling me from the first moment he spoke to me when running the Palermo marathon. It's not so much a danger as duplicity."

"Duplicity in the form of deception akin to seduction?"

Paul dwelled on her quest for clarification.

"No. Duplicity as in a fluctuation or deviation from a personal conviction, which is based on his interpretation of the Paladin myth. He has a personal agenda. We know that. And he uses duplicity as a strength to fulfil his agenda. We know that too."

"Do we need to guard our backs?" Alexandra asked.

"I'm not sensing a direct danger to either of us. I believe him when he said that he would be forever grateful to us for helping Francine, his Tanya. His voice resonated with conviction when he said that. But grateful is an emotion that doesn't necessarily translate into action. He didn't say that he would be there for us, to protect us, if push came to shove, unlike Marcel who unselfishly put his life on the line to save me in Compiègne."

"And as you did for Marcel in Sarajevo," Alexandra confirmed. "True comrades in arms beyond just bravado."

"Perhaps it is cultural. When we joined the EUI Unit, Daan said that our colleagues are only recruited from the initial six-member states of the European Union because we tend to be more alike in a common culture, conviction. Yusuf comes from a different culture," Paul concluded.

"Like you, I don't sense any direct threat or danger from Yusuf but instead just caution. You have mentioned a few times that the key to unlocking your memory about him could be Sarajevo. Perhaps the time is ripe certainly for you and Daan, and probably Marcel and Matthieu, to reminisce over a cognac as all of you served with the United Nations Protection Force in Sarajevo at the same time."

Paul held her gaze, thinking.

"You seem hesitant."

"Maybe I'm wrong," Alexandra considered. "Maybe he would be there for you, for us. Maybe the conviction of Paladin would rise to the challenge, the ethos of honour to be defended, to right the wrong."

"Perhaps." Paul repeated her qualification. "Perhaps."

CHAPTER 31

"How did you locate me, Monsieur Marchand?" Baird Durand asked. His smile was thin. His bearing was hesitant. His voice was welcoming yet skeptical. His stare was penetrating yet prudent. Throughout his adult life, he had rarely entertained cold contacts and then only when referred to by those in his inner circle with whom he had developed a life-long cloistered relationship. Herr Blosch was one of those very few steadfast colleagues. Baird and the other five members of the *Quer* had all received an introductory communiqué from Herr Blosch regarding the return of Claude Etien Marchand, the truant seventh member. The banker had described his credentials as impeccable.

"I have a network that specializes in finding those who do not want to be found, particularly those who have some affiliation with the Wewelsburg Castle," Claude Etien Marchand responded. "That led me to Herr Blosch and ultimately to you, although finding you was more challenging, I admit."

The reference to the Wewelsburg Castle, Reichsführer-SS Heinrich Himmler's lair, in addition to other Nazi SS affiliations Claude Etien Marchand had alluded to in his initial email, caused Baird to instinctively waver. He concluded that his heightened response was due to a combination of factors. He was acutely aware that his own introverted personality caused him to withdraw from the world beyond the bastions of his fortified home. He did not deal well with variances in his normal routine. Most concerning were the nightmarish images of his gagged and hooded colleagues with hands bound behind their backs pinned down on the plush carpeted floor of the yacht. Perhaps more perplexing was the unexplained

187

circumstances relating to the unexpected departure of Herr Blosch from his long-standing appointment as manager of one of the most prestigious banks in Switzerland. If ever there was a person who demanded routine, it was Herr Blosch. Finally, the disquieting and in some cases complete dearth of responses to his electronic requests for communiqués from the few administrators in the *Quer* caused his acid reflux to act up.

"What happened on the yacht? Why were you not captured with the others?" Baird pressed.

He had anticipated this question and had rehearsed the answer. "I was to meet Herr Blosch at the dock but as I was approaching, the yacht was raided by men wearing black clothes and balaclavas pulled over their faces. As I stood behind a tree, a group of men, hooded and cuffed, were speedily escorted away from the yacht to a van. I immediately went into hiding. I had no way of easily contacting other members of the *Quer*. Do you know what happened to Herr Blosch? I haven't been able to contact him since this incident on the yacht. The bank told me that he had become ill and had to retire unexpectedly. I thought it strange because he seemed in excellent health the evening before when we dined at the Il Vero restaurant in the Fairmont Grand Hotel Kempinski Geneva."

While listening to his guest's recollection of events, Baird carefully examined Claude Etien Marchand's ring with an inelastic stare. He had examined his own ring many times and had memorized every feature of the hand-engraved design. He had no doubt the ring he held was an original. It showed all the wear markings that Claude's ancestors would have subjected it to over the centuries. With reverence, he returned it to its rightful owner. His faint smile morphed into warm validation and acceptance. His anxiety abated slightly. His posture began to relax. His demeanour edged closer to becoming more hospitable. For the first time since he witnessed his colleagues being accosted on the yacht, he felt calmer.

He now had someone with whom he could engage in conversations that mattered, regarding strategic plans for the future of the *Quer*.

"I believe the others are being held prisoner somewhere. Rumour has it that they may be dead, including Herr Blosch. Recently, my son, Joseph, was killed. I haven't yet told his sister, Alana, because she is dealing with the trauma of her own messy divorce."

"Dead?" Claude Etien Marchand repeated in exasperation, which mirrored the shock and disbelief in his eyes.

"An existence of non-existence," Baird muttered in acceptance. His manner was shrouded in vain pride and a nuance of arrogant indifference. "It appears that we may be the surviving members of the *Quer*."

"I know virtually nothing of the history of the *Quer*. My father alluded to it when telling me stories of our family. He has since died. Herr Blosch briefed me on its broad purpose and some of the current activities. I appreciate that its heritage reaches back to the Gallic Celtic era but I know little of the detail."

"We will need to spend considerable time together. Some weeks. Is your calendar free?" Baird invited. He very much looked forward to the close companionship of a colleague, albeit distant.

"My calendar is completely clear. When do we begin?" Claude replied. He was surprised that Baird had not grilled him more regarding his heritage. He surmised that Baird was so eager for collegial company, as Alexandra had predicted, that he initially accepted him based on the verification of the authenticity of his ring and validation of his legitimacy as the truant member of the Quer as briefly outlined by Herr Blosch in his scripted introductory e-communiqué. Other questions would follow in the course of time.

"Now is as good a time as any," Baird began. "Tell me about your initial meeting with Herr Blosch."

Claude correctly assessed the calibre of the loaded question.

Baird was indeed testing him and would continue to do so, perhaps forever.

"Let me start with my preliminary impression. Herr Blosch had an almost pathological need for neatness and attention to the most minute detail."

Baird chuckled at this initial assessment of Herr Blosch and his almost compulsive behaviour regarding the exactness of his office.

"I agree that he was neat to the extreme. In fact, it bothered me at times because it interfered with discussions. Seemingly out of nowhere, Herr Blosch would rise from his chair to remove a speck of dust from something. He would then return to his seat and instruct me or one of my colleagues to continue with the conversation," Baird admitted. "A strength taken to an extreme becomes a weakness. I understand that bankers need to pay attention to detail but…" Baird interrupted himself. "I apologize. I digress. It has been a long time since I have had the opportunity to sit and chat, especially about our heritage."

For the balance of the morning, Baird listened intently as Claude Etien Marchand reiterated the details he had committed to memory, while his microphone relayed the details of their conversation that were being recorded meticulously by the EUI Technical Team and monitored live by Daan.

Over the next several days, Baird related the entire history of the *Quer* since its inception, and as it grew in influence and sophistication, including its affiliations. Of particular importance was the connection of the *Quer* to the Third and Fourth Reich, and Nazi stolen gold, art objects, shares and securities. Much allegedly remained hidden in Bavarian mines, Swiss banks, offshore accounts including a few nominal deposits in China, and smaller secreted caches in countries in Western Europe that had been occupied by the Third Reich during the war. Baird also identified numerous collaborators holding senior positions in governance and policing.

Alana's ex-husband had been one of those paid for his influence until he was fired mainly due to his loose tongue that became looser when he was under the influence of alcohol that recently had become more frequent. He had been cautioned but to no avail. He believed naïvely that he was untouchable due to his marital status, which he failed to appreciate and had ended with the divorce. Alana was not aware of the familial influence of her father's business transactions. Baird did not seem to know that his son had spied for the Russians in addition to at least one other nefarious player, only that he worked in Paris as a senior director in the General Directorate of Internal Security. The *Quer* fraternity had paved the road for dynastic employment opportunities and careers, which paid substantial dividends.

With the death of his son, Baird revealed that he no longer had a male offspring to inherit his position in the *Quer* and his considerable wealth. Alana could not occupy one of the seven positions because it must be paternal. More tellingly, Baird did not have faith in the sons of the other members of the *Quer*, the latter now assumed to be dead.

Claude commiserated with him. He revealed that he did not have a son either to inherit his newly acquired position and wealth. This common dilemma brought them closer as they debated the fate of the *Quer,* which might be leaderless at their deaths. Given the yet unconfirmed recent fatalities of the other members, there wasn't a great deal of time to envision let alone implement solutions.

Baird had been aware of Moscow's incursions throughout the Cold War. Only recently had he seriously considered the peril of the Beijing affiliations. Nominal deposits in the limited number of Chinese banks had become increasingly more difficult to access. When transactions were approved, the actual transfers of funds were exceedingly slow and then only in increments. Much of his banked financial assets in Switzerland appeared to have been frozen. This further limited his options, including his ability to protect Alana. Other accounts were currently being activated but the process was slow.

One of his Wewelsburg Castle associates had informed him that a female Chinese agent had assassinated his son. There was a high probability that Beijing had ordered the assassination of Herr Blosch and his *Quer* colleagues. Certainly, he and more than likely Alana were now in the crosshairs.

Claude Etien Marchand seized the initiative to propose an audacious plan, a merger or partnership with another organization that could bring considerable offensive and defensive resources to the table to counter the impending terminal threats from Beijing. Key among them were security and intelligence assets. Initially, Baird rebuffed the idea. But ultimately, he agreed in principle that it was a possible way out in the short term, especially in the absence of any other viable options. Heavy on his mind were the looming threats and shrinking financial resources. Claude reassured him that Alana could also benefit from the protective umbrella. Claude would arrange a meeting with a business associate – Daan Segers. Baird agreed guardedly.

⚐ ⚑

THE NEWS OF MATTHIEU'S SUCCESS playing the part of Claude Etien Marchand was greeted with jubilation by all, especially Yolina and a select few among her security colleagues, as a justification for the *raison d'être* of the creation of the EUI Unit. Its sole purpose was the protection of the European Union from internal and external threats. Bringing Baird Durand in from the cold, if even ever so slightly, met that mandate.

Alexandra celebrated with caution. She sensed that Baird's acquiescence was not wholly sincere. He had not disclosed the existence of the *Quer* Cyber Unit that was in the process of transferring financial resources. Jean's briefing on cyber crime and terrorist activities had confirmed otherwise.

Alexandra surmised that the root of all evil wasn't money. The *Quer* had amassed more wealth than the majority of nation states collectively held in their respective coffers. It could not be classified as evil in the same arena as Nazi Germany, Communist Russia, the Chinese Communist Party, or dictators of rogue states whose sole motivation was greed. What created and drove evil was fear. Fear of not getting what you want or losing what you have. So, what drove Baird Durand, the surviving member of the *Quer*? Was it his inflated vanity, his faith in his ability to ultimately succeed against all odds? Or was it fear of losing it all?

"Baird will need to be watched very carefully," Alexandra cautioned. "He has proven himself to be a survivor. The *Quer* is his birthright and he is happiest when in its womb. There is nothing more sacred to him, not even his daughter, Alana. Alone and under siege to fend off the hoards that are holding his *Jus Sanguinis* – his right of blood hostage is his worst-case scenario. If he perceives that there is no alternative, he could push the doomsday button and unleash Armageddon, propelling the New World Order into an unimaginable apocalypse."

Alexandra's sober analysis returned the mood of celebration to a more realistic plane. Matthieu observed Daan return to his introspective reflection as he had done so many times when they served with the United Nations Protective Force in Sarajevo. The secret world of intelligence, whether military or civilian, had that effect. The threat is never over until it is over, and it is never over. Like a virus, it morphs into more virulent variants. The *Quer* hadn't survived for centuries due to luck alone.

CHAPTER 32

"Did you sense you were being followed? Or was the Hotchkiss factory under surveillance and you just walked into the trap?" Alexandra asked.

"Both are possible," Francine replied. "I want to know the motivation of the shooter – killing me or getting hold of something I had or was after? If I were the shooter, I would set a trap and have the target come to me or ensnare them en route like the Moulins-lès-Metz ambush. But I would need to know in advance that the target was coming to the location and the approximate time."

"If the latter, who knew that you were en route to the Hotchkiss factory?" Alexandra asked. "Knowing that will narrow the field considerably." Alexandra considered the myriad of options, given Francine's extensive background in the mysterious world of espionage and intelligence gathering. The answer to the question of who would want her dead was long. It included many in the KGB and FSB, starting with those in her training cadre and colleagues who saw her as a threat to their own advancement opportunities. The higher you rose in the hierarchy, the more toes you would potentially have stepped on.

She was good at what she did, probably graduating at the top of her class. In a highly competitive environment, she would have been a natural target for most. She was physically attractive so less well-endowed and less-confident women would have seen her as a threat and competition for male liaisons in the cohort and other superiors. As a Soviet agent, she would have crossed paths with her Western counterparts, some of whom she would have wounded or scarred and were now facing an early retirement or dispatched to the great spy school in the sky.

"Apart from Yusuf, only one other person knew because he put me onto the scent. That was Dmitri. He might have ordered someone else to follow me and provide updates on my progress to the actual shooter." Francine became somber as she looked at Alexandra but reflected in her own mind on the events that had transpired at her last rendezvous with Dmitri on the Valencia beach. This latest wounding stank of his revenge for putting him in an uncomfortable position when she summoned Yusuf to make their twosome into a threesome meeting. In doing so, Dmitri was at a disadvantage. She knew it but may have misjudged the reaction of the venomous viper. It would have been his style to have someone else perform the deed, thereby maintaining his distance.

Alexandra looked at Yusuf. A faint smile of satisfaction lit his eyes and faded onto his lips. Nothing further needed to be said. She knew. He knew that she knew. Simply, move on. But Alexandra wanted verification. She looked at the Armenian Turk and said nothing.

"Someone got to him before me," Yusuf responded. "By the time I arrived at his apartment, he was dead. I spoke with the waiter from the café across the street. He told me he had found the body and called the police. Dmitri had been shot twice, double tap, a professional job. According to the police, the murder weapon was a Chinese pistol." Yusuf's accounting of the facts ended as abruptly as it had begun.

Paul carefully monitored Yusuf's matter-of-fact response. He would notify Daan that the surveillance team previously assigned to tail Dmitri could be reassigned.

Maintaining his eye contact with Yusuf, Paul enquired, "Were you walking north or south toward the Hotchkiss factory when Francine was shot?"

"North," Yusuf responded in a matter of fact manner and without the slightest hesitation.

His immediate reply caused Paul to wonder. *Was his quick response the result of prior knowledge of this latest ambush and preparedness for the question he anticipated? Alternatively, was his intent to mislead? Or did it come from his professional training in acute observation and strategic analysis?*

Paul and Alexandra exchanged a quick glance. Clearly, their deductions had brought them to the same possible explanation. The question they now faced was: Was their analytical process accurate or flawed because of cultural misinterpretation of East versus West or Armenian Turkish Middle-East versus French mid-Western European? They would hold that thought for a future discussion.

"Did you know exactly where in the Hotchkiss factory you were going?" Alexandra followed up with Francine. This interrogation tactic was consistent with their overall strategy. She would focus primarily on Francine while Paul directed his attention to Yusuf.

"No, not exactly," Francine replied. "I was hoping to find some deviation from the original building plans, which I had scanned in the city engineering archives. Numerous amateur treasure hunters would have traipsed around since Paris was liberated by Charles de Gaulle and his Free French Army in 1945. So, any obvious physical clues would have been raked over and taken as souvenirs, if there were any. I figured that my best bet would be architectural. I was told that most recently a wall had been blown out in a previously unrecorded room after a mysterious explosion. The hole that exposed the adjacent Metro station and rail tracks has since been boarded up."

Paul looked surprised. He was aware of the room and adjacent Metro station from personal unpleasant experience. In this regard, Francine's facts were accurate, which provided credence to other information she had related. In contrast, Yusuf remained the wild card and the details he related potentially more theatrical than evidence-based.

Francine continued to draw on her research acumen. "The verification of a subterranean network of inter-connected rooms validated previous intelligence that Herr Göring had built these structures as part of the Nazi vision for Hitler's Thousand-year Reich. Or, Herr Göring purposely constructed these rooms as warehousing annexes for his bounty of stolen treasures. If these facilities had interconnecting secret tunnels, as many had, he could stealthily access his private stash of riches in the years after the war. I surmise that he hadn't considered that the Third Reich might be defeated and he would be found guilty by a panel of military judges and sentenced to death. Perhaps poetic justice that he committed suicide while in custody," Francine grimaced. "That begs the question: Did Herr Göring actually use these underground rooms to store treasures still unaccounted for? If so, where are they now?"

Directing her attention toward Paul, Alexandra commented, "We need to go there. One of us should approach from the south while the other from the north."

"I'd like to accompany you," Francine said, "but I think I'll rest here a bit longer." With a tight smile, she glibly added, "Age seems to have caught up with me and I wouldn't want to slow you youngsters down."

"Probably a good idea," Alexandra chuckled as she reached for Francine's hand. This expression of compassion was acknowledged with a warm Parisian smile that did not go unnoticed. On this occasion, her grin mirrored that of an authentic Parisienne and not of an impostor who had only been schooled in the basics of proper French etiquette, not the subtle nuances which differentiate the two.

"I'm not happy with your suggestion to split up and approach from different directions," Paul countered. "If we do, we will both need backup from Delta Team members to shadow us. As Francine explained, apart from Yusuf, only Dmitri knew of her planned activity because he had her followed. That person had orchestrated the hit in real time. There is a high probability that no one is aware of the tentative plans we are now hatching."

"Fair enough," Alexandra conceded. "Best we brief Daan and have support close by."

※ ※

AS THEY LEFT THE SAFE house at Place du Tertre, a few steps from the Sacré-Coeur Basilica in Montmartre, Paul thought out loud: "Yusuf told us there was no need for Francine, for them, to return to Valencia. He must have known that Dmitri was dead. The question remains: Did Yusuf shoot Dmitri? Or did the waiter or a third party pull the trigger of the Chinese pistol? Was the shooter Chinese or did the shooter leave the Chinese firearm to misdirect police investigators' gaze east beyond Red Square toward the Great Wall of China?"

"It wouldn't be the first time," Alexandra agreed. "And?" she prompted, sensing he had more to add to his assessment.

"And when I was a junior lab technician, I recall my mentor telling me that if I found evidence at the scene of a crime or heard a sound, I should immediately look in another direction and only after that should I focus in detail on the immediate crime scene. More often than not, that helped me to solve the mystery of whodunit and identify the motivation. We live in a blaming culture and no more so than in the international political arena where the default move is to deceive and deflect."

"C'est très vrai," Alexandra validated his described behaviour. "I did the same as part of my own forensic approach to analysis. It worked many times for me, too." She stopped for a moment, looked up and then abruptly lowered her head. "A thought," she uttered. "I keep returning to our analysis of the Yusuf enigma and his characterization of Paladin, the knight-errant. It's in his character to right the wrong. But in doing so, would Paladin cover his tracks as a strategy to deceive?" After a moment of consideration, she answered her own question. "Perhaps if the deception were to increase the probability of catching the bad guy, righting the wrong?"

"I agree," Paul confirmed. "No doubt in my mind, he is playing the part of the Medieval knight-errant, the Western hero, Paladin. That was the ethos of the early days of the Hollywood Silver Screen when the good guys wore white hats and the bad guys wore black hats. The good guys adhered to the highest Christian-based ethical standards at all times. They never swore. Even after a fist fight, their clothes remained pristine. Today, Paladin's behaviour mirrors his own standards in which anything goes – survival of the fittest."

Alexandra considered Paul's assessment, which seemed to parallel her own.

"He had to have been the knight first, acting out the chivalric *noblesse oblige* before becoming the knight-errant. Given his Armenian Turkish background, anything is possible. The default mode – he is a survivor." An intriguing thought crossed her mind. "A survivor like Baird Durand."

Paul elaborated on the thought. "The knight lineage fits his persona, his conduct. In his eyes, he is Paladin. That is his *raison d'être*. To right the wrong is his mandate, his mantra, his ethos by virtue of his heritage, his heraldic standards passed down."

"I get the feeling that he doesn't care so much about commoners," Alexandra suggested. "He wouldn't jump on his white horse to rescue some peasant damsel in distress. That is not what motivates him. He would instruct the damsel to get off her lethargic butt, change her own circumstances and not depend on others. That is why he seems indifferent to everyday issues. From his perspective, his *raison d'être* is to kill the abusive sociopathic bully. That would right the wrong. If so, then that begs another question: Does he suffer from a multiple personality disorder? Or does he knowingly conduct a costume change, as needed, in order to right the wrong?"

"I'll leave that to the psychologist to answer," Paul retorted. "There is a twist in his Paladin identity though," he conjectured. "I sense that he, whoever he is – Yusuf or Paladin, or the knight-errant – truly loves Francine. But the American Western hero, Paladin, never had a wife nor a girlfriend, nor even a female in his company and certainly not a mistress on the side. The portrayal of the Medieval knight in contemporary literature and film, even the knight-errant, has always been without a wife, a betrothed, a female companion. Sex was a four-letter word. Caring deeply for Francine could be his constant dilemma. From his perspective, how can he be the true knight-errant, Paladin, and love Francine, his Tanya, at the same time?"

"If that is true, then Yusuf went to Valencia with one mission in mind, to kill Dmitri, the abusive psychopathic bully. He was motivated to do so by being Paladin."

"Now we have a dilemma of our own," Paul proposed. "Dmitri is dead. Baird has been located and tentatively convinced to work with us. Now, do we need Francine and Yusuf on the EUI Unit payroll? If not, they could become free agents with knowledge of the EUI Unit, conceivably working against us."

"Or ideally working for us, with us," Alexandra speculated. "An exit strategy. We haven't talked about this with Daan. We need to do so at the soonest opportunity."

"When I first proposed that Francine become the mongoose, I identified a challenge: When you sub-contract to another gladiator, you run the risk of giving up control over some aspects of the mission resulting in you becoming subservient to that gladiator in ways that only the gladiator may know. That moment may be fast approaching," Paul warned. "Who might be subservient to whom in our relationship with the duo of Francine, aka Tatyana, aka Tanya and Yusuf aka the Armenian Turk, aka Paladin, aka the knight-errant?"

Alexandra thought for a moment. "In the immediate term, there is still the Lucerne assassin who actually pulled the trigger, killing Dominique and Rudolf, and wounding Francine, on two occasions perhaps, as we don't know the identity of the Saint-Denis shooter. There is no doubt that Francine wants both assassins dead, as does the knight-errant, Paladin. I am also confident that she would have been happiest if she had pulled the trigger. Still happy if she had been present when Paladin righted the wrong. When Yusuf does tell her of Dmitri's demise, the news will bring a smile to her face. We have time while Francine is recovering, but not much."

"Strategy time with Daan and perhaps Yolina, given the short- and long-term implications," Paul suggested.

CHAPTER 33

Both Alexandra and Paul picked up text messages sent simultaneously from Marcel as they approached the Hotchkiss factory. "Yusuf appears to be following Alexandra."

Paul's heart jumped at the communiqué of a real and present threat. His hurried breathing mirrored the heightened alert. "Keep following him, Marcel. Alexandra, slow your pace and stop as if window shopping. Marcel, do the same. I will circle around and manoeuvre behind all of you as we did with Rudolf in Munich. Once I am in position, Marcel and I will conduct a pincer movement."

Yusuf assessed his situation but not quickly enough. He had been detected. His surveillance had been blown. Three sets of eyes now stared at him. None were smiling. Occasionally, even Paladin had been outmanoeuvred on the TV shows.

Yusuf was the first to speak, his voice confident. "I sense that you are wondering why I am following you."

"That would be a good start," Paul growled with no semblance of humour.

After frisking Yusuf and grasping hold of a Makarov PB 9mm pistol secreted in a holster behind his back and under his jacket, Marcel confirmed with a glance that the situation was safe. He was reluctant to remove the pistol altogether because of the high volume of pedestrian traffic on the sidewalk around them. Its presence was no longer a threat while secure and out of sight in his grip.

"Francine, my Tanya, was shot last time we were here. I figured that you might need another set of eyes. I wasn't aware but should have concluded that you would have your own surveillance on your approach to the Hotchkiss factory."

Paul continued to glare at him. His heightened sense of vigilance had not diminished after Yusuf's opening admission and brief explanation of his presence. The enigma of his persona continued to challenge Paul's confidence in him. One moment Paul trusted him and the next moment he questioned his honesty.

"I can appreciate your response, Paul. I apologize. I should have coordinated with you and your surveillance team."

"Probably a wise reflection in retrospect," Marcel replied, "else you could be joining Francine nursing wounds, that is, if you are feeling lucky, unlike Dmitri."

In a de-escalating tone, Alexandra asked, "I sense that you know details about what might be or what is in the old factory. Now would be a good time to talk." She leaned towards him and uttered in a low voice. "And carrying a Russian Makarov PB pistol which I might surmise is unregistered anywhere?"

He was acutely aware that neither Paul nor Marcel had relaxed their proximity to him. Marcel's hand was still clenching the pistol hidden in his waistline holster under his jacket.

Yusuf began his explanation in a forthright manner unperturbed by the circumstances in which he found himself. "Dmitri was ex-KGB, as you know. He was aware that Reichsmarschall Göring had hidden gold and other valuable artefacts somewhere close to or in the Hotchkiss factory, but he didn't know where. He had learned those details not from rumour but from his trainer, Uri Popov. Uri was one of the very few people Dmitri trusted – if one KGB agent can ever truly trust another agent."

"Then how did you find out?" Paul abruptly interrupted.

"Long story. I'll get to that later."

"Not later. Now," Paul demanded.

Yusuf continued, "In brief, I was in the Turkish Military

Intelligence. I attended the University of Rostov in southern Russia. My Turkish superiors knew that KGB agents were educated there. My job was to recruit Russian agents as informants. Tanya was one. Initially, I wasn't aware that she was there to recruit me to become a Russian agent. I played along. Eventually I met Dmitri and his trainer, Uri Popov. I learned about Reichsmarschall Göring's hidden treasures but had no details. One of Göring's strategies was to create a rumour mill about possible hiding places. They were all false, except the Hotchkiss factory."

"What led you to believe that Saint-Denis was not bogus?" Paul asked. He wanted to know the answer to this question as much as to gain an opportunity to confirm that Yusuf was telling the truth.

"Two factors. First, Francine had been sifting through the intelligence and was confident Saint-Denis was a viable location. Second, further analysis that I undertook suggested the Hotchkiss factory."

"And Dmitri?"

"Watching Dmitri all these years, I noticed that he rarely if ever went anywhere without his satchel in which he kept his sketching pencils and chalk for his caricatures. I concluded that he kept something else hidden in it. We talked many times. On one occasion, he spoke in more detail about the Hotchkiss factory. I guess that he liked me because he bequeathed his satchel to me. In it, I found a key and a non-descript diagram sewn into the lining. I think there is a hidden lock somewhere in the old Hotchkiss factory that matches the key. I have no idea what the diagram refers to."

"Who are you working for now? The Turks or the Russians, or yourself or someone else?" Alexandra asked in a slightly friendlier conciliatory manner.

"After the KGB merged into the FSB, I left their employment. Like Dmitri, I wasn't invited to transfer over. The president wanted to restrict the revised Federal Security Service of the Russian

Federation to homegrown agents. Fair enough. I left the Turkish Military Intelligence on my terms not long after and became an intelligence entrepreneur, a fast gun for hire." He looked at Marcel. "The Russian Makarov PB is my preferred handgun, or one of mine." *At least one of mine now that Dmitri no longer has any use for it,* he rationalized. "It's the best there is from my unbiased perspective."

"And the Chinese QSZ-92 pistol that the Spanish police located beside Dmitri's body?" Paul needed clarification.

"Substandard for long-distance but reasonably accurate for closeup targets, within spitting distance," Yusuf quipped. "Certainly not worth carrying, once used. A throw-away like a cheap single-use cellphone."

"You said that you merely left the Turkish Military Intelligence unit and just walked away. In layman's terms, just left the military is also called desertion. Most deserters have a bounty on their heads, shoot on sight. It was my understanding that once asked to join, you could only leave in a pine box. It was like being a member of a notorious motorcycle gang, never to fly your colours again, or any other colours."

"The KGB was good at hiding your tracks, falsifying annotated records of employment," he grinned. "My heritage goes back to a time when service to an organization earned respect and favours. In addition, my ancestry is linked through marriage to both the Cossacks and Caucasus. I died on paper and disappeared into my Cossack roots. The hierarchy of the KGB preferred it that way. They didn't want ex-KGB agents floating around hanging out their shingle as intelligence entrepreneurs. A few like Dmitri were the exception for some reason he never divulged, and I never found out."

"In your case, did someone in the KGB hierarchy think that

the combination of Cossacks and Caucasus could be used to their advantage? Is that why you were recruited or not killed?"

Yusuf shrugged. The details he continued to provide were purposefully vague. He had rehearsed his deceitful employment history so many times he could repeat it without fear of being tripped up under interrogation. The vagaries of lies had become tainted truths.

"Not sure," Yusuf stated with the same unblemished confidence as if he were reciting his mother's birthday. "The old KGB was the protégé of the NKVD, Stalin's paranoid spy network that tried to control every facet of life in the Soviet Union. It had eyes and ears everywhere and, as such, commanded obedience through fear countered with falsehoods. The current FSB is less obsessed with creating people who do not exist, like former Turkish Military Intelligence officers. But there still are those who chase after imaginary Trotskyites."

"And being a Cossack, how would that be an advantage to them?" Paul continued.

"I concluded early in my career with the Turkish Military Intelligence that most agents were incompetent, fraudulent and lazy. I quickly learned that mastering the art of pathological lying was a prerequisite for longevity in a relentlessly warping prism that was far too unstable for honesty. Add to that the reputation of Cossacks as fearless fighters. It seemed to meet the criteria for KGB agents schooled in Stalinist paranoia."

"And for whatever reason, unknown to you, you were not asked to transfer to the new FSB, like Dmitri, but unlike Francine, your Tanya. But you left the Turkish Military Intelligence on your own volition," Paul repeated with skepticism.

He again sidestepped Paul. "The lifestyle of the Austro-Hungarian Spartan warrior was not appealing to me. I sought better quality soundtracks in my life, as did Francine. It was a matter of timing for both of us. The Moulins-lès-Metz ambush tipped the scales. It provided an opportune moment for my Tanya to die and rise from the dead, especially with the assistance of the West as they provided a series of safe houses in exchange for first-hand timely intelligence. She passed up on extensive cosmetic surgery to alter her appearance in favor of other forms of less intrusive identity modification. I still recognize my Tanya where others who never had that lingering intimate relationship would not, even if they had her under surveillance. As you say in the West, the devil is in the detail."

Paul found it increasingly difficult to distinguish fact from fiction, provenance from myth. The irregularities in Yusuf's account indicated intrigue but also deception. It became increasingly apparent that Yusuf's default mode was survival, like Baird Durand, as Alexandra had suggested. In contrast, Dmitri never quite mastered the finesse for longevity as did the mythological steadfastly loyal companion of King Arthur – Merlin the magician. Perhaps Dmitri should have had his charcoal pencils dual-purposed as a wizard's wand.

Secrecy was seductive in an espionage fraternity. Seduction could mould robust yet artificial allegiances in a milieu of seemingly incompatible intelligence priorities. Like running marathons, successful intelligence gathering required endurance and stratagems of time management. Endurance he had but time was in short supply at the moment. The street-interrogation venue enhanced neither. Yusuf looked at Alexandra and Marcel for a sense of comradeship and collaboration.

"We will talk more later, Yusuf." Marcel filled the brief interlude of silence. "For now, we will all proceed to the Hotchkiss factory. Perhaps your bequeathed key and diagram will open a lock and shed some light on the as-yet unvalidated hidden treasure."

"I would feel much safer if I could keep my Markov PB pistol," he bargained. "This neighbourhood has a proven reputation for being decidedly unsafe."

Alexandra and Paul responded in unison with tentative smiles. With some reservation, Marcel released his grip on Yusuf's Makarov PB pistol that remained securely holstered in the beltline beneath Yusuf's jacket.

CHAPTER 34

How vast the thievery was that robbed Parisians of their masters and patrons of the arts, and of their prized possessions and cherished freedoms, Alexandra lamented. How devastating their loss of artefacts and citizens, the former transported with arrogance and contempt to private collections, and the latter with betrayal and anonymity to concentration camps, with unrecorded and unmarked graves.

Some of the secreted locales behind false façades and staging portals behind berms and barbed wire remained long after the Nazi retreat and subsequent defeat – like poppies in Flanders Fields, lest we forget. Alexandra had walked the tortured steps of temporary holding pens such as Velodrome d'Hiver in Paris and Fort de Queuleu in Metz. She had seen conditions much worse than enclosures for farm animals. She had heard the silent screams of its forgotten transient detainees, some of whom had once owned the artefacts.

"You can lock up the wolves but cannot silence the haunting howls." She was reminded of a distant past that plagued her in gnawing never-ending nightmares.

Now, again, she was viscerally experiencing the shame of the pilfered art and artefacts removed from walls and taken from easels, all mauled by greedy Teutonic hands, to become heirless assets, gloated over. Alexandra's tears of hatred and vitriol were the voices of the nameless who could no longer cry out themselves in witness to the atrocities. Nor could they counter the growing number of voices that vehemently denied the atrocities and massacres ever happened. *History is the record of bias and prejudice*, she conceded. *It is what both the raconteurs and readers experience through the spectrum of their prisms.*

Paul reached for her trembling hand. The trepidation arose from the core of her being, catapulted up her spine, grating the raw messaging nerves.

"Do you want to leave?" he whispered.

"No," she replied. "We have come this far. We need to travel beyond these walls constructed from blueprints etched with the evil of the architect's soul. There is a lock on a door that needs to be opened. Behind it, there are truths to be revealed, truths that my mother spoke of. She would remind me that my roots are those of Charlemagne and my dynasty Merovingian. In them, I would unearth the truths."

Alexandra stared into space, following the dizzying rotations of the compass needle that seemingly span out of control, driven by other forces through the degrees, minutes and seconds. The magnetized pointer came to a sudden halt with such abruptness that she had to refocus on the final image.

"Behind that wall is where you were slammed by your captors, knocking you semi-unconscious. I felt your pain and called out to you to stay with me, not to leave me." Tears filled her eyes and flowed down her cheeks.

"I heard you calling. I fought back against the dazed numbness and stayed conscious for you," Paul murmured. "You kept me alive, aware, focused."

Her emotionless face sagged. Her complexion became gaunt. Her entire being shrieked. Her stare bore through the stuccoed barrier encased in a second layer of mortared limestone itself quarried from the tunnels holding the catacombs with far fewer skeletal bones than the mass graves in Dachau, Auschwitz, and the others tombs of the unknown. "Behind that wall is a locked door," she declared with a certainty she had rarely before expressed.

Never before had she felt so sure of her *shrew*, her intuition that yelled at her with uncompromising clarity.

"We need to contact Commandant Parent. We need to remove the wall," she demanded. Her voice seemed not to be her own, but a chorus of others whose words had been silenced, whose freedoms had been denied, all those murdered by Thon including Madame Deschaume, her mother's tenant on rue Michel Welter in Luxembourg, and the mother and daughter in the house in Metz whose murder her father had investigated but was unable to solve, and the other members of the French Resistance, the *Maquis*, all victims of Thon's marauding rampage.

"The key I have, I believe it may be to the lock," Yusuf declared. "Dmitri left it for me, gave it to me as a token of our artificial affiliation. Uri Popov, his mentor, had passed it along to him without explanation. It is poetic justice if it opens the door to history." A narrow smile mirrored Yusuf's thought of his final encounter with Dmitri. *His tortured soul is rolling on the floor in the hallway adjacent to his apartment in Valencia where he gasped for his final breath, witnessed by his feline friend.* Yusuf's grin morphed into a frown as he recalled Dmitri's forewarning of a Chinese tourist, the Lucerne assassin, currently in Paris.

"What else might Dmitri have unknowingly left for you," Paul demanded, glaring at him in a way that left nothing to misinterpretation. He had no patience for cocktails of truths, partial truths and make-believe truths. Yusuf needed to understand the gravity of the circumstances. He had taken matters into his own hands after Francine had been wounded a second time on the street leading to the Hotchkiss factory. Paul was in command now. Marcel was his backup. Neither were smiling.

Yusuf met Paul's stare. He became acutely aware of the magnitude of Paul's communiqué. There was no room for mystique in masked chivalry to be negotiated by Paladin, the knight-errant, the double KGB and Turkish Military Intelligence agent, or whatever part Yusuf thought he was playing at this moment as he atoned for the attempted assassinations of Francine. There was no doubt that Paul meant business as he stood defiantly prepared to redress any intended or pretended offensive action by Yusuf against Alexandra.

⊰ ⊱

CROWDS THRONGED AROUND THE ENTRANCE to the Hotchkiss factory as the police carried out concealed non-descript wooden crates containing bearer bonds, gold bars, some embossed with swastikas, priceless art and artefacts, among sundry documents. Yet the spirits of their owners could neither be suppressed nor estranged. All the boxes were whisked away under a heavily armed escort. The factory was sealed up. Security guards remained.

Switzerland and Liechtenstein were two of Hitler's private repositories. There were others. The secreted rooms in the Hotchkiss factory were Reichsmarschall Göring's individual safe deposit boxes. There were others. The plunder therein attested to his personal greed devoid of guilt, if more evidence were needed.

Alexandra could only surmise that after robbing and hoarding so much wealth from a devastated city and trampled continent, Reichsmarschall Göring had become arrogantly myopic. Art defines civilization. He believed erroneously that he could steal art and become civilized. With this seizure, history would be rewritten by the historians, retold by the raconteurs and reinterpreted by the critically informed readers. The disbelievers would continue to challenge the facts with fabricated mistruths and arrogant denial.

Francine had attempted to survey the Hotchkiss factory in an effort to find conclusive evidence of Reichsmarschall Göring's treasures. Yusuf had followed up, *in flagrante delicto* – caught in the act. Clearly, they interpreted the accounts as factual like some of their former colleagues in the KGB including Dmitri and his trainer, Uri Popov. That begged the question: What made Francine and Yusuf different from others? Did they also have irrefutable evidence that a super code existed, like Dimitri? Francine had previously mentioned it. Yusuf had neither refuted nor reinforced Francine's contention.

CHAPTER 35

"Additional information has surfaced regarding Yusuf. I need to brief you on this update before Yolina says a few words regarding any ongoing relationship with Francine and Yusuf," Daan advised. "Intelligence suggests that his heritage goes back to The Most Venerable Order of the Hospital of Saint John of Jerusalem, later the Knights of Rhodes. After the Sultan Suleiman the Magnificent won the battle for Jerusalem, they took refuge on Malta. There is some indication that the ancestry with whom he identifies was affiliated to the Knights of Malta."

"This sheds some light on his Paladin persona in addition to his emerging knight-errant temperament," Alexandra suggested. "He had to have been a knight first before a knight-errant, which it now appears he was, or at least has the chivalric lineage. Yet he did not give any indication of this when we confronted him outside the Hotchkiss factory. After we entered, he took on a more passive role more than likely because he was outnumbered by Paul, Marcel and me."

"I agree," Marcel added. "Perhaps the environment wasn't conducive. I said we would talk more but later. It is opportune, given Daan's update, for more but later to be now."

"Lady and gentlemen, the floor is yours," Yolina addressed the meeting.

Paul recapped. "When we invited Francine to be the centurion, we acknowledged that Yusuf would be part of that equation. That was a given. I also mentioned the subservient factor. Baird Durand is now in our grasp thanks to the good work of Claude Etien Marchand. Alana mentioned that her father had befriended

Dmitri. So, there is a strong probability that Baird is aware that Dmitri has been killed like his son."

Alexandra followed up. "The immediate threat is the Lucerne assassin. We believe this person to be Chinese/Caucasian and female. I am confident that once Francine recovers, the assassin's days will be numbered."

"My question is: What is the exit strategy for Francine and Yusuf, if there is one?" Paul asked. "They remain an inseparable duo."

Alexandra added, "When we joined, Daan, you mentioned that members of the EUI Unit were drawn from the original members of the European Union because of the common culture. Does that criterion still apply? Would it apply to Francine and Yusuf?"

"Daan and I have debated this after the recent revelations," Yolina commented. "We have more confidence in Francine than Yusuf who remains a mysterious wild card. You are quite correct. One is not an option with this duo. Your thoughts, Paul?"

"Yusuf seems to be a knight-errant. But he can be an unpredictable loose cannon on the deck. On a positive note, he brings considerable knowledge, perspective and experience to the table. Unfortunately, it can be akin to a calm eye in the centre of the hurricane. That would be reassuring if he was more predictable. Perhaps my reservation comes from limited experience working with him. The stakes are high. So, I err on the side of caution."

"Alexandra, your thoughts?"

"Yusuf has Francine's best interests at heart. No doubt about that. As such, he would be the true knight saving Francine, the worthy damsel in distress. Dmitri's death demonstrates that commitment. But Yusuf tends to operate as a lone wolf, Paladin for certain. The question I ask is would he sacrifice anyone of us for his own sake, the sake of Francine, his Tanya, or another yet unknown loyalty? Like Paul, I am unsure at this time."

Yolina transferred her attention. "Marcel?"

"I agree with Paul and Alexandra. We have time on our side at least until Francine fully recovers and focuses her sniper sights on the Lucerne assassin. So, perhaps we interview, interrogate Yusuf further with a fixed agenda before we decide. Alexandra interviewed Francine with the aid of a forensic hypnosis. I recommend she do the same with Yusuf. At this juncture, he remains an unpredictable wild card and very much enigmatic."

"Matthieu?"

"The Lucerne assassin is as professional and as deadly as any we have come up against. That begs another question. If we are considering Francine as a future contracted centurion or colleague by any other definition, do we want to risk her being killed at this time? Similarly, for Yusuf? Having said that, the Lucerne assassin remains an imminent and deadly threat. Hence, she needs to be eliminated. My assessment would be to develop a comprehensive plan with all the EUI Unit resources focused on the Lucerne assassin. It would be prudent to send a reconnaissance team to Lucerne at the soonest opportunity. We could include Francine, and Yusuf, but on a tight leash."

"Thank you, all," Yolina acknowledged. "I agree with your collective observations and recommendations. Time is on our side regarding Francine until she fully recovers, and Yusuf by association. To some degree, we can control this wild card in the short term by moving Francine to a safer location where she can receive the best medical attention. Yusuf would accompany her as her bodyguard. I am considering a location in Canada, possibly Montreal. The probability of him heading off as a Paladin knight-errant and getting into trouble would be lower. In the interim, we find out everything there is to know about the Lucerne assassin. We develop a comprehensive strategic plan as Matthieu recommends."

"Paul, Alexandra, proceed with the interview of Yusuf," Daan directed. "Matthieu and Marcel, work with me and the Delta Team gathering as much intelligence as possible about the Lucerne assassin, and additional information on Yusuf."

⊰ ⊱

"YOU ARE CORRECT," YUSUF REMARKED lamely. "My heritage is intertwined with the Middle East and the Mediterranean." He remained elusive regarding details, as if the revelation of those associations was inconsequential or so dire that sharing any details would result in pandemic-like consequences. For either, the trajectory of the hollowness ran parallel to his impreciseness. Yet both seemed to grow in scope and sophistication as he responded to subsequent questions. Alternately, he could simply be shy and embarrassed to elaborate on his humble lineage. But that option was wholly inconsistent with everything that defined him – the Turkish Military Intelligence officer, the Russian double agent, the knight-errant and the mythical Paladin.

"When we first asked you whether you had heard about the *Quer*, you said you were vaguely aware but would have to do more research in a library. Was that your former employer's library, Turkish Military Intelligence, or another library, perhaps in Moscow?"

Yusuf held his gaze for a moment without replying. Paul surmised that follow-up questions would be needed to draw out the information he was seeking. The slim smile hinted at the imprecise parameters of his response. Although frustrating, Paul was coming to the realization that Paladin's persona was multi-dimensional, akin to Einstein's fuzzy theory of relativity. Paul had no control over Yusuf. What he did have control over was how he responded to him. He could get highly stressed or relaxed. He chose the latter.

"Closer to a personal library," Yusuf admitted almost reluctantly.

"Care to elaborate?" Paul probed on the heels of his cagey clarification.

"A branch of my family tree on my father's side reaches back to the Knights of Rhodes. Original family money came from business transactions in and around Jerusalem in which my knighted relative had been involved. Some funds and other convertible assets were transported to Malta after the Sultan defeated the Knights of Rhodes forcing them to leave Jerusalem. Other smaller caches remain hidden in the desert sands, so to speak, somewhere north of Bethlehem."

"And your Turkish heritage?" Paul pressed.

"That is my mother's side of the family. Malta is not far as the crow flies on a trade route to Rhodes. Her family were seafarers who mostly navigated the Dardanelles."

"And your personal family library references to the *Quer*? You seem to be vague on details."

"That's because there are few details. There was conflict in my family. My parents didn't talk about their past, especially not my father's family. One side backed Mustafa Kemal Atatürk but the other did not. It was my father's father who spoke to me privately about early Turkish history and heritage of the Knights of Rhodes, and later Malta. He alluded to security provided by a select few knights to a wealthy powerful secret society. He gave me a medallion that had been passed down over the centuries. With it came a strong warning not to mention it to anyone, which I never did."

"Were there any identifiable markings on it?" Paul asked.

"Yes, but they seem to be hieroglyphic, not Middle Eastern or Egyptian. Perhaps similar in some respects to Sanskrit but certainly not Sanskrit. More like a single symbol than a series of letters."

Paul inscribed a figure on a napkin and showed it to Yusuf whose mouth fell open in surprise. The Armenian Turk eyed his inquisitor. His father's words of warning echoed in his mind, "speak of this to no one unless you trust them wholeheartedly." The image on the napkin was too exact to be a mere figment of Paul's imagination. For the first time since meeting Paul at the Palermo marathon, he felt uneasy. He knew the longer he wavered, the more Paul would become suspicious.

"That looks very similar," Yusuf murmured hesitantly, in a barely audible voice.

Paul followed up immediately, not allowing him time to consider a strategic reply. He held the high ground for the first time and would maintain the momentum.

"What else did he tell you?"

"My father talked about a supposed relationship between the Knights of Malta and the Emperor, later the King of Spain. Apparently, my knighted forefather travelled through Spain, across the Pyrénées to the Carcassonne region. There he became what today we would refer to as a private security entrepreneur for this secret society. I just thought that his tales were mythical ramblings told by an absent-minded old man living in the past."

"What else did he tell you about this wealthy secret society?"

"I can't remember much more. I wish I had paid greater attention and made some notes. I was a teenager at the time, just preoccupied with girls."

Quick on the uptake to keep Yusuf on the defensive, Paul followed up, "Where is the medallion now?"

"It's hidden in a safe place," Yusuf replied. With abruptness in his tone accompanied by the merest glance, he replied to Paul's question with equal swiftness, "And it's staying hidden."

"It could be related to the shooting of Francine, your Tanya. Additional information could get us closer to eradicating the shooter, like Dmitri."

Yusuf thought for a moment. The hands-on circumstances

surrounding Dmitri's demise appealed to him. The kiss of the death adder was another option that was highly attractive.

"Could you bring it to me?"

Paul's reference to Francine's safety struck at the core of Paladin's *raison d'être*. "I suppose I could."

"How long?"

"Twenty-four hours if I left now and can be assured that my Tanya will not be left alone."

"Rest assured that she will have round-the-clock security. Alexandra will be no more than a whisper away. Arrangements are underway to provide her with the best of medical services in another very secure safehouse."

"Thank you." Yusuf uncharacteristically extended his hand and gave Paul a sincere handshake. It was the first time that Paul could recall seeing a smile of sincere gratitude. Yusuf had lived a nomadic lifestyle as an agent of the secret tradecraft devoid of permanent roots, akin to the nomadic routine of his knighted forefather. Deep down, he sought some sense of permanency. Francine, his Tanya, was all he had, all he cared about. He had dreamed about anonymously riding into the sunset like the black and white silver-screen heroes of the old American West. He sensed that Paul might be a ticket to that theatre. He would surrender the medallion if that would bring about such a final chapter to his story.

"Could we meet tomorrow in Strasbourg at the Salon de Café, at the south end of the Ponts Couverts?"

"Yes, especially if it will keep my Tanya safer."

"Rest assured, Yusuf." Paul replied. "I will have someone else with me to validate the provenance of the medallion. If it is what I think it is, he will introduce you to another party who, like Alexandra and me, will provide you with greater safety and security."

Yusuf looked at Paul whom he perceived to be more like the

older and wiser brother he'd never had than a new acquaintance with whom he had not yet established close bonds. He envied Paul and Alexandra for the intimacy and incontestable loyalty born out of true love nurtured since their youth. He sought that for himself and his Tanya. He no longer wanted to play the game of spies and espionage. With the perfection of Harry Houdini, he had planned his egress and disappearance from the Turkish Military Intelligence and the KGB. He would employ the same strategy to disappear into the sunset with his Tanya, without a trace.

CHAPTER 36

"Thoughts, *ma princesse*," Paul enquired.

"From Yusuf's perspective, the truth is a lie looking to be resolved, somehow. Yusuf is seeking a way out, a clean break from his Spartan upbringing where deception was a cultural code. He desperately wants to become Paladin, the mythical Western hero who lived in the Hotel Carlton in San Francisco as a *bon vivant* in some respects – a man who enjoyed the good things of life. With a lucrative contract, he could be enticed to ride into the lawless West as a knight-errant to eradicate abusive bullies and sadistic villains."

"I agree. He answered questions but the details were scant when it came to his background," Paul confirmed. "When I asked a close-ended question, I received a quasi-complete answer. Yes was never really yes. Instead, it was closer to maybe but that changed too sometimes but not always depending on the circumstances."

"So, why? What does he have to hide and from whom?" Alexandra queried.

In that reflected moment, Paul drifted away from Alexandra's assessment, wandering into another cerebral domain, alone. *I am not errant. Or am I?* He had risen in his career to head the crime lab because of his disciplined nature and strict adherence to policies and regulations. He had been reunited with his puppy love on the eve of his retirement. It was not her fault by any stretch of the imagination that he now found himself questioning policy and interpreting rules to fit the circumstances. On their first informal case working together, just before his recognized retirement date, he found himself furtively completing an analysis in his lab on Alexandra's request. He would never have done that before. It wasn't illegal, just a deviation of policy. Had he not deviated, he would never have been promoted or received all the awards and accolades including his recent induction as a Commandeur de l'Ordre National de la Légion d'Honneur that partially led to his recruitment into the European Union Intelligence Unit. And yet to be successful in his current position, he must acknowledge the New World Order and variances in the rule of law. Integrity, the ability to steadfastly adhere to moral standards, demanded discipline. But by whose standards were he and Alexandra now playing? And by whose standards were Yusuf and Francine playing, and Maria, and Sir James, and Major Mike, and Thomas Hunt, and Daan? He recalled mentioning to Jean when he was first studying history in school that there was not just one history, but many histories depending on interpretation, winners and losers. He reminded Jean on several occasions that victors get to write history.

"Your thoughts?" Alexandra probed.

"Thoughts?" Paul queried, puzzled by her question which seemed to come out of nowhere.

"You are off in Neverland with Peter Pan and Tinkerbell!" she jested.

"Sorry. Thoughts about what?"

"We were discussing Yusuf and his imagined role as Paladin."

Paul lingered not so much to recollect but to assess his own mental state, where he was and what had triggered his relapse into Neverland as Alexandra had accurately identified. Making peace with his past was not as simple as flipping a switch. Throughout his career, he had experienced nightmarish dreams that he could not shake off. Some extended into daydreams leaving him distracted and unable to fully concentrate. They would abandon him on their own terms and schedule, not his. He'd had no one to talk to, certainly not Suzette. Now, he had his own private psychologist.

Alexandra held his attention. She was getting used to his occasional excursions down the White Rabbit's hole in Lewis Carroll's
Alice in Wonderland. His digression was not clear but, instead,
murky and menacing. She sensed that sometimes he was deep in
thought as he attempted to sort through options. Other times, his
jaunts were motivated by escapism from disturbing recollections
like the little girl lying face-down in the ditch, her arms tied behind her back with barbed wire that had ripped into her wrists, and
blood oozing out of a bullet hole in the back of her head staining
the back of her light blue dress. Alexandra could not wave her
wand and magically eliminate the violent images nor rescue him,
but only be there with him.

"I tend to agree with Yusuf's assessment of the New World
Order," Paul confided with a reluctant sigh, still not completely
in the present. "There are some bad-ass actors who do not play by
civilized rules. They need to meet their maker sooner rather than
later."

Alexandra did not reply. Instead, she just looked at him with a
non-judgemental countenance as she massaged his cold, sweaty
hands. She would debrief him this evening after he had had time
to come to grips with the disquieting howls of the haunting wolves
that could be locked up but not completely silenced. That was just
who he was. Over the years, she had accumulated a double closet
full of her own skeletons of wolves who tended to bay at her on
their terms, not hers.

Paul broke the silence. "I think of Collette and Jean and hopefully someday our grandchildren and the world they will be facing.
That life will be very different from the world we have faced in the
last half of the 20th century that our parents left us."

"No argument from me, *mon colonel*," Alexandra replied
still holding his clammy hand. "The Second World War and the

subsequent Cold War defined my mother and all the other espionage protégés of that period."

"We have a mandate to leave this New World Order in better shape for the next generation," Paul continued. "As bad as the Nazis were, there were those leaders in the Third Reich who realized that Hitler was a psychopathic megalomaniac. They attempted to assassinate him in order to bring a modicum of sanity to war, if that was possible." His demeanour became somber. His perspective philosophical. "I never thought that I would ever say this." He stared blankly before expressing a conclusion. "There is a role for the knight-errant, like Yusuf."

Alexandra thought about his assessment, hoping to ground his pronouncement. "Is that why we have reservations about Yusuf, because he is the knight-errant, the Paladin who rights the wrong based on his standards? In the New World Order, there is a rule of law – just with different rules?"

"You are the psychologist. And once again, you are correct. *Je t'aime, ma princesse*. Thank you for being pragmatic. I need the balance."

She squeezed his hand in order to confirm the connection. "The original Paladin-like characters were the paramount warriors of Charlemagne's court. My mother reminded me on numerous occasions that my roots are those of Charlemagne and my dynasty Merovingian. In them, I would unearth the truths. Is Yusuf part of my destiny, part of that truth as a Paladin knight-errant? Is that my moral dilemma?"

"*Our* moral dilemma," Paul responded with direct assurance and validation of her mandate as she interpreted her mother's communiqué.

"If we sanction Yusuf as a colleague, are we endorsing the knight-errant, the Paladin who rights the wrong based on his standard? Is that a bridge too far? Or have we already crossed that point of no return?"

"Others have made similar decisions, based upon judgements deemed to be flexible guidelines and not unwavering canons," Paul replied tentatively.

Alexandra did not reply. Instead, she considered the realm of her own decisions to keep secrets. She quietly acknowledged, "Perhaps the ability to operate successfully demands that we must all adopt the cloak of the knight-errant at one time or another. The truth of Charlemagne has been revealed. It was the truth that my mother, Sir James and Major Mike became acutely aware of, and which defined their lives in the murky world of espionage on the edge of noir intelligence. Our fathers experienced the same as they doggedly pursued Thon, who managed to stay at least one step ahead. How frustrating that must have been for them to feel powerless as police investigators, as if condemned to wander in Thon's wake like an offshore fog bank devoid of references knowing that more female members of the French Resistance, the *Maquis,* and their daughters would fall victim to his murderous impulses. They did not have clinical psychologists to help them with their mental struggles."

CHAPTER 37

"**D**o you have it with you?" Paul asked.

Yusuf produced the medallion from a concealed pocket inside his jacket. The symbol was as he had acknowledged when Paul drew a derivative of the modern-day letter 'F' on the napkin.

"Are you aware of the origin of this symbol and the context in which it was developed?" Paul followed up with a reassuring voice.

"No," Yusuf replied, intrigued as to what he might learn from someone he had never considered to be conversant in the mythical chronicles of medieval and ancient cultures and folklore. Following the wary direction of his grandfather, he had spoken to no one about its existence. Thus, he was surprised when Paul replicated the design on the napkin. If Paul had become aware, there would be others who had too. This thought caused Yusuf to squint as he reached up with his hand and drew his index finger across his lips as if to reinforce the need for secrecy. He had never rehearsed this scenario because he had not conceived of an occasion when he might need to. He would have to carefully consider his response to questions.

"Before I begin, allow me to introduce you to a colleague, Claude Etien Marchand," Paul announced. "Please bear with me, Yusuf. Claude has a strong connection to what I am about to explain."

With reservations, Yusuf extended his hand. He had growing confidence in Paul. He would have to make his own decision to trust Claude Etien Marchand and, if so, to what degree.

Paul continued. "In the Runic alphabet, the character 'F' is like the old Anglo Saxon 'f' for feoh that is a symbol for cattle because they were the source of wealth and influence during the early Gallic Celtic period.

A class of elite males wore it to show their prosperity. Those in this select group became a tight-knit fraternity, which held considerable economic power and influence."

"I had no idea, more likely because I kept it hidden as directed by my grandfather," Yusuf openly acknowledged with a still cautious tone.

Yusuf judiciously returned the medallion to the concealed pocket inside his jacket. He kept his hand under his jacket as an added layer of safekeeping. His caution did not go unnoticed.

"It's OK, Yusuf. Trust me," Paul said calmly, acknowledging his heightened level of concern. "You will not come to any harm. Monsieur Marchand will take you next door to meet Monsieur Baird Durand who is a member of the secret society that your grandfather spoke about. Show this gentleman the medallion. I will not accompany you for reasons I will explain later."

Yusuf's anxiety subsided initially but only ever so slightly. Now learning that he would be introduced to yet another stranger caused it to rise to its previously heightened level, especially because Paul would not accompany him. He retained some solace knowing that Paul would be close by. His holstered Russian Makarov PB pistol was reassuring.

"Baird, may I introduce you to Aiolos Yusuf Dimir," Claude Etien Marchand said. "I am confident that he will address some of your immediate concerns."

Baird stared warily at Yusuf who returned his guarded glance like two contestants fresh to the arena. Neither shook hands. Instead, each maintained a respectful distance. Yusuf prudently scanned the room making note of furniture that might provide cover, and doors and other exits should a hasty retreat from this sanctuary be necessary under fire.

Following Claude's respectful request, Yusuf showed Baird the medallion. Baird stared in awe and with increasing concentration and reverence before extending a welcoming hand. It was readily apparent to Yusuf that the distinguished man in front of him was aware of its significance. Now there were three, Paul being the first and Claude being the second.

"A Knight of Malta. It is most timely that you present your credential," Baird uttered with confidence and gratitude. "I very much need your security services."

Baird relaxed to a level that he had not experienced for longer than he could remember, certainly more than he had felt in the last several weeks. He extended his hand a second time. On this occasion, the sincerity of his gesture was reinforced by a double grasp.

"Enter into my abode, Sir Yusuf," Baird beckoned warmly. "Please take a seat. We have much to talk about."

"After you," Yusuf replied to the hospitable gesture. His Makarov PB pistol seemed to seat itself lower in the gripping holster, sensing it may not be needed.

"Tell me about your medallion, Sir Yusuf," Baird asked. "It is the first that I have seen. My father explained its origin to me. That is as much as I know, but I am in awe and admiration of its existence and deeply humbled by your presence." Baird bowed slowly while maintaining eye contact with his honoured guest.

"It was given to me by my grandfather who described its heritage. He instructed me to present it only to a member of the secret society. My knowledge of the other knights who worked for the *Quer* is scant."

"Allow me to fill in a few details that were passed on to me by my father," Baird volunteered. "The *Quer* entered into what today we would call a personal service contract with a few of the

Knights of Malta to provide an enforcement and security contingent. Like the *Quer* and their passing of the ring from father to son, the medallion was passed down only through the male heirs of the knights. A knight would wear the medallion, which ensured him immediate access to the *Quer* council and the guarded respect of others. A disrespectful challenge of the wearer would result in instant regress and possibly bodily harm in the form of repeated lashings while in solitary confinement."

Baird showed Yusuf his ring with the Runic letter 'F' as did Claude Etien Marchand. He had studied the same letter on his medallion so many times, he could verify its authenticity by memory. Staring at the confirmed expressions on the faces of both Claude and Baird provided Yusuf with further validation. With this disclosure, Yusuf's anxiety all but returned to its normal state. He was among trusted honourable colleagues.

"What happened to the initial knight contingent?" Yusuf asked.

"The knights in service to us were affiliated with Freemasonry. Around the time that the King of France, in cahoots with the Pope, was purging France of the Knights Templar, they went into hiding for fear of being rounded up and murdered too. Thereafter, the Swiss provided protection for the *Quer* with the now famous Swiss Guards, the same that guard the Vatican today. This relationship paved the way for the *Quer* to deposit the lion's share of their accumulated wealth in Swiss banks."

"You and I have the honour of being affiliated with Monsieur Claude Etien Marchand," Yusuf stated as he turned his head and confirmed his presence as an equal member of the *Quer*.

"We are the final two directors of the *Quer* with roots back to its inception in the Gallic era. And yourself? How did you meet?"

Yusuf confidently explained, "I have spent a career in the realm of security and intelligence as has Monsieur Marchand. It is a relatively small world. In some respects, it is getting smaller, like the

Quer membership. But in other aspects, it is expanding its influence via the cyber world."

Baird huffed, "We seem to have that in common. I have in my employment a few very talented software programmers but do not have full confidence in them. Perhaps you could verify their loyalty to me and not to my competitors."

"Quite easily done, Baird. If you provide me with their identities, I can get back to you in the fullness of time."

Baird used a nearby laptop to email the names and related information to Yusuf, with a copy to Claude.

"Done, Sir Yusuf."

Baird looked directly at Claude Etien Marchand and pronounced with confidence, "With you and me, and now Sir Yusuf, the future of the *Quer* is secure. It is opportune that we move forward into the 21st century a smaller yet more robust *Quer.*"

CHAPTER 38

"I need to apologize to both of you, especially to you, Paul, for not letting you know sooner about Jean's promotion to head the new Anti-Terrorist Cyber Unit," Commandant Parent said. "We received confirmation from the Chief just moments before I called Yolina and Daan."

"Not a problem, Benoit. This case has been on the fast track since we initially established contact with Baird Durand," Paul replied. He gazed over at Jean. Nothing more needed to be said. A father could not be prouder of his son's accomplishments.

"Sorry that I couldn't say much, Dad," Jean added. "I also have to be selective and somewhat evasive about what I mention when Collette asks."

"The shoe is on the other foot for all the times when I asked you to conduct enquiries and analyses based on faith," Paul acknowledged with a congratulatory bow.

Jean elaborated, "Cyber crime involves the Dark Web. I can confirm that hackers, after breaking into major corporations, quietly sit like Cold War sleeper cells. Here, they focus on certain targets such as lucrative business transactions, technical blueprints and, on the defence side, high-tech weaponry. Sometimes, they simply monitor transactions, stealing data without leaving a calling card. I can see the day when underground cyber crime becomes a distinct, very profitable on-demand, service-driven economy. Dark Web software will command a reasonable price tag. But if cyber criminals demand a one-off custom-built program, that will be made available, but at a considerable outlay of cash."

"And the reaction?" Paul asked.

"The Dark Web was once the sole domain of hackers. More recently, law enforcement agencies have started playing catch-up. I predict that we will soon be in the same league. An increasing number of larger nation states that have already been targets of these hackers are countering in this new electronic battle space with recently formed legions of elite cyber enforcement warriors, like myself. We know when unauthorized eyes are merely watching and when they have crossed the line into covert criminal activities and cyber terrorism."

"What are we facing in the short term, Jean?" Paul asked with respect for the sensitivity of the information and the source. He was thinking about the impact it would have on the *Quer* and intelligence that had been revealed just recently.

"Governments and defence departments do not dread nuclear stockpiles as much today as they once did during the Cold War. Instead, they are fearful of an exponential increase in rogue internet service providers, ISPs, popping up in China and Russia, and increasingly in fledging African states, being used by hordes of renegade hackers."

"And your greatest concern?"

"That is easy but complex. My greatest concern is the fact that they currently hold the invisible high ground from where they are planning their attacks on civil societies such as interfering with national elections using phishing malware and botnets. This battlespace has no borders or even defined dimensions. As such, it has a quantum element. Those operating in this nebulous environment do not see their actions as an act of war. More problematically, they have complete disregard for the law of armed conflict or rules of engagement defined by the *Geneva Convention*. There is an absence of doctrine written for the jurisprudence of this evolving cyber space. I recall reading a Master of Law thesis written by an Air Force military lawyer about this phenomenon approximately forty years ago. His thesis wasn't about cyber space, so to speak, but the more encompassing concept of just who owns space. He had been an RAF pilot during the Second World War and was a visionary. Was it serendipitous that this officer had served with the Canadian Air Force in Metz during the early days of the Cold War on the eve of the first flight into space by the Russian astronaut, Yuri Gagarin? Was it also fortuitous that Metz was the seat of power for Charlemagne?" Jean summarized his assessment. "Welcome to the perhaps not so new, yet new e-world."

"The next generation of Typhoon Eurofighter jets has replaced the World War I Sopwith Camel biplane in the new multi-dimensional electronic air war," Paul muttered.

"Good analogy, Dad." Before he could comment further, Jean's cell phone buzzed. "We are pregnant! Call soon. Love you so much."

"Excuse me, Benoit. I need to make a personal phone call before we begin our update."

In seconds, Alexandra's phone buzzed. "I am pregnant, Mom!"

"Will call as soon as possible, dear," she eagerly keyed in her reply.

Alexandra showed Paul the message.

"Exciting!" he whispered as he reached for her hand. *Jean's promotion, now news of a grandchild on the way.*

Alexandra pulled her hand away before he could gauge a sense of her underlying anxiety. She returned his beaming smile but did not immediately comment as if there was nothing to celebrate, only trepidation to contain. Thoughts of Collette sobbing into her cell phone with news of her miscarriage overcame any joy. What if…? She wanted to be, needed to be with Collette at this moment. But she couldn't be. She wanted to be, needed to be completely honest with Paul at this moment. But she couldn't be. She had to say something.

"Absolutely exciting," Alexandra countered. Her fabricated excitement was tempered with emptiness that untold secrets evoke after they surface and immediately sink again into the abysses of the tormented soul. She had always been truthful with her mother but her mother had not always been honest with her. Her mother had intercepted her letters to Paul and Paul's letters to her in which they had declared their puppy love to each other. Both had felt deeply scarred and rejected, as a direct result. That duplicity had twisted all her future relationships, most poignantly her disastrous decision to marry André, which robbed her of decades of true happiness. It had done the same to Paul in his decision to marry Suzette for all the wrong reasons. It was only after reading her mother's letter, left in her safety deposit box, admitting to interfering in that budding relationship that she and Paul could start afresh. They promised each other never to lie, always to be completely honest. But she had reneged on that commitment.

Now, history was repeating itself. She was not being wholly honest with Paul. Their relationship was in jeopardy. As her mother had not been honest with her father, had kept the news of her pregnancy with Alexandra from him, she was hiding truths from Paul. Her mother's words resonated in her mind: *Your roots are those of Charlemagne and your destiny Merovingian. The truths of those times are masked in the mists of the Moselle. In them, you will discover your strengths and unearth the truths.* She pined for those strengths, to be completely honest with her puppy love, to reaffirm those vows of trustworthiness, to reveal all the truths of Charlemagne and her Merovingian destiny. Her heart ached with pain; tears flowed inside.

Paul was too excited to notice any discrepancy in her reaction, to see beyond her smile, however feigned.

"Sorry for the interruption, Benoit," Paul blurted out. "Collette and Jean are pregnant and we are grandparents-to-be."

"Congratulations!" Benoit replied as he extended his hand. "I'll keep this discussion short as I am sure you want to celebrate with the jubilant parents-to-be."

At Jean's return, Benoit revealed that Daan had requested Jean's assistance. He had asked Jean to interview Baird Durand regarding the *Quer*'s development of a criminal cyber cell. Hackers were on the *Quer* payroll. Despite the fact that Baird had not willingly acknowledged the *Quer*'s involvement in cyber crime, the newly created Anti-Terrorist Cyber Unit had evidence that hackers had written intrusive software for the *Quer*."

"Baird had admitted initially to its existence but denied any direct knowledge of who the hackers were except to Sir Yusuf, Knight of Malta and Claude Etien Marchand of the *Quer*," Jean explained. "He said that one of the assassinated *Quer* members had dealt with the Cyber Unit. He later acknowledged the identity of these *Quer* cyber contractors."

Benoit added, "More concerning was the fact that Baird had used the software to electronically steal funds from major offshore corporations and transfer them into newly created bank accounts on behalf of the *Quer*, yet solely in his own name. To date, two banks have been identified, one in Liechtenstein and the other in Luxembourg. Additional offshore financial institutions have also been implicated."

Benoit's voice dropped. "Baird Durand had initially involved the Chinese in these nefarious financial transactions but then double-crossed them by keeping all the transferred funds for himself. Word on the street is that a Beijing assassin is on his trail and will place in the crosshairs anyone remotely associated with Baird."

Joy of the news of the pregnancy was immediately replaced by concern for Jean's safety as a result of his interview with Baird. Paul's heart sank. *If killed by the assassin, Jean would never know the delight of holding his own child as I had done. But if Jean's*

child follows in the footsteps of his uncle, Yvon, Jean would not es-
cape the guilt that had plagued me with incessant nightmares and
anxiety associated with the circumstances of Yvon's death.

It became acutely evident to Paul that the revelation would scar
Jean's marriage, perhaps beyond any chance of reconciliation. And
then there was Paul's relationship with Alexandra. A second nup-
tial, a fortuitous opportunity at happiness, marred a second time by
the bedevilled progeny of his first union with Suzette in the eyes
of his God. The horror, the utter horror. How could he live with
the truth should it be exposed? He needed to speak to Father Luke,
whose own sins left him eminently qualified not to judge lest ye be
judged, but instead to listen and provide counsel to a parishioner
in need.

Alexandra had never seen Paul in this state. His stare was not
just that of a man tackling Dickens's ghost of a Christmas Past but
struggling with ghouls riding in unison with the Horsemen of the
Apocalypse, capable of delivering unfathomable consequences.

"Ghosts?" Alexandra whispered.

He whispered, "Sarajevo." Any greater gesture or louder response would cause reverberating head pain, nausea, and blurred
vision – symptoms that were all too familiar. He was consumed
with images of the little girl lying face down in the ditch, her thin
arms tied behind her back with barbed wire that had ripped into
her wrists, and her light blue dress stained in blood that had oozed
out of a bullet hole in the back of her head. His mouth dried as his
heart pounded, battling for space with his lungs that fought back in
his ever-tightening chest. It had been a long while since an episode
this debilitating had riveted him to this extent. At this moment, he
needed to be still, quiet, alone with himself. Tears from the sheer
physical pain filled his eyes.

Du calme, du calme, Paul repeated to himself as he took slow
deliberate breaths in an attempt to wrestle for possession of his

mind and his soul. But those breaths felt like the explosions of artillery shells. He became light-headed. In the depth of such mental duels, he was unable to concentrate on the matter at hand. Yet he could describe every vivid detail of the emaciated little girl wearing the blood-stained light blue dress.

"Thank you again for understanding," Benoit repeated. "I suspect that you will want to celebrate this announcement with Jean and Collette."

Alexandra reached over and tightly grasped Paul's cold, clammy hand. Her presence provided a beacon for him to return to. She surmised that the news of Collette's pregnancy had triggered him somehow. She needed to remain fully focused on him yet find the space to speak with her daughter. The circumstances leading up to Collette's previous miscarriage continued to agitate her. The details of the assault had become even more haunting.

Jean held her apprehensive stare. He had seen his father in a similar detached state of mind before. On those occasions, Paul had withdrawn into the darkness of his own room. He would emerge sometimes hours later, delicate but on the road to recovery. With a degree of confidence, Alexandra assured him that his father would be safe. They just needed some quiet time.

"I'll tell Collette that you will call as soon as you can," Jean softly responded as he departed with Benoit.

Alexandra smiled. Her eyes confirmed her divided sentiment. Her main priority sat beside her. Jean's priority was with his wife-to-be, mother-to-be. The transfer of allegiances was established in that moment. She would draw on her strengths and reveal the truths of her Merovingian destiny.

In every adversity, there are the seeds of its opposite, Paul recognized. He had sunk to these depths before and always found the fortitude to rise from the ashes like the phoenix.

CHAPTER 39

Paul sighed as he read the email from the senior administrator at the retirement home in Paris. "Deeply regret to inform you that your father has died." *The double-edged sword*, he reflected. *One email announcing the pending birth of my first grandchild, a new generation, while the other foretold the calling of the Grim Reaper and the passing of the previous generation.* He recalled his father talking with absolute love and devotion about Paul's mother. They would now be together again, holding hands as they always had when they walked side by side. That closeness was absent with Suzette. He now yearned for the wholeness of that experience with Alexandra.

How proud he was to have been his father's son and so gratified by how his father smiled inwardly at each of his accomplishments, culminating most recently with his appointment as a Commandeur de la Légion d'Honneur at the Élysée Palace. And now his father joins Alexandra's mother, Sir James and the other noble warriors of the Cold War with its deadly consequences in the aftermath of the Second World War. His father had been a decorated hero. Yet Paul found himself continually challenged to grapple with ghosts from a United Nations mission in the Former Republic of Yugoslavia and subsequent nightmarish scenes of war crime investigative forays. *Was morality only measured by one's ability to deal with the consequences? Did my father set the standard that I fell short of achieving? And how honoured I am by Jean's accomplishments and recent appointment as the leader of the new legion of cyber law enforcement warriors with the Anti-Terrorist Cyber Unit.*

"I would like to have Father Luke handle the funeral service,"

Paul's email to Jean read. He would take the opportunity to speak privately to Father Luke after the service. No one would think otherwise, not that that was a concern. It would not be a confession so much as a request for spiritual guidance to help him navigate through the murkiness marred by the moral ambiguity required of him as an agent of the European Union Intelligence Unit.

⇥ ⇤

THE FUNERAL SERVICE WAS ATTENDED by over one hundred, as many as Maria's service, in contrast with his wife's and eldest son's, combined. His relationship with Suzette had been a mistake even before they were married. He recalled his father's words that the Pope wasn't always right and he should divorce Suzette. He chuckled at the fact that his father could not remember Suzette's name on an increasing number of occasions. Perhaps a Freudian slip, perhaps dementia, more likely purposeful convenience in not wanting to remember.

Father Luke had previously assured him that he could not be held responsible for Yvon, whose soul had been beset by the devil at his moment of birth. *How could Suzette be so wrong and Alexandra, his puppy love, be so right? How could Yvon be so wrong and Jean be so right? How could he make such seemingly arbitrary judgements? Was his father correct when he reiterated that the Pope wasn't always right?*

"A toast to another great soldier in the war against criminal insurgence," Marcel murmured to Paul at the funeral reception.

"Thank you, my friend," Paul replied. "We spoke those words of our fallen comrades at too many ramp ceremonies in the former Republic of Yugoslavia, and more recently of our EUI Unit colleagues who died when I was taken hostage, and subsequently when you rescued me in Compiègne."

"Just repaying you for saving my butt when I was wounded in

Sarajevo," Marcel replied with undeniable gratitude yet gnawing guilt. Untold truths have a way of plaguing the sorcerer at inopportune moments. Although riddled with remorse, he could still look his colonel straight in the eye. He had behaved in more unethical ways but not by much. He had spoken with Daan when the howling of those wolves had become too disturbing. Thereafter, the haunting sounds had subsided. He knew they would return and again he would make peace, if only temporarily, with his soul.

"Death brings with it a time for reflection," Paul conceded. "Especially when ties are broken by a paternal passing. I am reminded of Yvon's drowning and funeral, which bears no comparison to this funeral service for my father." A frown masked his feelings, which caused Marcel to inhale with hesitation.

After a brief hiatus, Paul rejoined, "I never thought that I would say this of my own flesh and blood and I will only say this once and deny that these words ever rolled off my lips."

Marcel had rehearsed several responses in preparation for the one looming revelation that could erupt at any time. Only he, Matthieu and Daan were aware of the details pertaining to Yvon's drowning, or so he thought. There was always a chance there could have been a witness who might come forward. This funeral service was the least opportune moment to be forced to address the consequences of his actions.

Paul broke the silence. "Yvon was an evil person. As such, I lament even repeating his name in the same context as my father or his brother. Yvon was a loser who abused others, especially women. In addition, he consistently failed to take responsibility for his self-imposed malevolent lot in life. He deserved what he got as do all those who fail to honour a moral canon."

Paul said nothing as he stared in earnest at Marcel.

Marcel's mouth went dry. His heart began to beat faster. Part of his strategy to explain his actions would be to meet and hold Paul's gaze. Such was the oath of obligation of comrades in arms.

Paul's frown merged into a quiet smile. His stare confirmed his loyalty. His voice softened. "In complete contrast, you are more of a son to me than Yvon ever was."

Marcel calmed down with the pronouncement of those words by his colonel, his colleague, his comrade in arms, and his friend. Sometimes unforeseen candour eliminates repentance. This was one of those bonding moments.

"I am deeply honoured by your gracious invitation to be your honorary son," Marcel whispered. "Enough said. We move on." He had not rehearsed this reply, yet it was appropriate.

They raised glasses to seal the covenant of comrades.

Funerals were not Alexandra's favourite cultural events marking the passage from this world to another. Her mother's funeral service was still too recent, too raw. The faint scent of trepidation and grief surfaced as she thought about her mother and their quasi-estranged relationship. Paul seemed to have had a closer rapport with his Papa who returned from work most nights in time for dinner and his Maman who was a loving stay-at-home wife and mother. Each evening, his father and mother would embrace and repeat their respective vows of adoration. He missed that moment.

There were the nights when Alexandra did not sleep, would not allow herself to close her eyelids. As long as she could remain awake thinking about her Maman, she would not lose her. She would not be left to fend for herself like a fawn that had witnessed a hunter take its mother for its flesh. The law of the jungle. Rise to the circumstance or fall prey. She was her mother's daughter – *de l'audace, encore de l'audace, toujours de l'audace. What about Collette, her daughter*, she pondered. *Would Collette be a nurturing mother to her children, or abandon them to well-meaning nannies?*

Alexandra had felt safe growing up with her uncle and aunt who loved her as if she were their own daughter. But she was not. She had missed her mother and yearned for the warmth of her touch during those long periods of separation. She mostly missed those tender moments when her mother would lovingly brush her hair while softly singing fairy-tale verses from her own childhood.

Alexandra allowed the uneasiness to settle. Yet her doubts remained and with them the threads of lingering apprehension. *How can I support Collette and still be with Paul?* Most pressing would be the revelation of all those secrets.

She held Collette's hand. Nothing could be said that would communicate the sentiment expressed with the tears that now flowed from her eyes. "We need to take very good care of you and the baby," she whispered. The sincerity of her tone left nothing to misinterpretation.

"Yes, Maman. Don't worry. I'll be OK. I have a feeling I will make it to full term this time," Collette whispered in a barely audible voice.

"*We* is the collective we," Jo piped up. "I won't let her out of my sight. Imposing on my librarian skills, I will scrutinize every bit of validated research on what expectant mothers need to know and do. So, while you and Paul are off fighting crime, I will be the dutiful honorary aunt watching over the home front."

"Thank you, Jo, I expected you would step up," Alexandra replied with grateful enthusiasm and confidence. "I would not have anticipated anything less from my oldest and dearest friend." She wondered whether her uncle and aunt had expressed the same sentiment to her mother on the eve of Maria's counterintelligence forays, which were referred to casually as business trips. *Would Collette think the same?*

Collette caught and held her mother's concerns. She understood the implicit communication.

"Yes, Maman," she quietly confirmed again as they hugged as only a Maman and *fille enceinte* could.

Intuition had always been a strength in Collette's relationship with her mother. That is what made it so special. She loved Jean but he was her intimate partner. With her mother, there were bonds forged by maternal conversations both tacit and explicit. They were akin to what her grandmother, Maria, had had with colleagues from the French Resistance during the World War and French Counterintelligence during the Cold War. She was born into a life of impenetrable mysteries, nurtured by a mother and grandmother who had also been raised in the synergy of the covert. Their resolve had been tested and found sufficient. Collette's mettle would also endure.

CHAPTER 40

P aul's father had made countless friends, many of whom were present at the funeral. He had also accrued his share of unsavoury adversaries both within and outside the policing service. Paul and Alexandra, in the relatively brief time that they had been working with the EUI Unit, had attracted fewer but exponentially more toxic antagonists who operated on the fringes of intelligence and espionage.

As with her mother's funeral, there were invisible eyes with nefarious intentions present at this service and reception. Most worrying among them was the impending appearance of the Lucerne assassin whose identity was still unknown. The never-ending game of cat and mouse was playing out with masked surveillance tracking these self-invited guests who were doggedly seeking clues to the whereabouts of Maria's elusive code under the guise of somber condolences.

The code had acquired the potency of an elegant enigma despite the fact it had been developed decades earlier during the disquiet of the early days of the Cold War. Its life and utility had not yet succumbed to the onslaught of supposedly superior technological analysis in rogue as opposed to revisionist states. That fact alone had made it even more alluring. The re-emergence of the rumours of its existence had fostered renewed interest. Moscow now had competition from Beijing for intelligence regarding both the code and the *Quer*, initially thought to be unrelated but now suspected of being inextricably linked.

"It would have been convenient to have had Francine and Yusuf here with their collective experience to vet the guests for ulterior motives," Daan reflected. "We may have dispatched her and her bodyguard too early to the safe house in Montreal. But she should recover more quickly with the best of Canadian health care."

Matthieu reassured his boss. "The safe house in Montreal is a relatively short direct flight to Paris. We may have to bring the Knight of Malta back temporarily to set Baird's mind at ease, to reassure him that he is secure in his own Alsatian safe house at the south end of the Ponts Couverts under the protection of the knight-errant. At their first meeting, Yusuf had committed to confirming the loyalty of Baird's cyber programmers. One had been stealthily eliminated and replaced by an operative from Commandant Parent's Cyber Anti-Terrorist Unit. Like a Trojan virus, this agent had inserted a clandestine GPS-worm into the illicit software, which will signal us each time it is used for criminal purposes or copied and passed on to another rogue proprietor. It is currently making its rounds in the backrooms and boardrooms of Manila, Hong Kong and Saint Petersburg."

"Don't you just love tattletale technology when it tracks the bad guys," Daan chuckled.

The smile on Daan's face faded as he became unexpectedly quiet and withdrawn. Matthieu had witnessed this transformation on several occasions throughout their relationship, but more so in the past few weeks. His concerns were less worrying than curious. When they first met a decade earlier at the headquarters of the United Nations Protection Force in Sarajevo, Daan would invite Matthieu to walk around the courtyard of what had been Tito's palace to debate intelligence issues. Occasionally, Daan would stop suddenly and stare seemingly at everything yet at nothing. These pauses were purposeful, constructive. Matthieu knew not to interrupt but to await Daan's deliberation. Lately, his stares appeared less focused on weighing debated options and more concentrated on vetting eclipsed events from his past, perhaps from Sarajevo, perhaps elsewhere. The consequences of not finding what he was seeking seemed onerous beyond any moral ambiguity to abandon the mission of clearing his memory fog.

"I'm missing something," Daan declared in a troubled voice. "It's right in front of me and I can't see it, can't recognize it." Being responsible for every member of his team was the greatest weight he carried. Even with the most accurate and timely intelligence, he knew that occasionally intervening variables pop up on the radar that could not be anticipated. That was when intuition from individual agents had to take over. But when an unknown gnawed at him, as he was experiencing at this time, he could only express his concerns and direct his colleagues to take extra caution. Matthieu was the best sounding board he had to eke out the nebulous from their hiding places in the recesses of his mind. But even now, Matthieu's presence was insufficient.

"Talk to me, Matthieu," Daan asked. "We have known each other, worked together, since before Sarajevo. In those waters that have flowed under the bridges of all the cases we have worked on together, there is a virus like a sleeper cell, poised to awaken." He hesitated while Matthieu followed his searching eyes. "An army commander never wants to leave enemy forces in his rear echelon as he advances. I feel as though I have done just that. What was different about this mission as opposed to other UN missions we served on?"

Daan had repeatedly mentioned Sarajevo. That would be Matthieu's starting point. "A bit similar but different, there was no peace to keep for peacekeepers. It had spawned other conflicts. With the support of some former allies in the former Austro-Hungarian Empire, Slovenia had been granted independent status as a nation state by the United Nations with a relatively peaceful transition. Kosovo, in contrast, witnessed devastating loss of lives and damage to property from continued open conflict. Perhaps both because of their relative closeness to Serbia."

Daan sat in silence with his chin balanced on his steepled fingers. His eyes slowly traced the images in the interconnected web that Matthieu had spun.

Matthieu reached further afield still reflecting on the United Nations mission in the Former Republic of Yugoslavia. "As a permanent member of the UN Security Council, Russian troops had been deployed as blue beret peacekeepers in Sierra Leone, Western Sahara, and the Sudan. I always found it odd that they had served in Bosnia and Herzegovina, in addition to Kosovo."

With the mention of Russian troops serving as UN peacekeepers, Daan moved his attention from images portrayed on the monitor of his mind to Matthieu's stare.

"Why did you find it odd?" Daan asked. "Under Marshall Tito, the Socialist Federal Republic of Yugoslavia had become a satellite state of the USSR."

Matthieu grimaced as he scratched his balding head. "Tito had been taken prisoner by the Russians during the First World War and sent to a work camp in the Ural Mountains. Something transpired there. During World War II, he led the Yugoslav partisans against the Nazis. Thereafter, he became prime minister, then president for life and Marshal of Yugoslavia. I just found it ironic that his palace in Sarajevo became our headquarters, where we worked alongside the Russians."

Daan's posture changed from relaxed and pensive to alert and enquiring. Something that Matthieu had said had ignited his attention. He stood up and beckoned Matthieu to accompany him as he strode along with purpose.

"Hold that thought, Matthieu," he uttered with renewed energy.

Matthieu watched as Daan's eyes came alive. He then stopped and stared at Matthieu.

"The Russians planted a sleeper cell, left an agent in our rear echelon, while we were distracted by the violence that had erupted in the Former Republic of Yugoslavia. Tito still walks the corridors of his opulent palace in Sarajevo. I just have to figure out where and, most importantly, who the embedded agent is."

CHAPTER 41

"**M**any moons have passed since I received an email from the service manager for urgent maintenance due on my Harley," Alexandra commented to Paul with some apprehension. Previous contacts had been shrouded in the mystique of the messenger as much as the connotations of the communiqué itself.

"With Tom Hunt's death, it can only mean that Helena LeDuc has some crucial information for our ears only," Paul replied. "Her request to meet is more than likely a result of her own initiative, a personal commitment, and not one of agency to agency consistent with the terms and conditions of a memorandum of understanding which does not formally exist between the Central Intelligence Agency and the European Union Intelligence Unit. That begs the question: Why would the CIA be requesting a meeting or perhaps a séance to communicate with Tom's departed soul? We will need clearance from Daan, and a wire installed by our techies."

"In the immortal words of Lewis Carroll as *Alice in Wonderland* cried out, 'curiouser and curiouser,'" Alexandra laughed.

⚅ ⚅

"HELENA, IT HAS BEEN A long time since you delivered Tom's antiquarian book collection that he kindly bequeathed to us. Are you still brushing up on your German at the University of Frankfurt?" Alexander asked as both she and Paul assessed her body language. Alexandra was the more astute mentor and Paul still her protégé in such ethereal techniques. She had spent as much time observing people as Paul had done gazing at samples in petri dishes. Same discipline in discerning skills, different foci.

"Finished my classes and now working out of our Embassy in Berlin," Helena replied in as welcoming and respectful a tone as the question had been posed. "It is very good to see both of you again. I enjoyed our time together, brief as it was. I recall how respectful of my cultural background you were when we first met at the CIA headquarters in Langley."

"You sent me an urgent request from the Harley Davidson service manager?" Alexandra enquired.

"When we briefly spoke just after Tom's murder, I promised to advise you of any new developments that might pose a threat to either of you. I had advised my supervisor that I would be meeting with you and mentioned the general subject matter. For your information, he didn't object but didn't much care one way or the other."

Paul replied, piqued by both the intelligence she was about to pass on and the apparent attitude of her superior. "You have our undivided attention."

"A Russian agent recently crossed the border from the Province of Quebec into New York State. He is known to have worked with a female FSB agent, formally KGB, who had infiltrated French Internal Intelligence. We know this because she had been on Tom's radar."

"That is too close to home. Did she know about our relationship with Tom or with you?" Alexandra enquired.

"We don't believe so because your association with Tom was just beginning and we hadn't yet met," Helena replied. She picked up on Alexandra's level of concern.

"That is reassuring," Alexandra acknowledged with a sigh although she had not broken eye contact. She sensed that this tidbit of information was not all that Helena had travelled this distance to divulge.

Helena continued, "The French General Directorate for Internal

Security confirmed that this female FSB agent had been killed in an ambush south of Metz. Yet, we have information from another source suggesting she is alive. She was supposedly seen meeting the two of you at the EU Parliament in Strasbourg a few weeks ago. Subsequent to this alleged meeting, she was reported to have been shot in Paris by a Beijing assassin, while in the company of the male Russian agent. How and when he ended up in Canada is not known. He triggered our file when he crossed the border from Quebec into New York State. It is a small and increasingly dangerous world. The two of you need to be careful."

"And the name of this Russian Agent who crossed the border?" Alexandra asked.

"His name is Anatoly Gorky."

"And the female Russian agent who supposedly died but has nine lives like a feral alley cat?" Paul probed.

"Her name was or is Tatyana Sokolov."

Paul grimaced. "I haven't heard either name bantered around in the Third or Fourth Reich context, which is where we have been focusing our enquiries, following up on the work we did for Tom and yourself. Do you have any photos of them? Perhaps we have crossed paths but they used other names."

"He sometimes uses a code name of Rakici. Tatyana's French name is Francine Myette," Helena suggested more nonchalantly than informing, as if baiting Paul and Alexandra into acknowledging a close connection.

Paul slowly shook his head from side to side as he looked at Alexandra for confirmation. She responded with a similar negative gesture.

"No recent photos of him. The CCTV camera photo at the border is imprecise as it was late evening when he crossed and he was wearing a low-brimmed fedora." Helena qualified. "Our customs and immigration folks believed he was probing for a reaction."

"Probing for what?" Paul needed additional details.

"Not sure," Helena replied.

Alexandra followed up, but with the intention to shift the topic. "We have heard rumours about a Beijing assassin. Do you have any information or photos?"

"There are two assassins I am aware of but no photos," Helena responded. "Both are females. The senior is reported to be deadly accurate when she has a target in her crosshairs, top of her class, never missing a shot. Her protégé was apparently not that skilled. I use the past tense because she was killed in a shoot-out with French police in Strasbourg. The French media reported the incident as a thwarted terrorist attack on the EU Parliament. We doubt that because the Chinese do not have a track record of engaging in such a blatant manner. Their attacks are increasingly cyber-related, cyber-terrorism, cyber-war, cyber-espionage, and cyber-crime like intellectual property theft, or simply searching for vulnerabilities. That's not to say that the assassin might not have been Chinese by cultural appearance and contracted to pull the trigger by another party. It's the Wild West all over again." Helena shrugged her shoulders in resignation implying that everything old is new again. "You don't know what you don't know. It is relatively inexpensive just to snoop and probe. But we could be mistaken on this occasion as these sources are new to the game. As a result, they may be too eager to please their new masters with deep pockets."

"We very much appreciate your words of caution and the information regarding the Beijing assassins," Alexandra replied earnestly. "Please keep in contact if your travels bring you to Paris."

"And the same to you if your hunt for Nazi gold and artefacts takes you into my backyard. *Auf Wiedersehen meine freunde und sei vorsichtig* – goodbye my friends and be careful."

"NICELY PLAYED, FOLKS, REGARDING IDENTIFICATION of Francine and Yusuf," Daan remarked. "Information on the gender of the Lucerne assassin being female narrows the field. But the most damning intelligence is the security breach in the EU Parliament. Could it have been Baird's daughter, Alana?"

"That would be my first guess," Alexandra replied.

Paul responded, "I am not sure that Alana saw us with Francine and Yusuf. I am confident that the CCTV inside the building would have recorded us, though. The security guards, especially the Head of Security, would certainly have been monitoring the movements of all occupants. I go back to Herr Blosch's final statement when we were being hooded and gagged on the yacht: "We have people in high places in policing and governance." That leads me to believe the breach in security is elsewhere."

"Oh, that is worrying," Daan uttered. "And what is Yusuf doing venturing away from the safe house in Montreal, where he is supposedly guarding Francine, his Tanya? Why would he be driving south to the United States?"

"That's it!" Paul exclaimed. That's it!"

"What's it?" Alexandra asked.

"That's where I saw Yusuf – in Sarajevo in 1994! It was in Sarajevo at the United Nations Protection Force headquarters of the Russian battalion."

"Yes," Daan confirmed. "Yes. I've been racking my memory to place him. He was in civilian attire, a fly on the wall. I never saw him in any uniform. Yet he strangely did not seem solely committed to the Russian mandate. He would wander away for no apparent reason. As a result, we deemed him to be untrustworthy and didn't accord him security clearance. Instead, we thought he was a security threat. Like Yusuf today, he seemed to have an ulterior motive in Sarajevo. If he was just probing, seemingly observing, then for what?"

"That's what has been bugging me too," Paul agreed.

"So, today is he a Russian FSB formerly a KGB agent like Francine, or a Turkish Military Intelligence officer, or just a freelance espionage entrepreneur?" Daan queried.

"Or all of the above and perhaps more, a loose cannon on the deck?" Paul proposed. "And, as you ask, what is Yusuf doing driving south from Montreal to the U.S. border, venturing away from the safe house where he is supposed to be guarding Francine, his Tanya? It's as if he had an underlying motive to accompany Francine to the new safe house in Canada, wanting to be present but not seen, like the proverbial camouflaged fly on the wall. Why would he be presenting a false façade?"

Alexandra sat back, hesitant, withdrawn. *Have I misread my shrew, my intuition? Have I made a fatal error in judgement about Yusuf? About others? As a result, have I placed any of us in the crosshairs of an assassin's gun, tricked by a traitor? And my Collette? The baby?* She second-guessed herself as she wrestled with doubt.

"Comments, Alexandra?" Daan asked.

"Nothing to add," she responded ostensibly disengaged as in another dimension, from another time and space. When her mother had returned home after her business trips, she would sometimes greet Alexandra with warm yet absent hugs, and expressions of endearment devoid of sentiment despite the long-awaited reunion. Words and actions had been incongruent from Alexandra's perspective. They had left her feeling deflated, more alone than if her mother had never returned, only to abandon her again, to force her to fend for herself in the make-believe world of her imaginative mind where confidence was tentative.

Alexandra knew she was at work, not at home though in her own mind she was at home and not at work. Yet she had no home, so to speak, only houses she had temporarily passed through like voyages of the *Starship Enterprise* through far-off cognitive galaxies. The escapism of work had become the transient nature of a home. Such was the life of a nomad with a mind torn between priorities in time and space. Daan had asked an explicit question and she had provided an implicit answer but devoid of honesty linked to the present, just like her mother's words and actions on those occasional fleeting reunions.

Paul glanced at her, puzzled. She always had critical analyses to add, propositions to suggest, recommendations to make. At this moment, she felt vulnerable, threatened, and distant like a little girl alone seeking sanctuary from ghoulies and ghosties and long-leggedy beasties and things that go bump in the night, Good Lord deliver us, as the old Scottish bedtime prayer wove a protective spell. Yet, she wasn't holding her amulet.

De l'audace, encore de l'audace, et toujours de l'audace. Here, now, a complete dearth of audacity, a noted deficiency in confidence. Paul had never seen her in such an apprehensive and detached state.

In Greek mythology, Kassandra was Apollo's wife. On their wedding day, he had given her the gift of envisioning the future and convincing others who were in the path of misfortune to take evasive action. When Kassandra rebuffed his amorous advances, Apollo withdrew her ability to convince others of the impending disasters. Kassandra went mad without the confidence to protect. Was this the fate of Alexandra? Had the amulet that hung around her neck been drained of its ancient powers like had happened to the Walt Disney cartoon character, Dumbo, who no longer had the confidence to fly after he lost his feather?

CHAPTER 42

"A re you OK?" Paul asked in a quiet, concerned voice as he reached over and held her close. She remained distant, detached, indifferent.

"Fine. Why do you ask?" Alexandra replied as if out of defensive habit and devoid of emotion.

"You seem to be elsewhere."

"Just tired," she replied, with a fabricated smile.

Paul awaited a more engaging response in a space where exclusion had replaced explanation, and empty words were rapidly being veiled by an increasingly dense fog of isolation. His barren relationship with Suzette had been his compass for so many years, a deceptive beacon from a desolate lighthouse. He sensed that he stood unaccompanied beside Alexandra Vanessa, married but without a true partner just like his relationship with Suzette. "The Pope isn't always right," his father's words reminded him of his wedding vows to his first wife.

Alexandra pulled back and returned his stare. Tears filled her eyes and rolled down her cheeks with the realization that she had caused him to withdraw as a direct result of her detached response to his concern for her wellbeing. *Where had that come from? Who was this insensitive bedevilled person inside me?* It had driven a wedge between them. She had hurt the first and only person she had ever loved and who loved her unconditionally. She embraced him in a hug as she had never done before but had dreamed about countless times since their first kiss all those years ago as young teenagers.

"I'm so sorry. Please forgive me," she whispered in a trembling voice and then repeated, "I'm so sorry. Please forgive me. Promise that you will never leave me, never abandon me."

She moved closer to him and into his embrace and stared at him with her nose touching his.

"Promise you will never leave me, never abandon me," she pleaded again.

"I promise," he pledged, still perplexed by her change in manner.

As they maintained the closest of that physical and emotional proximity, he asked himself: *What have I done or what have I said that would cause her to believe that I would ever leave, abandon her?* Now was not the time to enquire.

"We need to talk, soon," she whispered. Her words were both a request and a declaration.

The intimacy of the renewed embrace confirmed his response. They would talk about what they both had on their minds, but later.

⊲ ⊳

"I spoke with Yolina about the security breach at the EU Parliament," Daan announced. "Not surprisingly, she was outraged. She would normally have asked the Head of Security to initiate an investigation. But for obvious reasons, she has deferred to a contact in the German Federal Intelligence Service, the BND, to make discrete enquiries. It is a high priority. I pass this along because Baird Durand may be involved. Alexandra, please contact Alana and make subtle enquiries."

"For your information, Baird contacted me and asked if I could help Alana because her ex has been bothering her," she replied. "I could meet under this context. How much should I probe? How subtle should I be?"

"I leave that to your discretion," Daan replied. He looked at her but more at Paul with a perplexed expression. Why had she become indecisive? Since joining the European Union Intelligence Unit, he had always admired her for her ability to make timely decisions within the strategic context. She had spent a career as a forensic psychologist assessing the motivation and behaviour of depraved criminals. In comparison, making subtle enquiries regarding someone's knowledge of an event was hardly an overwhelming task.

Paul held Daan's enquiring look with equal curiosity. He sensed that Alexandra's hesitation had something to do with her emotional response to his own enquiry about what he perceived to be her indifferent withdrawal. He deduced that the recent change was premised on events unknown to him that had occurred in her youth. He did not have a lifetime of shared experiences with her to draw upon, which might suggest an explanation or remedy. He tilted his head slightly and subtly raised his eyebrows, suggesting that he shared Daan's concern.

"Get back to me tomorrow, Alexandra," Daan directed more as a commander and less as a colleague. He felt uncomfortable in doing so. It had never been his preferred style of leading, especially with highly qualified professionals with whom he had developed a strong working relationship. He was confident she would resolve whatever issues were interfering with her abilities either alone or with Paul's support. In the interim, he needed answers.

"Do you have a moment, Daan?" Matthieu asked on the heels of his brief visual communiqué with Alexandra.

"Certainly. Let's go for java now." Matthieu didn't make such requests often. When he did, it was important enough to follow his lead for a tête-à-tête. Café points tended to be more productive than fixed agenda items.

Both Daan and Matthieu followed Alexandra with a puzzled gaze as she and Paul left. They appeared to be together as usual but distant. Paul occasionally looked at her yet she did not reciprocate with any sense of acknowledgement. Instead, she walked in solemn contemplation with her head down and shoulders heavy.

"I am bothered by the inexplicable variance in Alexandra's behaviour that you are noticing," Matthieu murmured. "It doesn't appear to be a new issue, but one that has been simmering over time and has recently boiled over."

"You know her perhaps better than I," Daan suggested. "Can you have a chat before I do? There could be serious ramifications at this juncture in the investigation if she remains distracted."

"That was going to be my suggestion," Matthieu replied. "It could just be related to her daughter becoming pregnant. I suspect rather more so because of Collette's previous miscarriage."

Daan confessed, "If the latter, I am concerned with the link to the circumstances of the miscarriage, especially with Paul's eldest son, Yvon, and his subsequent drowning. I will speak with Marcel. I know he had a long talk with Paul at his father's funeral. Marcel came away appearing more relaxed than I have seen him since before the drowning."

"This may be just a bump in the road which we suspected might occur. Alternately, it could be something unrelated to the miscarriage. Regardless, we need to get her refocused on the mission at hand," Matthieu asserted.

"I sincerely hope so," Daan replied. "But we had best monitor closely. Paul appeared as surprised as we were with her indecisiveness today. That suggests that whatever the issue is, it is more than likely hers to resolve and not something between them. I will have a chat with him also."

⚐ ⚐

"HAVE YOU MET WITH ALANA?" Daan's text to Alexandra read.

Alexandra's response was heartening to Daan because it demonstrated a higher level of analysis and engagement.

"Not yet," she replied, "but Baird Durand contacted me again and reiterated his concern and urgency that I chat with Alana soon. Baird apparently spoke with Alana's ex and suggested that his harassing conduct was unacceptable. Why do you ask?"

"I will call you," he concluded the text message.

"What's going on?" Alexandra asked. She preferred face-to-face than text or emails. Voice-to-voice was the best compromise. Her resistance to the least-personal approach was on the rise.

"Good to hear your cheerful voice," Daan welcomed her. He noted an increase in her energy. "Yolina's contact in the BND advised that Alana's ex was found floating in Lake Geneva. It appears that he was drunk, fell off a boat and drowned. I encourage you not to break this news to Alana, but instead just provide stress counselling regarding her divorce."

"Fell off a boat drunk, and drowned?" Alexandra repeated sceptically. "There has to be more."

Thoughts raced through Alexandra's mind. *Yvon had also drowned, not impaired by alcohol but supposedly too high on drugs to save himself. A coincidence? Perhaps. He was merely an abusive loser, as both Paul and Jean had described him. Or was he?* These thoughts were not rational and she knew it. Secrets were seductive and seduction was the antithesis of loyalty. Secrets contributed to her divorce from André. She vowed not to do the same with Paul. Yet here she was harbouring secrets, dancing around the circle of deceit like fairies pirouetting around late-night mushroom circles. She needed to have that honest talk with Paul, and sooner rather than later.

Daan continued. "Alana's ex has been on the BND radar as a low-level Russian informant for several years. He had been having an affair with one of the executive support staff in the EU Parliament in Strasbourg before Alana started working there. So, Alana's claim of being stalked was incorrect in this context but valid in perceived circumstance. The BND have reason to believe that Baird arranged the party on the boat. Someone played the role of the gracious host and got Alana's husband drunk with a mixture of lethal drugs and alcohol, and secretly pushed him overboard when he was nearly unconscious."

"Thank you for this update, Daan. "That makes more sense," Alexandra replied. "I will be seeing Alana this evening and will report back to you tomorrow morning at the latest."

"Just your mother checking in," read Alexandra's text to Collette.

"Need to talk… over cognac," read her subsequent text to Paul.

⊰ ⊱

"The counselling session with Alana went well," Alexandra reported to Daan. "I didn't feel she was aware her ex was deceased. Neither did I get a sense she was aware of any security leak in the EU Parliament. She was just distressed about the ongoing divorce process and her ex's daily presence which she interpreted as harassment. She mentioned she had spoken to Baird who assured her that all would be resolved shortly as if referring to the legal divorce."

"Thank you for your prompt response," Daan acknowledged. He surmised that whatever the issue that had prompted Alexandra to withdraw had been resolved or decompressed to a manageable level. Either way, she was back on track.

"One other point, she added. "After this case is complete, I would like to take a leave of absence until Collette has delivered and perhaps sometime thereafter."

"OK. Once this case is wrapped up, we can certainly explore options. Take care of yourself in the meantime."

Daan inhaled slowly. Then exhaled. He needed to consider all options.

CHAPTER 43

"An operational issue. Alexandra has asked to take a leave of absence," Daan announced pensively as he held Matthieu's gaze. There was no mistaking his concern. Other members of the European Union Intelligence Unit had submitted their letters of resignation but rarely in the middle of a case. Although valuable resources for the expertise they brought, none had been sought after by foreign agencies for the depth of knowledge they possessed.

"Hmm," Matthieu murmured. "That will have complications, certainly implications." Daan did not have to elaborate. Both she and Paul had become integral players in the *Quer* investigation. Matthieu had never worked with two people who were so synchronistic in their thinking. More alarmingly, if Alexandra took a leave of absence, would Paul follow suit? It was more than likely.

"We need to talk about the ramifications of such a hiatus on security surrounding Maria's code, among other related matters," Daan proposed. "Moscow and Beijing are still actively looking for the code, perhaps more because of its perceived mystique than its possible use, which was considerable in itself. Nonetheless, we still need to ensure it doesn't change hands. We have the physical codebook locked up. But Alexandra has it memorized. That means we would need to keep Alexandra secure while she is on her leave of absence. Thoughts, my friend?"

"Therein lies the dilemma," Matthieu proclaimed. "The methodical Teutonic mind was its own worst enemy because their codes were too orderly, not all related to the Fibonacci sequence, but still possibly broken if Alexandra was interrogated under duress such as a threat to Collette and the baby. Even the extreme complexity of the German Enigma Code during the Second World War was eventually solved. Maria's code is an elegant enigma in comparison, the complete opposite in its convoluted simplicity. Our techies predict that the probability of someone deciphering it is smaller, but still possible, especially with the aid of AI algorithms combined with the exponential speed of today's system technology. That just leaves one question. How secure do we want to or need to be, to ensure the knowledge that Alexandra has acquired remains safe?"

Daan's assessment was unambiguous. "If it was just the paper copy of the code, my response would be different. Alexandra, as a resource, is exponentially more valuable. So, I assess the need to keep her secure is as high as it is for you and me," Daan emphasized. "I have not yet had this conversation with Yolina."

"I agree. Having said that, we do not have the resources to provide 24-hour security and I doubt Yolina will think highly of us if you plead with her for a budget increase at that level, even in the short term," Matthieu concluded.

"And you are suggesting?" Daan pressed, hoping that his colleague would pull more than a rabbit with deep pockets out of the hat.

"I am suggesting that I, you, we speak with Alexandra."

"And speak with Paul alone, and preferably the two of them together," Daan added with greater emphasis on Matthieu's playing a significant role. Daan never found it necessary to have formal job descriptions. But if he did, personnel matters like this would undoubtedly fall to Matthieu. At this moment, his warm smile and inclusive expression left nothing to misinterpretation. Matthieu would take the lead.

"When I last spoke with Alexandra, I got the sense that her request to be close to Collette while she is pregnant and immediately thereafter was not negotiable," Matthieu added. "Her conundrum relates to her estranged relationship with her own mother. Alexandra does not want to become a surrogate mother like her aunt and uncle were to her because Maria travelled so much while employed with French Counterintelligence. I am confident that is the underlying reason or motivator for Alexandra's desire to step back."

"We are omitting the Paul factor," Daan suggested. "Paul and Alexandra are partners, two peas in a single pod, in the truest sense. But secrets make for bad bed partners."

"I think I know where you are going with this and the waters get murky," Matthieu acknowledged. "We don't want to pull back the layers of the onion skin if we don't have to and I think we don't have to. It is imperative that we clearly understand Alexandra's motivation and only deal with that factor."

"Marcel mentioned that he and Paul had a frank discussion at his father's funeral regarding Yvon's drowning. Without openly acknowledging his involvement or our involvement in the drowning, Paul toasted their tight-knit mutual relationship as brothers-in-arms. He went so far as to say that Marcel was more of a son to him than Yvon had ever been. I'm confident that Paul and Marcel will work through that in the fullness of time. The unresolved issue for Alexandra relates to Yvon's sexual assault of Collette and her subsequent miscarriage. That is where we need to provide the support without involving more people than is absolutely necessary. If it was someone else on the team, I would have Alexandra provide the psychological and emotional support." Daan held Matthieu's gaze. "How comfortable would you be in taking on that role?"

"There is no definitive proof that the assault caused or directly contributed to the miscarriage," Matthieu stated. "But perception premised on emotions can be more influential than proven facts, even for a seasoned forensic psychologist like Alexandra."

"Correct. This is where the waters get muddy. Alexandra has kept that secret from Paul out of fear that their relationship might not survive the strain if Paul found out. This is a related impetus for Alexandra's decision to take a leave of absence. So, this is what we have to address. I welcome your thoughts. Recommendations?" Daan stated.

Like his superior, Matthieu stared at everything yet focused on nothing. He wasn't comfortable with the idea of taking on the mantle of a clinical psychologist. He had been present when Collette related the circumstances of Yvon's attack. Alexandra had sworn him to secrecy and he had agreed. With that oral commitment, a bond had been sealed between them. Nothing further needed to be said. Each time the issue regarding Collette's safety raised its ugly head, they would exchange subtle nods confirming that all was OK.

Matthieu confirmed his analysis. "Alexandra has made her decision to take a leave of absence. We cannot nor should not attempt to change her mind in the short term. It has to be her decision."

"My turn to agree," Daan committed.

"Two scenarios," Matthieu proposed. "First, if Collette miscarries again with this second pregnancy, then Alexandra can more readily accept the fact that her daughter is one of those unfortunate women who has difficulty carrying a fetus to full term. Under this scenario, there is a high probability that Alexandra will accept that Yvon's assault, as terrible as it was, did not directly contribute to the first miscarriage. Second, if Collette carries the fetus to full term and ideally the baby is healthy, the secret of Yvon's assault will no longer have as much weight with the perceived irreputable harm to her marriage with Paul. The grandparents will become even closer. Either way, I predict that Alexandra will return to our happy family of sisters- and brothers-in-arms. In the interim, we offer her continued part-time employment in our Paris office with the option of working her own hours."

"I agree and I like your plan," Daan confided. "That solves the security dilemma regarding Alexandra's intimate knowledge of Maria's code. I will propose it to Alexandra and Paul and inform Yolina."

CHAPTER 44

"Helena, I just want to thank you again for your concern and the information about the Russian agents in our backyard," Alexandra said. Her voice was sincere. The intent of her message less so. Both she and Helena were aware of the rules of the game of espionage and intelligence-gathering in which there were truths, partial truths, make-believe truths. Hence, there was no excuse for impoliteness or disrespect among equals who were occasionally on different sides of the same side, or at best at oblique angles. Trust could be earned like honesty shared between Maria, Sir James and Major Mike but that was rare.

"You are welcome. I hope that you will reciprocate," Helena replied, her tone reassuring. She prepared to weigh the veracity of Alexandra's pending information.

"We seem to have a bad connection or is there background interference from nearby construction?" Alexandra commented. "May I surmise that you are not calling from the Harley-Davidson dealership or other similar location?"

"I will have to register a complaint with my service provider," Helena replied after a brief pause. *Alexandra is as astute as I hoped she would be,* she concluded.

Alexandra trusted Helena from the moment they first met at the CIA headquarters in Langley, Virginia. Helena appeared genuine when Alexandra enquired about her American Indian heritage, or as Helena referred to it, Canadian First Nations. When they met again at the Harley-Davidson dealership in Paris, their mutual trust became more entrenched. Helena's caginess in her current greeting suggested that Alexandra needed to be careful with what she divulged. Building trustworthiness occasionally took a circuitous route. Alexandra would not mention specifics.

"We checked with French Intelligence who confirmed that the Russian agent had in fact been killed in an ambush south of Metz. You said that her name was Tatyana Sokolov. The source that supposedly saw her with Paul and me at the EU Parliament was a low-level unreliable snitch for the FSB. He had huge gambling debts and was feeding false information to get whatever payoff he could. I say *was* because he is now confirmed dead, drowned in Lake Geneva. Deception can be seductive, but only if the deceived is a willing partner. Suffice it to say, his Russian handler was not willing to play that game and is, today, not lamenting a great loss to the FSB intelligence network."

"I very much appreciate the feedback," Helena replied. "For your information, I return to Montreal once in a while to visit my family whose traditional lands are nearby. If you are looking for a different holiday venue, I could be your personal tourist guide. Just a thought."

"Always looking for exotic holiday locations. *Jusque là*," Alexandra acknowledged her invitation. On her own turf, Helena could be assured of greater privacy. It would be an opportune venue to develop their relationship if they continue to be on different sides of the same side.

⊲ ⊳

"Daan, I just got off the phone with Helena LeDuc. Do you have a moment to discuss an opportunity for a possibly beneficial scenario?"

"Always, Alexandra. What do you have?" Daan was encouraged by her upbeat pitch and strategic perspective. Whatever it was that had hobbled her before seemed to have corrected itself. He would confirm his assessment with Matthieu and continue to monitor her performance. Paul had always been audacious without being fool-hardy with his proposals. That was one of the characteristics Daan admired about him from when they first met in Sarajevo. Although they had only been working together for a relatively short time, Alexandra was readily adopting his style.

"As you directed, I confirmed with Helena that Francine had been killed in an ambush just south of Metz. I also verified that the source of intelligence that supposedly connected Paul and me with Francine and Yusuf at the EU Parliament was a low-level unreliable Russian informant, now deceased. Helena seemed to accept my accounting of those two events that she had previously mentioned."

"Did you get the sense that Helena was playing along? You thought she might have been throwing out some bait when she called you."

"I believe she was being sincere. When Helena delivered Tom Hunt's antique book collection which he had bequeathed to Paul and me, I concluded she was being honest and forthright. Our te-chies checked the books to ascertain if a bug had been planted either by Helena or the CIA unbeknown to her. There was none. Unlike the mythical Trojan Horse, Helena's overture was not a deceptive stratagem. I am confident that she was being truthful with me on both occasions. I could be wrong but I don't think so."

"Fair enough," Daan replied. "I trust your judgement as al-ways." His confirmation was as much a validation of her intuitive-ness as it was a statement of confidence, which seemed to have waned when last they met.

"The plot thickens, so to speak," Alexandra added. "Helena then invited me to let her know if I was considering Montreal as a holiday venue. I got the idea she was aware that Francine was in a safe house there. She did not mention Yusuf." Alexandra recalled the previous discussions she had had with her. "She mentioned

Yusuf when last we spoke, stating that he had attempted to enter the United States at the border crossing south of Montreal. I'm thinking that her interest is with Francine rather than Yusuf, at least at this time. Perhaps she has been ordered by her superiors to focus all her attention on Francine while someone else tracks Yusuf."

"Curious," Daan noted. "The elusive Knight of Malta. Yusuf and Francine are a team like you and Paul. Follow one, you follow the other. Find one and you find the other. Concerning Helena's invitation to be your private tourist guide in Montreal, accept her offer. Without violating your growing mutual trust, find out what you can. I leave it to your discretion as to how much to share and when. Francine and Yusuf are on our current radar but there could be longer-term benefits to the European Union from your growing relationship with Helena for future cases."

"One last point of concern. Helena could have been probing me. I am unsure if she was also baiting us regarding the security leak at the EU Parliament? In addition to being a low-level Russian informant, according to Yolina's BND source, was Alana's ex also an informant for the CIA?"

"Well, isn't that an interesting scenario – the CIA actively spying on the EU and our Intelligence Unit. It wouldn't be the first time. Montreal isn't Liechtenstein. A short vacation in Montreal is certainly warranted."

CHAPTER 45

"URGENT," the text subject line read. "Lucerne assassin tentatively identified by one of Commandant Parent's informants. Photo attached. Assassin is en route to Strasbourg, due to arrive shortly."

"Intelligence from Helena appears to be accurate. The photo confirms an Asian female," Paul noted. "She is only carrying what appears to be a large purse. So, not planning an overnight stay."

"May not be a purse, but a satchel for her weapon," Alexandra countered. "Eurorail service doesn't have the same high level of security regarding weapons as Swiss Air commuter flights would have. That suggests she wants to keep her profile as low as possible."

"URGENT – MORE," the updated text read. "Intercepted communiqué states intended primary target is Baird Durand and secondary is his daughter, Alana. Be on the lookout for a backup to the Lucerne assassin, also Asian female."

"Alexandra and Paul, set up surveillance at the north end of Ponts Couverts. Matthieu and Marcel cover Baird's home at the south end. Delta Team en route," Daan advised.

"The assassin's train has just arrived at the Gare de Strasbourg. No sign of her backup but that doesn't mean that the backup isn't already in situ. It is highly unlikely her assistant would have travelled with her because two Asian females would be twice as obvious. The Lucerne assassin would want to hit and run. So, the probability of her assistant following would be infinitely small."

"Switching to voice communications," Paul confirmed. "Will be in position within two minutes. I will be adjacent to the middle tower. Alexandra will be behind me at the north entrance to the bridge close to the north tower."

"Marcel and I are at the Café de Thé, adjacent to the entrance and south tower," Matthieu confirmed.

"Suspect is approaching my location," Alexandra announced.

"Hello, Alexandra," Alana said as she walked along the bridge heading toward her father's home.

Aghast at the sound of her voice in such close proximity, Alexandra immediately looked in her direction. Her wide-eyed stare and startled expression signalled to Alana that she had entered an unsafe zone.

"Beside Alana," Alexandra exclaimed into her microphone in a startled voice. "Yusuf is nearby! What is he doing here? I thought he was supposed to be in Montreal guarding Francine."

"On him," Paul replied. *Were both Alana and Yusuf now placing Alexandra in increased danger?*

"Target is approaching you from behind at a rapid pace, Paul," Marcel warned. "She has her hand inside her satchel. She is pulling a weapon out. It looks like an Uzi."

The assassin swivelled toward Alana as she squeezed the trigger but not before Alexandra pushed Alana aside. Bullets creased Alexandra's left side as she fell to the bridge deck, her own pistol knocked from her hand temporarily preventing her from returning fire.

Some tourists ran for cover in both directions. Others retreated behind the tower turrets. Still others lay flat on the ground in an attempt to become less of a collateral target. Screams of terror filled the air which drew the attention of others seated at the Au Petit Bois Vert café.

Alerted by the hail of bullets and screams to the attack on his daughter, Baird leapt from his seat at the café and sprinted toward Alana with his own pistol drawn, shouting, "HALT! HALT!"

The assassin adjusted her aim from Alana and Alexandra toward Baird.

Simultaneously Yusuf rushed toward the assassin yelling in an effort to distract her while shooting in her direction. His aim was deadly. The assassin's body swivelled toward him, collapsing to the ground as bullets sprayed erratically from her Uzi. Her disciplined salvo struck Yusuf, causing him to tumble backwards over the bridge railing and into the water.

Baird stood face-to-face with Alexandra who had managed to stand upright. His gun held in both hands pointed directly at her. Her pistol pointed downward. He had the draw on her. He debated the dilemma of the ethos of his upbringing as the senior member of the *Quer* or fleeting loyalty to his potential association with the EUI Unit. The Malta Knight had sacrificed himself in his defence, Baird concluded. He was once again without tangible support. His heritage pushed him to default to his Celtic roots. He turned away from Alexandra and ran back over the bridge toward the sanctuary of his home.

His hasty retreat was immediately halted by a second hail of bullets from another source, another female Asian, this time the backup for the Lucerne assassin. The bullets found their mark.

Matthieu's lethal aim brought an end to this gunfire as the backup assassin fell to the ground, the recipient of a tight grouping of shots to her neck and head.

Paul sprinted to Alexandra's side. "Taking a break while everyone else does all the work?" he jested.

"I'd hug you," she replied, "but it hurts too much. We do need to talk about an important matter before it is too late," she exclaimed, almost pleading.

"About Collette and Yvon?" Paul interjected.

Alexandra stared at him. *He had known. But how?*

Paul smiled and reassured her that all was OK. "Nothing will ever come between us," he whispered. "I promised I would never leave you, never abandon you. Never."

Alexandra sensed a change, a difference in him, but not a threat to their marriage in the eyes of God. *The Pope may not be always right but their own wedding vows were*, she concluded.

The shooting spree had stopped. Patrons in the Au Petit Bois Vert café were stunned and silent, many still kneeling down behind their tables. The increasing volume of two-tone sirens announced the rapid approach of emergency vehicles.

Alexandra admitted to herself, *Yusuf may have been a knight-errant, but he was a true knight after all. There was honour to be defended, a need to right the wrong, a vein of veracity in the myth of the Wild West after all. Ultimately, the ethos of Paladin prevailed.*

"And you were correct in your assessment of Yusuf. Your *shrew* was accurate once again, as always. Never doubt it." Paul praised her. "*Mirabilis es* – you are miraculous. Perhaps not your best pose wedged against the bridge railing with pistol in hand at the moment, but you are no doubt a foxy lady. *Candens es* – you are hot."

"I appreciate the lighthearted compliment but feeling less than foxy at the moment."

CHAPTER 46

"That was unbelievably brave of you to stand in front of Baird with his gun pointed at you," Daan said to Alexandra with a mix of compliment and criticism in his tone. "In the future, I would very much prefer you not deliver a repeat performance because you are far too valuable an asset to lose to a stray bullet."

A sheepish smile brightened her face.

"I have recommended you for the *Ordre National du Mérit*," Daan followed up. "It seems to run in your family, both past and present."

"Thank you," Alexandra quietly replied with a humble bow. "Perhaps not as brave as well informed, augmented with an understanding of human behaviour."

"You have always expressed caution when providing an analysis of how Baird Durand might behave." Daan reacted with an inquisitive expression. "Care to explain? It might help me to deal with my overactive acid reflux that is causing me considerable discomfort at this moment."

"You are correct and that motivated me to examine the factors leading up to my reaction, why I felt there was a need to be only wary. I surmised that Baird thought and acted as an individual, a natural anarchist. In one respect, his personality has been consistent with that aspect of the Celtic warrior culture."

Daan stared blankly at her. "Please elaborate."

"Back in the day, the Romans were able to defeat the Celts in battle, because the Celts defaulted to individualism, where the Romans steadfastly held ranks as a disciplined cohesive military force."

"I'm not following your logic," Daan stated.

"The Celts believed in the afterlife. Thus, they had no fear of death. But Baird was fearful of death. He was paranoid. As an individual, he trusted no one. That is why he used more aliases than the most devout Catholic has Christian names, Brennus, Brennos and Banona, Brennen and Bary."

Daan acknowledged her explanation but continued to seek the connection with her assessment that Baird would not pull his trigger.

"Traditional Celtic leaders would step out from the ranks and challenge the most valiant champion among the enemy to one-on-one combat. The victor took all. Unlike his forefathers, I was confident Baird would not stand and defend his ground, his Celtic culture. Instead, he would camouflage himself like a chameleon and, at the first opportune moment, run away, which is exactly what he did."

Daan summarized her analysis with scepticism, still seeking to connect all the dots, some of which remained hidden in his mental fog bank. "Baird initially challenged you on the bridge. But he presented a false front. He ran away because he was not a traditional Celt. Is that the extent of your reasoning?"

"That's basically it," Alexandra replied.

"Slim analysis to risk your life on," Daan concluded. "That took a lot of intestinal fortitude."

"It wasn't that evaluation alone. Baird based his prowess on the image of the French battleship, *Brennus*, which was one of the aliases he used. This was illusory bravado, a false façade because the *Brennus* was never tested in action against an enemy. Instead, the battleship was only used as a training ship for naval reservists. By 1914, it had become outdated, so ended up as scrap before the guns of August formally rang out."

Daan evaluated the logic of Alexandra's full analysis, which led to her decision to confidently stand in front of Baird's gun. "There is no doubt in my mind that you displayed courage above and beyond. That is why I have recommended you for the *Ordre National du Mérit* which, by the way, Yolina has endorsed. You are your mother's daughter," he concluded with sincere admiration for her gallantry, tenacity and tacit wisdom.

Her mother's strident voice resonated in her mind, "*Run ... that was a shot in a million ... you are a natural sharpshooter.*" Her voice then softened, "*I am so very proud of you.*" Alexandra's breathing slowed. Her palm remained sweaty as she squeezed her fist on the imaginary pistol grip. Her diminishing confidence had reversed its downward trajectory. "*I have taught you well, daughter,*" her mother reminded her.

The press reported another thwarted attack on the EU Parliament. Credits were awarded to the Strasbourg Police Department and the newly formed French Anti-Terrorist Unit. For security purposes, no names were disclosed.

CHAPTER 47

"Helena, we have wrapped up the current case and will be taking a little down time. Is your invitation to be my personal tourist guide in Montreal still open?" Alexandra enquired on an upbeat note.

"Absolutely. Down time can be the best time," Helena replied. She would update her employer. Depending on the level of intelligence Alexandra might pass along, she would be selective regarding the details she would include in her report. As her field trainer, Tom Hunt, had repeatedly reminded her, you never ask a question that you don't know the answer to or at minimum you have sufficient knowledge of in order to determine the truthfulness of the target's response. That would always include her superiors when they tasked her to interview someone. She needed to be aware that there were those in her own organization who would always be testing her reliability. And more worrying, conspiring to set her up. Tom had also counselled her on how to cultivate long-term trustworthy relationships as he had with his trainer, Major Mike Murphy, and Major Mike had with Sir James in the British Secret Intelligence Service and Alexandra's mother, Maria Belliveau in French Counterintelligence, formerly of the French resistance, the *Maquis*.

Alexandra turned to Paul. "Looks as though we'll be taking a brief vacation in Montreal, compliments of our employer, but on separate flights. I will explain to my tourist guide that you became ill at the last moment but will be joining me later. While Helena is showing me the sights and we play cat and mouse with whatever information each of us divulges, you can meet with Francine/

Tatyana and relate the circumstances of Yusuf's fate, although his body is still missing."

"Thanks. Remind me to reciprocate," he replied in a tone mixed with sombre jest. He held her gaze with wary concern. Images of her being wounded by the Lucerne assassin on the Ponts Couverts in Strasbourg and Baird Durand aiming his pistol at her point blank flashed in his mind. If he could not be by her side, having an experienced CIA agent with her would be second best. He gained additional confidence knowing that Tom Hunt had trained Helena. Slightly more comforting was the fact that Helena would be on her own turf in Montreal where she had been employed by the Royal Canadian Mounted Police with their Watcher Service. He would not have that home-game advantage but would be close by.

⚐ ⚑

PAUL CLIMBED THE LAST STAIRS to his rendezvous with Francine in the shadow of the cross at the summit of Mount Royal, which seemed to best reflect the solemn tone of his message. As a couple, he and Alexandra had established a working relationship with Francine and Yusuf as a couple. That affiliation had crossed the line into quasi-friendship. Throughout, Yusuf had remained an enigma, a balance between the knight-errant and Paladin whose gun holster had been embossed with the symbol of the knight chess piece. Yusuf was as loyal and dedicated to Francine, his Tanya, as Paul was to Alexandra. How would he feel had Alexandra been killed on the Ponts Couverts? He couldn't imagine. How would Francine be feeling? The full extent of those emotions escaped him. At least having a body to bury would provide some solace. But at this moment, Yusuf remained missing. He would always wonder about Yusuf in the final analysis.

"The view of Montreal from this vantage point is like the vista of Paris from the Sacré Coeur Basilica Montmartre," a familiar voice commented.

Paul harrumphed in comic relief as he glanced toward the source. Yusuf stood a short distance away. The broad brim of his fedora masked his face. Paul's immediate reaction was to reach over and give him a warm hardy double handshake and a gratified grin. Instead, he smiled subtly but with every muscle in his face. His brother-in-arms had beat the odds once again.

"The Malta Knight, still coming to the rescue of maidens in distress," Paul acknowledged with a respectful bow. "You and Francine/Tanya have one more characteristic in common. You both have nine lives like a cat."

"Yes, but felines tend not to come in from the cold," Francine added with a suggestion that they had made such a career change.

"Correct to some degree," Yusuf smirked. "I am neutral to all supposed maidens in distress. Nor should I concern myself with their predicaments. The weak need to accept responsibility for their own self-imposed lot in life. They need to get off their lazy asses and defend themselves. My *raison d'être* is to confront the bullies. I hate hubris, smug tyrants and tormenters who think they can get away with being abusive."

Paul raised his eyebrows in response to Yusuf's diatribe. His rant brought more clarity to his ever-emerging personality. But Paul was more interested in his presence on the Ponts Couverts. "And returning to Strasbourg instead of remaining here in Montreal with Tatyana?" he retorted.

"My source was timelier than yours." He gingerly wrapped his arm around Francine, still nursing the pain from his own injuries. "My motivation was more personal. Had the Lucerne assassin listened to Dmitri, the Lucerne assassin and her assistant might still be alive today."

"You were wounded on the Ponts Couverts," Paul countered.

"I saw you fall back and over the stone railing. You didn't surface. Obviously, my eyesight failed me."

"In all decisions, there is a path taken and a path declined, despite serendipitous circumstances. Being shot was an opportune moment. I needed to create a new persona. I needed to die in order to be alive," Yusuf summed it up bluntly.

That somewhat convoluted rationalization brought an inquisitive response from Paul. "And your aborted attempt to enter the United States?"

"I drove to the New York State border to test the post-9/11 security response. It became evident that anywhere in the United States, particularly the Pacific coast, would not be accessible to me with my espionage track record."

"Why the Pacific coast?" Paul queried. "That's a long way from the U.S. eastern seaboard, even further from Strasbourg, France, the European Union...."

"Paladin's base of operations was the Carleton Hotel in San Francisco. If I couldn't use that location, the closest replication would be a 19th century private club in Victoria on the Pacific coast of Canada. Francine and I will relocate to Victoria to this private club where we will set up our own intelligence consulting organization as the 21st century Mr. and Mrs. Paladin. There, I will sip raki with friends and play backgammon with worthy opponents. Our business cards will not read: Wire Paladin, San Francisco. Instead, they will state: E-mail Mr. and Mrs. Paladin, Victoria."

"*We* will sip raki and *we* will play backgammon," Francine corrected him with an emphasis on the collective *we*.

"Yes, dear," Yusuf humbly acquiesced with a smile of domesticity that Paul had never before witnessed. This Knight of Malta had redefined the bachelor image of his forefathers. The 21st century knight-errant would be more subservient and less independent. As an intelligence consulting duo, they could not follow in the footsteps of Dmitri and his lonely spartan lifestyle.

"We have made the conscious decision to step back from the paranoia of the tradecraft and the unrelenting onslaught of the munitions," Francine added. "We are acutely aware that in the duplicitous world of espionage and intelligence, nothing exists in the absence of context. More importantly, intelligence and context are askew in the world of espionage where there are truths, partial truths, and make-believe truths. We especially do not want to have to second-guess the menace of invisible shadows and having to stare at nothing while being wary of everything." She concluded her proclamation with a sharp nod. "That reality is no longer our reality."

Yusuf added, "Please advise Daan and Yolina that we are not interested in formally joining the European Union Intelligence Unit. Instead, if you would like to contract us to undertake certain intelligence-related projects, we would consider such a request with its related compensation."

Alexandra and I should consider following their example, Paul pondered as he watched them standing beside each other and holding hands as his parents had done and as he and Alexandra took every opportunity to do. *One certainly can teach old dogs new tricks,* he concluded with a sheepish grin.

⊨ ⊨

"How was your short vacation in Montreal in the company of a personal tourist guide?" Daan enquired.

"It was as I expected, pleasant but business-like. Helena was definitely probing not so much for information but for a possible future relationship with undisclosed mutual benefits."

"Fair enough," Daan replied. "Keep in contact with Helena as there certainly could be benefits."

Glancing over to Paul, he followed up, "And how did Francine reply to your accounting of Yusuf's final moments on the Ponts Couverts?"

Paul reiterated his conversations with Francine and Yusuf under the shadow of the Mount Royal Cross.

Daan pondered as he stared at Paul. "I hearken back to Sarajevo when we both first laid eyes on Yusuf dressed in civilian attire, not in the Russian combat uniform of his colleagues. He was a fly on the wall attempting to be inconspicuous but was prominent by virtue of the fact that he was a purple cow among a herd of Mongolian Kalmyk cattle. He was different and, as a result, I recall thinking we would meet again more as allies than enemies pretending to be colleagues-in-arms working to maintain a tenuous peace. I can only imagine how his superiors in the Turkish Military Intelligence would have assessed his performance and, more perplexingly, what his supervisors in the Kremlin would have thought of this Caucasian Cossack."

With an equally complex reflection, Paul replied with his own recollection of the fateful day at the Russian headquarters in Sarajevo when the three encountered and assessed each other in that politically fragile environment. "The persona of the Knight-errant of Malta with his roots embedded in the sands surrounding Jerusalem and later the Island of Rhodes would have been transformative. It remains a fundamental part of his 21st century espionage DNA. It is, perhaps, a bit ironic that Yusuf and Francine met on the campus of the University of Rostov, both with the intent of converting the other. I am confident that, ultimately, they were both successful in their respective missions. They are now Mr. and Mrs. Paladin, committed to each other in a common cause."

CHAPTER 48

"Thank you all for attending this final briefing regarding the *Quer* case," Daan announced. "There are a few summary points I would like to make and a few outstanding issues that are still on our plate. Because Commandant Benoit Parent and Jean Bernard have been involved since we started down this path, I have asked them to attend. You all know Yolina."

Benoit, Jean and Yolina acknowledged the invitation.

Daan began his briefing. "First, the Beijing Moscow factors. The elusive waiter at the Café de Thé in Strasbourg was a Beijing agent. His sole purpose was to intercept messages from the Moscow spy ring, which was composed of café waiters and headed by Danielle Caron, the file room supervisor in Paris. Danielle was reporting directly to the same Russian handler as Joseph Durand and Francine Myette. Although the Russian agents were not supposed to know each other, only their handler, Francine made the connection and shared that information with us."

"Sorry to interrupt, Daan. Where is the file room supervisor now? What is her status?" Alexandra asked.

"Her security clearance has been revoked and she has been moved to another position where she has no access to any classified information. She is being kept under surveillance and all her activities and contacts are being recorded. We know that since Dmitri's death, the Valencia waiter has disappeared off our radar screen and does not appear to be a planet in her orbit. We could be wrong, though."

"How many more Beijing waiters are there?" Alexandra asked.

"Not certain," Daan replied. "The General Directorate of

Internal Security is following up and they are tight-lipped. Understandably, they are a bit embarrassed. We can expect Beijing to follow up with renewed infiltration in addition to aggressive retaliation for eliminating their two assassins."

Paul speculated, "Another mythical Hydra from the depths of Lake Lerna."

"If we consider our track record with the *Quer*, a Beijing Hydra may not be so mythical," Daan predicted.

"Speaking of Dmitri," Matthieu interjected, "Yusuf found a key and a map in Dmitri's sketching satchel. The key opened the door in the Hotchkiss factory but we have not been able to connect the map with anything related to that locale. If there is a connection, it remains a mystery. Baird travelled to the Island of Crete where he had a yacht anchored in Heraklion harbour. One source suggested the map could be related to more stolen Nazi gold hidden there during the Nazi occupation of the Greek Island, but that is just supposition at this time."

"Thank you, Matthieu. Any other follow-up points or questions?" Daan asked.

No one spoke.

"The second point relates to the *Quer*'s flock of governance and security informants," Daan continued. "*We have people in high places including the police department.* These were the last words that Herr Blosch said to Paul as they were being gagged and hooded on the yacht. Baird divulged the names of these informants to Claude Etien Marchand. We have neutralized some of these confederates and will be dealing with others in due course."

"We know that Alana's ex was squeezing one of the senior executive staff," Paul said. "Were there any others in the EU Parliament?"

"Benoit, would you like to respond?" Daan asked.

"The short answer is yes. At least one was reporting directly to Baird Durand. This investigation is ongoing so few details are available at this time. I can say with great relief that the Head of Security in the EU Parliament is clean."

Daan continued, "The third point goes back to our pursuit of stolen Nazi gold and the antiquarian trail that led us to the book binding shop in Graz. Jean, can you brief us on the work you have undertaken regarding the cyber crime activities of the Fourth Reich?"

"I can say with confidence that the good guys in the white hats have taken control of the commanding heights although the war is far from won," Jean announced. "Unlike the Cold War when the various espionage and intelligence agencies tended not to share all information openly, and I understand why, the current ranks of cyber warriors are sharing programming methodologies. We have infiltrated the Fourth Reich criminal cyber cell. Instead of closing it down, we have planted GPS worms to neutralize their efforts to transfer stolen funds. More importantly, we can now follow their e-trails which illuminate their strategic intentions."

"Thank you, Jean."

"One final point," Jean added, "I have just digitally converted the relative coordinates of the features on the map that Dmitri had hidden in his sketching satchel, and will attempt to identify its location somewhere on this continent. This is an enormous task that could take a very long time. When all else fails, it is our best investment."

"We may find the lair of Hydra and the source of the myth of Lake Lerna, after all," Paul commented as he proudly bowed to Jean for all to notice.

"Incredible, Jean," Yolina complimented him.

"I second Yolina's expression of gratitude," Daan added. "I have one final point to make before we adjourn. Membership of the *Quer* has passed down from father to son since its inception.

We have identified the sons and de facto paternal benefactors. They are aware that their fathers are missing and assumed dead. Two factors in our favour. First, unlike their fathers, they do not have access to the wealth, and we will ensure that they never will. Second, they have not been mentored as a team and, as a result, are operating as individuals, and we will ensure that they always will. There is an expression: the grandparents created the organization, the parents ran the organization, and the grandchildren destroyed the organization."

"Just one follow-up point," Benoit added, "the media have reported that the body of the missing terrorist gunman who fell off the Ponts Couverts has been recovered. His identity has not been confirmed."

"Well done to all," Yolina announced. "I can assure you that my colleagues in Brussels will have no qualms about authorizing future budget requests."

CHAPTER 49

Alexandra and Paul sat in the plush Bavarian high-backed chairs, without words, caressing each other's fingers while being serenaded by the crackling sounds of burning logs in the gargantuan stone fireplace of their favourite Lichtenstein hotel. The shadows of the flames danced lazily around the warming façade like pirouetting otters on the ebb of currents. Sounds of stillness silently embraced the ambience as the sun set over the silhouette of the Swiss Alps.

Alexandra gradually turned her head and drew Paul into focus. "Last time we sat enjoying this view, we asked ourselves why we were just here recuperating as guests when the inheritance from the Marchand estate could have changed all that." A moment later, she asked, "Regrets?"

"No regrets, *ma princesse*," Paul whispered.

"It was first about my mother," Alexandra reaffirmed. "Finishing what she had started. Putting an end to Thon's murderous marauding. Then avenging Sir James's poisoning. Perhaps avenging is an inappropriate word. Redressing a perfidious misdeed might explain my motivation more accurately. And then there was Tom's death. My mother's work seems never ending as the old KGB and its successor, the FSB, remain a menacing reality. And now we add the Beijing factor to the mix of those external forces bent on dismantling the envied culture of the European Union."

"But should it be our responsibility, our standard to carry?" Paul responded.

Alexandra allowed the silence to fill the space before again expressing her thoughts. "Allow me to answer that question with a question. You continue to mention your ghosts of Sarajevo?"

With that observation, Paul released her hand momentarily. "Images of those Muslim children being killed by their own people, and the little girl lying face down in the ditch with her tiny wrists bound behind her back with barbed wire that had ripped into her wrists and her light blue dress stained with blood that had oozed out of the bullet hole in the back of her head will remain a lasting part of who I am. I entered the black abyss of my own tortured soul and experienced the insanity of the psychotic hell of civil war. But I have returned a stronger person. The children no longer haunt me, although I still think of them."

"More so lately with the pending arrival of our first grandchild?" Alexandra asked with sincere concern.

"Yes, for certain. Like you, I want to be closer to the baby, and to Collette and Jean. I continue to be reminded of the words of Ralph Waldo Emerson in his poem about success, *to know that even one life has breathed easier because you lived.* That was my motivation to carry on before. Now we will have one more life to help breathe easier."

"So, can we find a balance?" Alexandra asked. "To carry on with the tenacity of warriors and also to sit by the fire together holding hands in the tranquility of intimacy? We still have to complete our inaugural retirement ride on our Harley-Davidsons. We planned to research a Second World War ace named Kurt Welter, just to keep our minds occupied. We feared we might otherwise be bored!"

Paul chuckled and resumed his tender massage of her fingers. "Let's propose that to Daan. Then, like Mr. and Mrs. Paladin, we will work on cases with the greatest potential to ensure that every peaceful life breathes easier."

"And to know that those despicable individuals who market carnage and suffering breathe much harder or, ideally, not at all," Alexandra quietly whispered as she snuggled closer.

"What about your leave of absence?" Paul asked.

"I can't move in with Collette and Jean to become their permanent surrogate like my aunt and uncle were to me. Nor should I. The baby needs its own mother. Collette can pursue her e-career from a home office which will allow her to sing fairy-tale songs and brush the baby's hair every night."

Collette's voice interrupted the ambience as she and Jean strolled into the lounge. "We will very much enjoy the amenities of the spa and Principality Suite each time we come to escape the stresses of work in Paris."

"Although not the hot tub until after the baby is born," Jean commented in a protective, fatherly tone, "and no alcohol either."

Paul smiled as he looked up at Jean and asked, "How is the beta test of your new kinesiology software coming along? Are you enjoying the collaboration on that, Collette? Have you been able to identify any criminality traits?"

Jean stared at his father from the depths of foreboding. Before responding, he scanned the room for any patrons who might be listening as spies of multiple loyalties would have done in decades past. He noted none.

"How well do you know Commissionaire Poulin, Commandant Parent's immediate superior?" he whispered. "My software has been using AI – artificial intelligence – to analyze 12 months of internal CCTV security footage isolating Baird Durand's son, Joseph Brennus Durand, to look for specific gestures and postures that might identify other KGB informants. The kinesiology analyses by the AI could take some months to complete. But meanwhile we have found video showing Joseph meeting surreptitiously with Commissionaire Poulin on more than a few occasions…."

Alexandra and Paul stared aghast at one another. Would they ever get to take that retirement ride?

– F I N –

Manufactured by Amazon.ca
Acheson, AB

15742002R00164